THE WALK-IN

THE WALK-IN

GARY BERNTSEN

AND

RALPH PEZZULLO

Crown Publishers
New York

Copyright © 2008 by Gary Berntsen and Ralph Pezzullo

Published in the United States by Crown Publishers, an imprint of the Crown Publishing Group, a division of Random House, Inc., New York.

www.crownpublishing.com

CROWN and the Crown colophon are registered trademarks of Random House, Inc.

Library of Congress Cataloging-in-Publication Data
Berntsen, Gary.
   The walk-in / by Gary Berntsen and Ralph Pezzullo.—1st ed.
      p. cm.
   1. Terrorism—Prevention—Fiction. I. Pezzullo, Ralph. II. Title.

PS3602.E7633W35 2008
813'.6—dc22

                                        2008002978

ISBN 978-0-307-39481-1

Printed in the United States of America

Design by Level C

10 9 8 7 6 5 4 3 2 1

First Edition

The authors would like to thank editor Rick Horgan, Amy Boorstein, Mary Anne Stewart, and, especially, Julian Pavia of Crown for their keen intelligence, passion, and editorial insight. We would also like to express our appreciation to our agent Heather Mitchell of Gelfman-Schneider and manager Michael Garnett of Leverage for their expert guidance.

The writing of this book would not have been possible without the love and support of our families, especially our wives and children. We dedicate this book to them.

THE WALK-IN

CHAPTER ONE

September 4–5

Maggie's *going to be disappointed,* he thought as he pushed through Muscat's narrow, crowded, dusty Ruwi High Street, brushing white-robed Arabs and South Asian laborers from Pakistan and Bangladesh, dodging white and orange taxis that crept through the pedestrian melee. *And I don't blame her.* It was 7:45 PM exactly, a little more than four hours till the fifth.

Air conditioners straining to cool the jewelry and electronic shops along the souk exhaled stale hot air, adding more bite to the rabid ninety-five-degree heat. September in the Sultanate of Oman was a bitch.

Matt Freed took a quick glance over his shoulder to check that dark-haired Cody still followed on the other side of the street. They'd been on foot for more than an hour. Neither had detected hostile surveillance.

At thirty-eight, Matt was a solid six foot one with sandy hair and light brown eyes. An intense high-kilowatt current seemed to run through his body and beam from his eyes. Otherwise he was unremarkable—nice looking, but not handsome; alert, but not studied; conventionally dressed in a short-sleeved cotton shirt and khakis.

He could easily pass for an Irish oil field worker, Swedish SAS pilot, American engineer, German businessman—and had used all four identities.

At a kebab stand, Matt made a sharp turn into an alley, jostling the loaded Glock he carried in his canvas briefcase. Almost immediately a young Arab man in a white IZOD shirt standing outside of Big Apple Electronics looked up from his cell phone. The two men made eye contact as the big American closed the space between them.

This better be my man, Matt thought.

It was. He and the Arab exchanged no words, just an electronic key inside a paper cover. The cover read Al Bustan Palace Hotel; room number 723 was written in pencil. Smoothly, without stopping, Matt continued through the alley, exiting back onto Ruwi High Street. His partner stood waiting on the other side of the street. Matt flagged down a cab, and tall, pencil-thin Cody slid in.

"Take us up the corniche, then down into Old Muscat. My friend wants to see the Sultan Qaboos's palace," Cody said in Egyptian-accented Arabic.

"*Naam,*" responded the driver.

"We're clean," Cody said out of the side of his mouth.

Matt pointed to the tattoo of a blonde peaking from under the sleeve of Cody's short-sleeved shirt. "Who's Gayle?"

"An ex-girlfriend. A mistake."

"We've all made a few of those."

As sleek new high-rises and apartment buildings greeted them, Matt relaxed into the back of the seat. After two tours with CIA Operations and five years with the National Counterterrorism Service (NCTS), this was old hat.

The U.S. Army major "on loan" to him remained tense while Matt's mind oscillated between his oldest daughter, Maggie, and the economic development of Oman. He admired both—Maggie for her grace and spirit, the Sultan of Oman for all he had achieved under his benevolent dictatorship.

Entering the coast road, the corniche, the taxi swerved right. To their right, a row of three-story buildings decorated with Islamic filigree and arches. To their left, past the lights, modern commercial vessels mingled with Arab-style dhows in the harbor.

They sat in silence admiring the serene beauty of the landscape. Matt rehearsed the mission ahead. He was interrupted by Cody's humming a tune and drumming on the armrest.

"Focus," Matt warned.

"I was thinking about this girl back home who sent me this download of her dancing to the song 'Polaris.' "

"I need your full attention."

"You got it, sir. I just love watching women dance."

The hills they entered were honeycombed and sucked by the sun of every bit of moisture. After climbing for five minutes, the taxi descended a slope into Old Muscat, past a sheer cliff topped with an ancient Portuguese fortress. The driver hung a right and stopped.

Cody handed him some rials and the two men stepped out. There were no tourists in sight—only a small number of Omanis milling about.

Matt felt exposed. "Let's move."

The gentle breeze off the Persian Gulf carried a hint of poet's jasmine as they passed the palace, its large, flat entrance protruding like a huge concrete tongue. At the next corner, Matt hailed a second cab. "Al Bustan Hotel."

This driver, a Bedouin, took off leisurely, scattering the cigarette ashes that littered every surface of the cab. Picturesque Old Muscat and the coast bounced by again.

After jostling through several villages, they approached a traffic circle with a dhow in the middle. The resplendent Al Bustan Palace Hotel glittered to their left.

They'd be meeting Manochehr Moshiri, a former general in the Iranian Army now living in exile. As a young man, Moshiri had made a name for himself fighting the Iraqis. He had once been loyal to the mullahs. But no more.

The lobby dripped with luxury, from the rich handwoven carpets over marble to the jewel-effulgent eighty-foot dome. Packs of rich Omanis and other Arabs lounged in stuffed chairs discussing business in hushed tones.

Exiting the elevator was a stocky man with short-cropped white hair, dressed in an Omani dishdasha, the traditional long white robe. His skin was a shade lighter than the average Arab's, and he had a C-shaped scar on his neck. *Iranian,* Matt thought as he inserted the plastic card in the elevator security panel and pressed "7." *What's he doing here?*

Later he'd be paying the general's bill, which would run at least $800 a night. For a year now the general had provided Matt and his employer with valuable information regarding the Iranian armed forces and the Islamic Revolutionary Guards Corps (IRGC). On two separate occasions he'd helped thwart attacks on U.S. interests in the Persian Gulf. Clearly, the general had a highly placed source within the IRGC. Matt speculated that it was a member of Moshiri's extended family.

They followed the plush carpet past a dozen doors and stopped. Matt knocked and waited. He knocked again. *I bet he fell asleep.*

Two men in white robes exited a room down the hall. Matt waited until the elevator swallowed them before inserting the electronic key and letting himself in. The room was pitch black. The plastic key placed in the wall system changed that.

As soon as the lights came on, both men noticed signs of a struggle—a chair knocked over, the contents of the minibar spilled across the floor. Then Matt saw the general, facedown on the carpet in a pool of blood.

Silently they drew their guns. Matt moved toward the body and pointed Cody to the bedroom.

One bullet hole above the right eye, a second below the left, four in the general's light blue silk shirt. Matt figured: *.22 caliber, suppressed.* He found no pulse.

"Nobody in the bathroom or closet," Cody said.

"Holster your weapon, look through the eyepiece, make sure there's no one in the hall. Then put out the Do Not Disturb sign and throw the dead bolt. Company's the last thing we want."

Matt continued the search, discovering a cell phone charger, which was empty. Tearing through the dead man's luggage, he found July's *Playboy*, a bottle of Lipitor, a gold bracelet, but little else besides clothes.

Pulling a notebook out of his pocket, he was starting to dial a number when a cell phone rang. Simultaneously he and Cody traced the sound to the sofa. They found the cell behind a pillow.

"Whoever killed Moshiri got everything else," Matt said, scrolling through the numbers. He stopped at a prefix he recognized, then used the hotel phone to dial.

A deep voice on the other end answered in Farsi: "*Salaam.*"

Matt recognized it immediately. "Cyrus, this is Robert," he said. "The general wasn't in. Where are you now?"

"That's odd. He was at the hotel when I left. He knows you're coming."

Matt cut to the chase. "Look, I'm in a hurry. I have something to give you. Meet me across the street from the Sheraton Hotel. You know where that is?"

"Yes. But—"

"I'll see you there in ten minutes."

As soon as he hung up, Matt crossed to the bathroom to get a washcloth, which he used to wipe the phone.

"What's next?" Cody asked.

"We need to get out of the country, pronto. We need to get the general's nephew, Cyrus, out of here, too."

"Why?"

"Because the Omanis will pounce on him, and he'll tell them that we were here talking to opponents of the Iranian regime. Sultan Qaboos won't like that. The Iranians helped the Omanis during the Dhofar War in the '70s. Even though it wasn't the Islamic Republic that helped the Sultan, the Omanis and Iranians are still friends."

"Won't they suspect he was meeting with us?"

"They can suspect all they want," Matt said as he wiped the inside of the door and the handle around the Do Not Disturb sign. "Let's go."

A family of Arabs rode down with them to the lobby, the boys demanding an immediate return to the swimming pool. "The water is refrigerated and cool like the ocean!" one of them exclaimed.

The taxi sped down a double-lane highway cut through the stony hills. Matt's mind raced. He knew who'd done this. The Islamic

Republic of Iran made a habit of murdering political opponents. The question was whether this was the work of the Ministry of Intelligence and Security (MOIS) or the Revolutionary Guards Corps (IRGC).

They were several blocks from the Sheraton when Matt ordered the driver to stop. They found Cyrus standing under a sodium streetlight in a plaid cotton shirt, smoking a Camel. Matt introduced Cody as "my associate, Bob."

The three men shook hands.

Matt took the young Persian's arm. "Cyrus, let's walk."

Moshiri's nephew knotted his dark brows. A light wind rippled his shirt.

"The general is dead," Matt said calmly.

The young man stopped in his tracks and seemed to sink into the pavement. "What do you mean?"

"I mean your uncle is dead. We found him on the floor of his hotel room. He's been shot."

The young Iranian let the cigarette burn his fingers, flinched with pain, and dropped the butt.

"What else was the general doing in Muscat?" Matt asked. "Who was he meeting?"

Cyrus took a deep breath. "We arrived two days ago. He met with someone yesterday. I don't know who." As he finished, he began to sob.

"Cyrus," Matt began, "your uncle was a great man. I'm very sorry."

A handkerchief over Cyrus's mouth muffled his "Yes."

"You need to get out of Muscat immediately. You don't want to be taken into custody. The Omanis will hold you for months."

Cyrus shook his head and said, "The mullahs," in a broken voice.

Matt pulled him close so their noses almost met. "Where are you staying?"

"The Intercontinental."

"What airline did you use?"

"British Airways. We were scheduled to leave late tomorrow night."

Matt did some quick calculations. "Go to your hotel, check out. Then proceed directly to Seeb International Airport. You still have time to catch the midnight flight to London."

"Who will take care of the general?"

Matt held both of Cyrus's shoulders for emphasis. "The general's in God's hands now."

This brought more tears and a nod.

Matt continued, "My object is to keep you out of jail. Go. Now!"

Cyrus wiped his eyes on his wrist and blew his nose.

"I'll call the general's brother Ahmad and have him meet you at Heathrow. Speak to no one until you're in London. You understand?"

He responded through fresh tears, "Yes."

Matt squeezed his hand. "I'm so sorry for your loss, Cyrus. I really am." Then he waved down a cab and Cyrus was gone. Watching the red taillights, Matt took out his cell and dialed. A woman answered in accented English.

"Hello, this is Mr. O'Rourke," Matt said. "I'm sorry to be bothering you at this hour, but I understand you're selling a car. Is there any possibility I could see the car tomorrow?"

The woman answered without hesitation: "My husband is out right now. Can you call again in an hour?"

"Thank you very much." He snapped the cell shut and turned to Cody. "We need to hurry. The moment Cyrus's plane takes off, he'll probably be on the phone telling the world."

Cody nodded. "I kinda figured that, too."

"I'll tell headquarters you're not as dumb as you look."

"Thanks."

They walked in sync another three hundred meters and flagged down a cab. Their destination this time was an upscale shopping center in an area called Medinat Qaboos. Matt instructed the driver to pull up behind a white four-door Nissan Pathfinder parked at the curb. Seated casually behind the wheel was an attractive Middle Eastern woman in her thirties—raven haired, sharp dark eyes, full confident lips outlined in pink.

"Nice to see you this evening, gentlemen," said Leila—the woman

Matt had called about the car. She was a Lebanese Christian who had immigrated to America as a teenager. Like Matt, she was currently employed by the National Counterterrorism Service (NCTS).

"We have a problem," Matt said urgently. "Axelrod One was murdered in his hotel room."

Her narrow black eyes widened. "You mean you went to the hotel?"

"Yes, we went to the hotel."

"You saw the body?"

"With six bullet holes in it. Axelrod Five's on his way to the airport now. I need you to inform Axelrod Two to meet Axelrod Five at Heathrow and make arrangements to recover the body."

She held out her long-fingered hand. "Give me your weapons and holsters."

Without hesitation they handed over their Glocks and extra magazines, which she zipped into a canvas diplomatic pouch and placed on the seat.

"The Omanis are gonna be pissed," she remarked out of the side of her mouth.

"They'll be watching the airports," Matt reasoned. "We need a vehicle so we can make a beeline for the United Arab Emirates."

"What about papers?" She was quick.

Cody held a resident permit from Dubai, which would get him across the border. Matt had none, so he'd have to hide in the trunk.

"My boss is gonna love this," she said firing the engine.

Matt passed the general's cell through the open driver's window. "Have your tech people download the numbers. Send them to Odysseus base and headquarters."

"Done."

Within an hour the two men were on the road in a new white Toyota Corolla with a full tank of gas. Cody, at the wheel, kept an eye out for stray camels while Matt listened to Iranian radio stations broadcasting from the other side of the Persian Gulf.

"See if you can find the White Stripes," Cody drawled.

"Shut up and watch the road."

They changed positions twice during the night. As the sun began to spread its fingers over the desert, Cody pulled to the side of the road.

"It's time, boss."

Matt transferred their luggage to the backseat and climbed into the trunk. As Cody covered him with a blanket, he said: "Don't let the bedbugs bite."

"Up yours."

Twenty minutes later, as Cody slowed to a halt, Matt was sweating bullets in the trunk.

He heard Cody talk in Arabic, then shut off the engine. The car door opened and shut. Footsteps, then more conversation between Cody and an Omani official.

Finally, the car door closed again and the vehicle lurched forward. Fifteen seconds later it stopped.

That's when Matt started feeling sick. It had to be at least a hundred degrees in the trunk. Craving water, he occupied himself by remembering the names and ages of his various cousins. He was up to his second cousin Lucille, who lived somewhere in Tennessee, when the car jerked forward again.

Hurry up, pal, before I get out and kick your butt.

CODY HALF-NOTICED the silver Ford Explorer rounding a curve in front of them. With one hand on the wheel, he gunned the car down the asphalt, thinking about how relieved he was going to be to return to base in the UAE and maybe hook up with the young radar technician with the light blue eyes he'd met at the PX. He half-noticed a quick movement ahead to his right.

A spray of six bullets splattered the side window and windshield. Ducking behind the dash, he turned hard right, past the white-haired man firing the AK-47, directly into the Ford Explorer, now blocking the road at a forty-five-degree angle. Precisely at the moment of impact, he yanked the wheel left the way he'd been trained.

The Corolla slammed into the bigger vehicle and fishtailed.

Poking his head above the dash, Cody saw the Explorer turn over and the man behind it jump back.

He hit the gas and prayed. The Corolla responded. After swerving left, then right, he got it under control. With bullets whizzing through the swirl of dust, he found the asphalt and raced, his heart beating a tattoo in his throat.

Ten minutes later, his blood still pounding, he pulled over and let Matt out of the trunk.

"Nice fucking driving," Matt groaned, gulping fresh air. Then he threw up.

"Same son-of-a-bitch we saw getting out of the elevator in the Bustan Palace Hotel."

"The guy with the white hair?"

"Yeah."

"You sure?"

"Eighty percent."

"Sounded like two shooters."

"I didn't get a look at the other dude."

The two Americans didn't have time to inspect the damage. As Cody drove, Matt cleaned himself, changed his clothes, turned the air-conditioning up to full, then dialed his cell phone.

It was 9:45 AM on September 5 when they stopped at the gate of Al Dafra Air Base. Two members of the U.S. Air Force Office of Special Investigations (OSI) stood waiting in civilian clothes. Once inside, Cody and Matt both started shaking. It took a six-pack each to calm their nerves.

APPROXIMATELY THREE HOURS later, the C-17 transport touched down on Araxos Air Base just outside Athens. Bright sun stung Matt's eyes. Waiting on the tarmac was his boss, Alan (Moses) Beckman, with a full head of longish gray hair and a beard.

Beckman was the head of Odysseus base, one of the National Counterterrorism Service's most important overseas teams. The unit consisted of eight officers, two communications specialists, and two technicians. They were responsible for recruiting sources within jihadist terrorist groups and governments deemed state sponsors of terror, which included Syria and Iran.

As soon as Matt stepped off with his luggage, Alan started: "What have I taught you about leaving dead bodies on other people's operational territory and stirring up a hornet's nest?"

Matt smiled. "Which commandment is that?"

Alan, who was fifteen years older, liked Matt's attitude but wished he'd learn to cut authority a little more slack. "The body was found early this morning. The border posts were closed an hour after you crossed."

As the SUV sped through the front gate, Matt glanced at his watch. It was almost 5 PM on Monday, September 5.

Alan passed him an envelope. "Here are your true-name documents. I'll drop you off at home."

They were on Kydatheneon, approaching the Plaka, home to endless tourists shops, jewelry merchants, tavernas, country girls selling flowers, street musicians. The glorious Acropolis loomed above.

For the first time in a week, Matt turned his full attention to his wife and three girls. He had an uncanny knack of compartmentalizing things, which allowed him to do his job.

"Alan, you mind if we stop here for a moment? It's Maggie's birthday and I've got to pick something up."

FIFTEEN MILES NORTH in cooler Kifissia, smoke continued to pour out of Liz's ears. The party was already two hours old. Twenty eight-year-olds had eaten pizza, been entertained by the hired clown, had their faces painted, and played games. Their parents would be arriving in a few minutes to collect them. But Maggie still refused to cut the cake.

"I'm waiting for Daddy," she insisted. "He'll be here any minute. I know."

She could be stubborn, just like her father—a trait that didn't endear her to her mom.

Still, Liz was trying to be patient. "Look, honey," she started.

"No. No!" screamed the solid little eight-year-old as she climbed on the sofa, turned her back, and looked out the front window.

"At least go play with your friends."

"NO!!!!"

Liz retreated to the kitchen, her blood pressure rising, repeating to herself over and over, "I can't live like this anymore. I can't." Seeing the cake melting on the white tile counter, she resolved to call her mother back in Cockeysville, Maryland, and break the bad news. Then she heard a scream from the front room.

Liz flew through the passageway, sure that one of the kids had been hurt, already castigating herself for taking her eyes off them when she saw Matt smiling in the doorway. Maggie had her arms around him, hugging with all her might. Sunlight streamed through the open door, casting father and daughter in an otherworldly glow.

"Daddy! Daddy!" Maggie shouted. "Now we can cut the cake!"

CHAPTER TWO

September 5–6

"**D**on't shut me out!" she screamed in his face, her hot breath smelling of pizza.

He clamped a big hand over her mouth. "The kids."

Liz stabbed him with her eyes until he pulled his hand away. "They can't hear us, Matt. They're watching *Cars.*" She was referring to their daughters—Maggie (eight), Samantha (six), and Nadia (three). The birthday guests had already been picked up.

That was some relief to Matt. "Look—"

She cut him off. "No, *you* look. You're weeks away from home, doing your thing, and I'm supposed to sit in Athens pretending like we're a normal family while my husband is God knows where, doing God knows what, with God knows who."

The fire in her blue eyes, the way her face twisted into something completely different, showed him how much she cared. He pulled her close so her breasts flattened against his chest. "It's the job," he said.

"Maybe you like it more than you like us."

"Come on."

"Maybe we don't give you the same rush."

Matt squeezed her and grinned. In some ways Liz was smarter than he was. When they'd met at the CIA Farm twelve years before, she was a budding analyst fluent in Russian, Spanish, and French.

He'd just completed a stint in the U.S. Marines. "You're challenging in your own way," he said.

"What's that mean?"

He sighed heavily with exhaustion. "Go ahead, girl. Ask me anything."

She stopped breathing for a second because he'd caught her by surprise. She always felt more attractive in his presence, which confused her sometimes. "All right, Matt. Where'd you sleep last night?"

"The Holiday Inn in Dubai."

"With whom?"

"I shared a room with a U.S. Army major named Cody."

She said the first thing that came into her head: "Are you in love with him?"

The absurdity of her question brought a smile to his face. "No." He loved her ability to transition from tragedy to comedy so smoothly. "But maybe I should be."

"What's that mean?"

"It's classified, baby."

"Stop calling me that."

"Baby, baby, baby. You asked the question."

She stood on her toes and gently bit his lip.

"Ouch!"

"You selfish prick." She was a pretty woman with a wide, open Irish face who liked to play games: charades, gin rummy, Monopoly, tennis, volleyball, et cetera. It made it easier to forget herself.

"You're looking to get spanked." Matt deeply loved his wife and daughters. They provided the emotional grounding he needed to do his job. Without them he'd work himself to exhaustion. That's how driven he was to succeed.

"You're completely self-centered." She ran her hand across his chest. "Admit it."

"I'm more complicated than that."

Liz was, too—an interesting combination of modern feminist and '50s wife, committed to her own self-realization and her husband's happiness at the same time. She said, "I bet you barely think about us when you're away."

It was true and he knew it, but he said, "Wrong!"

Her hand slid over his hard stomach and stopped. "I'm not like you. I can't turn my feelings off."

She was starting to piss him off. Tired, his mind muddled, repelled by the web of guilt she'd started to spin around him, he shouted: "Dammit, Liz. I'm doing the goddamn best I can!"

"I want us to be happy together, our kids to have a good life, to know their father!"

His blood surged so boldly he had to hold himself back. "Why are you bugging me like this? I just got back!"

She pounded her fists against his chest. "Because I don't want your body turning up on some dark street of Karachi or Tirana!"

He squeezed her harder. "Get a grip on yourself!"

"This isn't what I signed up for!"

He shook her by the shoulders. "Listen!"

She slapped him hard across the face. "Stop trying to save the world!"

She could feel the surge of energy coursing through his body, then into hers. She didn't give herself up to it completely; she tried to meet it. And did. All the weeks of frustration, all the doubt-filled nights, fears, and anger issued forth in one molten force.

Buttons gave way; fabric ripped. They clawed, kissed, and fucked to the core of each other and ended up fifteen minutes later in a sweat-and-semen-scented ball on the floor.

LIZ WAS CAREENING backward, dreaming she was playing volleyball in college. As she followed the seams of the white ball over the net, she heard the playful gong of the front door. "What?" she asked, half awake, grabbing for the sheet and covering herself.

The scrape of wood against tile and eight-year-old Maggie's voice brought her smack into the present. "Matt!"

He snored against her chest, his lips soft and rubbery, his arms thick and strong.

"Matt, wake up!"

Maggie called again, closer. "Mommy!"

"Don't come in here!" Then, in her sweetest voice, "What is it, honey?"

"Uncle Alan needs to talk to Daddy."

That set off alarm bells in her head. "Not now!"

"YOU GOTTA BE kidding," Matt growled at his boss as he stared into the petal pattern in the living room rug, thinking it reminded him of something else. "I haven't even unpacked."

Matt watched as the older man stroked his beard into a point. "Sorry, Matt. You're the best Farsi speaker we've got."

Alan Beckman unfolded the paper in his hand and offered it to his deputy. It was a typed note to the U.S. ambassador to Romania from a man who claimed to be a member of the Iranian intelligence service saying he would return to the U.S. Embassy in Bucharest 9 AM Tuesday morning, the sixth.

"That's tomorrow," Matt groaned.

Alan reached into the inside pocket of his linen jacket and produced a ticket. "I've booked you on the red-eye to Frankfurt, which leaves in two hours."

"I thought you said Romania."

"You'll be catching a connecting flight in Frankfurt and arrive in Bucharest at seven AM."

Next, Alan handed him a passport and wallet. "You're traveling under the name of John Paul Morgan."

"I need to spend at least a day with my family."

"When you get back, I'll give you some time off."

Matt blurted out the first thing that came to mind. "Maybe I'd be better off sitting on my ass in headquarters."

Alan's jaw tightened. As much as he liked his younger lieutenant, and even admired his guts, he was running out of patience. "This is a real bad time to bellyache."

"I'm not bellyaching, Alan."

"Then what would you call it?"

"Expressing my frustration. I keep sticking my neck out for you guys and don't seem to get a lot back."

"Your frustration is noted." Alan summoned his most authoritative voice. "I've said this before. I'm going to say it again. You've got courage, which we need more of in this service, and you're remarkably dedicated. But it takes more than that."

Matt clenched his teeth. "Don't start lecturing me about how to play the game."

"Learn to control your enthusiasm."

"Even when headquarters is making bad decisions?"

Alan was frustrated, too. He'd grown tired of defending his junior officer and cleaning up his messes. "Look. A man you've been handling just got shot."

"What about it?"

"I'm not saying it's your fault, Matt. But it doesn't look good."

Matt wanted to scream. "Haven't I been warning headquarters about the Iranians? Haven't I been saying that they're getting more aggressive?" He and Liz talked about this all the time: the gap between the bureaucrats and policymakers in Washington who set the agenda and the operatives on the ground who dealt with realities.

With a dinner to get ready for, Alan didn't have time to debate. He said, "The men who tried to ambush you . . . You think you can identify them?"

"I was in the friggin' trunk."

"Your friend Cody said he's pretty sure it was the same man you saw at the hotel—white hair, prominent scar on his neck."

"Could be."

"Why do you think he fired at you?"

"Maybe he thought we were following him."

Alan considered. "Good answer. I'll send an FBI sketch artist to Dubai to sit down with Cody."

"What is headquarters going to do? Stick it in their files?"

Alan stopped him. "You're a damn good officer, Matt. Don't make things harder for yourself."

Matt stuck the ticket in his pocket. "I'm trying not to."

"Self-respect is supposed to be its own reward."

Matt grinned sideways. "Whatever you say, Moses."

"One more thing . . . Grow up."

•   •   •

MATT WAS LEFT with the unpleasant task of informing Liz, who wasn't the least bit happy.

"Again!" she exclaimed.

"Liz, please. I'm trying to manage everyone's expectations." He was on his way to see the girls, who were waiting with *One Fish, Two Fish*, by Dr. Seuss.

"Is that what you're doing?" she asked.

"If you really want to know, I'm trying to save my job."

Blocking the hallway, hands on her hips, she cut straight through the dross: "Is it worth it, Matt?"

It was a good question. He promised to return by Wednesday, Thursday at the latest, at which time he would talk to Alan and ask for a new assignment. After two years with Odysseus it was time to move on.

"You and the girls mean everything to me," he said. And he meant it.

An hour later, he sat in a Business Class seat of the Olympic Airlines jet as it banked over the Aegean, considering his options. He was a fluent Persian speaker with a degree in Middle Eastern studies from the University of Virginia. If he left NCTS, he'd have prospects. But the thought of quitting, or being asked to leave, made him sick. If the example of his father's life had taught him anything, it was not to shy away from challenges and hide from the world.

Besides, he loved his job and what he considered the privilege of serving his country. To his mind, the United States was the hope of the planet because of what it offered: an opportunity to create one's own life without disabling social, economic, and political barriers.

It pained him that sometimes his government was clumsy and stupid. That was one of the things he'd like to change.

As the flight attendant handed him a Mythos lager, he noticed a long-legged woman with shoulder-length auburn hair sitting on the aisle several rows behind him in Coach. They'd made eye contact in the terminal in Athens as he was buying a copy of the *International Herald Tribune*.

The Mythos helped him close his eyes. Soon he was back on Ruwi High Street in Oman bargaining over a rug with an elderly, bearded merchant with a jagged, protruding Adam's apple. He had him down to a few rials when he realized he had no money in his pocket.

Next thing he remembered was being roused by the flight attendant's voice. "We'll be landing in Frankfurt in fifteen minutes, sir."

He was still willing himself to full consciousness as a train whisked him from Terminal A to Terminal C. Entering the Lufthansa 727 for Bucharest, he spotted the auburn-haired woman in the queue behind him. He liked her tan high heels.

This time he opened a dog-eared copy of *An Introduction to Persian*, by Professor W. M. Thackston of Harvard, and studied. Matt had made it a personal goal to master not only colloquial Persian, but Farsi grammar as well. Language was an important tool in his trade, and he was obsessive about mastering skills.

The sun was trying to burn its way through low clouds when they touched down at Bucharest, a city Matt hadn't been to in years. He remembered that the airport, once known as Otopeni, was north of the city. It had been renamed Henri Coandă after the man who invented the first jet airplane.

His rubber-soled Rockports squeaked across the tile floor, past the concourse clock that read 8:03 AM. In French, he instructed the driver of the ancient Mercedes 190E to drive him to the U.S. Embassy. He wanted to stop at the hotel for a shower, but time was short.

Minutes, hours, years pressed around him. He saw them in the juxtaposition of modern and dirt-poor Romania that flew by his window—wooden carts pulled by horses carrying fresh produce past billboards selling cell phones with Bluetooth Internet service.

Technology had also left its mark on the black-tiled U.S. Embassy roof. Sundry antennas and satellite dishes showed that it was connected to the world. He thought the building itself, with its dark brick and turrets, looked like something from *The Munsters* TV show.

A young blond-haired man in an ill-fitting suit greeted him at the door. "Mr. Morgan, my name is Seth Bradley. I'm here to assist you."

Bradley led him past the local guards through U.S. Marine Post One, up an elevator, and into a third-floor room with no windows. Matt measured all four hundred square feet of it with his eyes— hardwood floors, a bookcase against one wall, a wooden table, and two chairs. "This will do."

Setting his black nylon suitcase in the corner, he removed a yellow pad, pencils, and a Persian-English dictionary from his briefcase.

Bradley spoke from the door. "I'm going back to the front gate to wait for the walk-in. I'll remain outside this door the whole time should you need me. And, by the way, I'm armed."

"Good to know," Matt said, looking down at his cell phone, checking to see that it was fully charged.

Bradley wasn't finished. "When you're done, you can use this room for your write-up," he said. "I'll handle the encrypted transmission. If you need anything else, just ask."

"A shower and shave would be nice."

"Sir?"

"I'm good to go."

At two minutes to nine, Bradley watched a middle-aged man in gray dress slacks and a pressed white cotton shirt approach the gate carrying a worn leather agenda. He had straight military bearing, short-cropped salt-and-pepper hair, and a neatly trimmed beard and mustache. While Bradley took a few quick puffs on his Marlboro, he overheard a local guard ask the man if he was applying for a visa.

When the man proffered an Iranian passport, Bradley stepped forward. "This gentleman has a meeting with the Economic Section," Bradley interjected in Romanian. "I'm here to escort him."

Crushing out his cigarette, he took the passport from the FSN guard and read the name inside: Fariel Golpaghani.

"This way, Mr. Golpaghani."

The young American escorted the Iranian toward the bulletproof glass booth. A nod from Bradley signaled the marine inside to push a button, which electronically opened the secure blast doors.

MATT STOOD UP behind the table and offered the customary Persian greeting: *"Hale shoma chetorin."*

"Khubaem merci."

Bradley handed the passport to Matt and left.

"Your protection?" the Iranian asked in English, referring to Bradley.

Matt responded coolly: "I have a short temper. He's here to protect you from me."

Mr. Golpaghani raised an eyebrow as Matt barked, *"Beshanid."*

"I speak English," the Iranian offered with a grin.

"Congratulations," Matt said leafing through the Iranian's passport. A tense minute passed before he scratched his chin and asked: "What can I do for you, Agha Golpaghani, if that is in fact your real name?"

The Iranian smiled, revealing perfect white teeth. "It's what I can do for you that should interest you."

"Why?"

Matt noted that he wore a simple wedding band and a Bulova wristwatch. His left arm had been badly burned.

"I believe you are Matt Freed, born in Fredericksburg, Virginia, on June fifth, your wife's name is Elizabeth Anne. She was born in Cockeysville, Maryland. You have three children, all girls. You are currently employed by the CIA and live in Athens. Your last overseas assignment was in Afghanistan. Your current boss is Alan Beckman, who turns fifty-four this December."

Matt noted that the Iranian didn't differentiate between the NCTS and the CIA. Still, hearing the information about himself and his family unsettled him. He resisted the impulse to grab Golpaghani by the throat. "You still haven't told me what you can do for me."

"For you personally?" the poker-faced Iranian asked.

Matt felt his cell phone vibrate. He quickly snapped it out of the leather holder on his belt and read the text message: "I'm at the club. Love J.J."

J.J. was the code name for the auburn-haired woman on the plane. She was telling him that she'd spotted hostile surveillance outside the embassy.

Alarm bells went off in Matt's head. Pointing his chin at the Iranian, he said sharply, "What can you do for me?"

Golpaghani leaned forward confidently. "I can save your life."

Matt didn't flinch. "From whom?"

"I was sent here with a team to identify you and kill you." He emphasized the word *kill*.

Matt's mind immediately flashed to the general dead on the hotel room floor. "You're targeting me specifically?"

"You are one of several of your officers who we thought might show up. We couldn't know for sure. Any of you would have made an acceptable target."

"Who are you really, and why are you telling me this?"

The Iranian fixed his eyes on Matt and lowered his voice. "I am Moshen Kourani from the Sepah-e Pasdaran [the Islamic Revolutionary Guards Corps—IRGC]." he said.

Matt recognized the name immediately. Moshen Kourani was not only a member of the Sepah-e Pasdaran, he was deputy director of the Qods Force—the terrorist element of the Islamic Revolutionary Guards Corps (IRGC).

The man now revealed as Kourani continued: "The assassination operation is the means I've used to come here and tell you something else."

"Without the knowledge of your government?"

Kourani nodded. "An event is about to occur that could lead our countries into a terrible war that could consume the whole Middle

East. I'm a soldier like you are. But a U.S.-Sunni-Shiite war to me is senseless. Millions of people will be killed."

Matt leaned back and stared at Kourani as the consequence of what had just been said sank in. Two days ago, his top asset, Axelrod One, had been killed; yesterday he'd been ambushed and almost murdered crossing the border into the Emirates. Now this.

He pushed all emotion aside and got to work. "Agha," he asked. "How much time do you have before you need to leave this embassy?"

"I have a little less than three hours. At noon my colleagues who are watching the embassy expect me to exit. The plan is for me to provide a detailed description of you. They'll kill you tonight at your hotel."

CHAPTER THREE

September 6

This could be big, Matt thought, checking his reflection in the men's room mirror, then splashing cold water on his face. The word *promotion* wanted to push itself forward. Instead he flipped open his cell phone and punched out a message: "J.J. You're not alone. There's a team of four in close. All men 24–35. Exercise your best judgment. J.P.M."

He lived for moments like these—the chance to match wits—and knew the Iranians were tricky. *The general,* he thought. *General Moshiri.* There was a connection between his murder and this meeting. *What?*

Dismissing the slight nausea in his stomach, he slid past Bradley, who stood guard outside the conference room door.

Moshen Kourani sat like a statue with his hands folded across his knee.

After cracking open a bottle of water and drinking, Matt asked in Persian: "Why have you decided to share this information with me?"

Kourani didn't bat an eye. "Because I need your help."

Sure, you do, Matt thought. *But . . . why? What's the catch?* Shifting gears, he said: "I remember a Hamid Kourani, an officer of your Ministry of Intelligence and Security, who was murdered by the Taliban when they seized Mazar-e Sharif in August 1998."

Moshen Kourani nodded solemnly and lowered his head. "My older brother."

Matt pressed. "How do you know my name?"

The Iranian continued muttering to himself, an expletive directed at the Taliban followed by something about people who murdered for sport.

"How do you know my name?" Matt repeated.

There was anger in Kourani's brown eyes, which were rimmed with gold. His deep voice was steady. "You first came to our attention, Mr. Freed, when you and a team of Americans entered Jalalabad, Afghanistan, in 2001. One of our people took a picture of you and your colleagues outside the governor's office. Six months ago you traveled to Dhaka, Bangladesh, and checked into the Pan Pacific Sonargaon Hotel using your true name. We obtained a copy of your passport from a hotel clerk. The individual you debriefed at your embassy during that trip, Mohammad Aziz, was someone I directed at you."

"I remember Aziz."

"You didn't believe he was telling the truth, Mr. Freed. You were correct."

A picture of Mohammad Aziz flashed in Matt's head—odd gnomelike features and big burning eyes. He leaned forward and asked, "What do you want?"

A note of urgency entered Kourani's voice. "There's planning going on right now in Iraq for a major attack against the U.S. in the Persian Gulf. Something very big. It will be followed by something even bigger in the United States. If these events occur, our two nations are likely to enter into war."

"Who specifically is planning these attacks?"

"A group of Sunni radicals operating in Anbar Province."

"Al-Qaeda?"

"They might call themselves al-Qaeda, but the name is not important."

"I need details."

"Their ultimate intention is to kill more than a million of your countrymen on Eid al-Fitr."

Eid al-Fitr was the feast that marked the end of Ramadan. It oc-
curred on the first day of the month of Shawwal. By Matt's quick
calculation it was less than two weeks away. He gnawed his lip and
said, "I'm going to need more specifics."

The determination etched into Kourani's hard face underlined
what he said. "I'm prepared to share information about the first attack against your forces in the Persian Gulf. All I know about the
second is the date, September nineteenth, the beginning of Eid al-
Fitr, and where it will take place."

Matt knew that the end of Ramadan began at sundown on September 18, but let that pass. "Tell me."

"The target is several midsized U.S. cities."

Matt sat up. "I need to know more about that."

"Our sources include a low-level security officer inside the group.
I will give you further details when I get them."

"If your information is correct, we don't have much time."

"Thirteen days to be exact."

Matt resisted the impulse to call someone. *Who?* The CIA station
chief in Bucharest was a pompous warhorse who knew nothing
about the Middle East. Alan Beckman would reason in concentric
circles before telling him to use his best judgment.

Kourani continued: "It's important that you raise the vigilance in
your midsized cities immediately. Secure water supplies, food, port
and airport facilities. It's critical that you believe me and know that
Iran is not the source of this threat."

For a moment Matt felt like they were working together. "What
is it that you want in return?" he asked.

"Five million dollars."

"That's a lot of money."

"Five million and resettlement. That amount will allow me to
take care of my family and cover the loss of properties that will be
seized when my government learns that I've defected."

"We won't announce your defection."

Kourani flashed a sly grin. "You know as well as I do, Mr. Freed,
that it's always in one's political interest to leak an intelligence success. I read your newspapers. I study your White House."

"I need to know what type of attack is being planned."

"The group will conduct a series of car bomb attacks on a U.S. military facility in the Persian Gulf. These will be followed up by larger attacks in the U.S."

"Where will the U.S. attacks take place?" Matt asked sharply.

"I told you what I know so far: midsized cities in the United States."

"I need the exact locations."

The Iranian paused before he spoke. "Mr. Freed, I don't have their full plan yet."

A hundred separate thoughts collided in Matt's head. He took a deep breath and considered a different approach.

Kourani continued: "I realize that this information will cause your government great concern. But if you act immediately and cause me, or my family, to be arrested, I won't be able to help you. I can't, under any circumstances, put my family at risk."

Matt nodded. "I understand."

"Your people must control themselves."

"We will," Matt said bluntly. He didn't like this foreigner telling him what to do.

"I'm not asking for money from you today. I'll make arrangements to meet with you again."

Shifting gears, Matt said: "Your passport reads Fariel Golpaghani, but you say you're Moshen Kourani." The only way he'd be able to confirm that the man before him was who he claimed to be was to get him to talk about his past.

The Iranian was caught midgesture. He lowered his arms. "My name is Moshen Kourani."

"Where were you born?"

"Shiraz, Iran."

"When?"

"1959."

"Where did you attend school?"

"I attended school primarily in Shiraz, but we lived in Hamburg, Germany, from 1964 to 1968, and then again from 1973 to 1978. That's where I learned German and English."

"Why did your family leave Iran?"

"My father felt that the Shah was arrogant, pompous, and uncaring about ordinary people. He also had inherited a farm, which was seized by friends of the Shah. My father's older brother was already in Hamburg, so they supported us when we arrived."

"Was your father a religious man?"

"He was very thoughtful. I would call him a philosopher."

"Did you attend the Islamic Center in Hamburg?"

"Regularly, yes. The great Ayatollah Beheshti was the leader of the mosque in the early 1960s and, as you know, a powerful opponent of the Shah. Beheshti and my father were close friends. I accompanied Beheshti when he flew to Tehran in 1979, after the Shah fled and Khomeini returned. I was nineteen years old and served as his aide."

"For how long?"

"One year."

"Then what?"

"I left his service because he encouraged me to join the Sepah-e Pasdaran. He was close to Khomeini and became the most powerful member of the Revolutionary Council. Beheshti wanted someone he trusted inside the organization."

"How often did you report back to him?"

"Every day."

"So you were his eyes."

"More than that. When Ayatollah Ozma Kazen Shariatmadari and his Muslim People's Republican Party revolted against Khomeini and rioting began in Tabriz, I was part of the group of Pasdars [Revolutionary Guards] sent there to quell the violence. We retook television and radio stations. We were devastating. Beheshti was the force that drove us. Had he not acted, civil war would have ripped our country apart and hundreds of thousands would have died."

"Did you take part in the Revolutionary trials?"

"No, but other Pasdars close to me supported Sadegh Khalkhali, the chief justice of the Revolutionary Courts who locked himself in

Evin Prison and began executing prisoners, including the Shah's prime minister."

"Did you feel that the actions of Beheshti and Khalkhali were excessive?"

Anger flashed in Kourani's eyes. "In the early 1960s the Shah's secret police murdered hundreds of Khomeini supporters by tying their hands behind their backs and throwing them in a river. When Beheshti was arrested, they tortured him and urinated in his face!"

Kourani was about to slam the table but stopped. Realizing that he was being baited, he reached toward his jacket pocket and asked: "Do you mind if I smoke?"

Matt left without saying a word. Three minutes later he returned with an ashtray. As Kourani lit up, he said, "Tell me about Beheshti's death."

The Iranian was momentarily lost in a big cloud of white smoke. "It was June 1981. We were at war with the Iraqis. Ayatollah Beheshti was attending a meeting of the Islamic Republic Party when a bomb exploded, killing him and seventy others. It was the work of the opposition, the Mujahideen al-Khalq, the radical students, perhaps with the help of Iraq."

"Where were you when you learned that he was dead?"

"I was in Abadan, where we have our refineries. My Pasdaran unit resisted the Iraqis. Six thousand of their soldiers died. Later that year we began Operation Samen-ol Aemeh and counterattacked into Iraq."

"How long did you fight?"

Kourani drew on the unfiltered cigarette and held up four fingers. "Four years. Then I was put in charge of procurement."

"What kind?"

"Spare parts for jet engines, radar systems, weapons. All our equipment was American. We had procurement offices in Dubai, Frankfurt, Singapore. Even though your government had imposed an international embargo against us, we were able to buy enough spare parts."

"How did you injure your arm?"

"Napalm," answered Kourani, leaning back and directing a stream of smoke at the fluorescent light overhead. "I was leading a group of Basijis [volunteers] across the southern marshes into Iraq. Saddam had brought in large pumps and flooded the area. We built pontoon bridges by hand. The Iraqis shot at us with helicopters and bombed us with napalm. When they destroyed the bridges, we'd go back and build them again."

"How many men did you lose?"

"Eighty percent of the brigade." He smashed out the cigarette and immediately started another. "You Americans don't understand war. You watch from a distance. You lose three or four thousand and want to go home. We would lose that many in a day."

The Iranian's arrogance was starting to rankle Matt, who said: "Khomeini could have stopped the war and spared half a million lives."

"A wise man doesn't leave a devil panting at his door."

There was no point arguing about Saddam Hussein. Matt thought: *Everything he's said so far fits. Either this guy is who he says he is, or he's been superbly prepared. Is he for real, or is he playing us? What possible motive could the Iranians have for getting us wound up about a fake al-Qaeda plot?* Matt asked, "Who killed General Moshiri in Muscat two days ago?"

Kourani seemed genuinely perplexed. "It must have been the work of the MOIS [Ministry of Intelligence and Security]," he answered, "because it wasn't the Qods Force."

Matt knew that the Qods Force and MOIS were considered competitors. The Qods Force was the external intelligence apparatus of the Islamic Revolutionary Guards and derived their power directly from the mullahs, while the MOIS was a branch—a ruthless and powerful arm—of the Islamic Republic.

"In my opinion, it was Tabatabai, their chief of special operations."

Matt thought that was a reasonable conclusion. He asked: "How did you get to Romania?"

Kourani glanced at his watch. "Mr. Freed, I know you must

confirm that I am, in fact, Moshen Kourani. But we're wasting precious time."

"Answer the question," Matt said sharply.

"I arrived here two days ago, Iran Air to Frankfurt, then Lufthansa to Bucharest. We're all carrying commercial documents. After shooting you, the plan is to drive east to the coast of the Black Sea. A boat will then transport us to Istanbul, where officials from our embassy will provide us with diplomatic passports. We will travel overland to Iran, so we can't be traced."

"Why target a member of my service?"

"Leaders in my country want to show your government that there will be consequences for meddling in the Middle East. You happen to be one of a half-dozen Farsi speakers who respond to this type of approach."

Matt looked at the man across from him and nodded his appreciation. Kourani was clearly a talented and highly trusted operative with insight into how his government worked. He was not unlike Matt.

Kourani lowered his voice. "Mr. Freed, I must warn you. You cannot under any circumstances leave this building today or tomorrow."

"Is that a threat?"

"If you leave and I find you, I will have no alternative but to fulfill the mission I was sent on."

"Why don't you describe someone who doesn't exist?"

"Do you think that's wise, Mr. Freed? Would you want me to risk raising the suspicion of my own people?"

"Do you think your people want the war that could result from these terrorist attacks?"

"Many of them, yes. I consider them shortsighted, even stupid. But they see this as an opportunity. A major terrorist attack by Sunni radicals will surely inspire a strong counterattack by the U.S. My government and allied Shias will take advantage of this situation to make their own advances. Some feel we would be fulfilling the word of the Prophet."

Matt understood that the Sunni-Shia split in Islam originated soon after the death of the prophet Muhammad in 632. Most of Muhammad's followers wanted the community of Muslims to choose a successor to be the first caliph. They became known as Sunnis. A smaller group (the Shia, who now make up only 10 to 15 percent of the world's Muslim population) felt that someone from the prophet's family should assume the mantle and favored his cousin and son-in-law, Ali. Over a thousand years later, the two factions still struggled to define local Middle Eastern politics and the relationship between the Islamic world and the West.

Matt asked, "When will it be safe for me to leave?"

"If we can't find you by nightfall tomorrow, we will abort the mission. With the mission a failure, I can return to Iran and include myself on a team traveling to New York City for the opening of the United Nations General Assembly on September nineteenth."

"That gives us no time before Eid al-Fitr."

"I'll make arrangements to arrive in New York City the afternoon of the eighteenth. We'll meet at that time, and I'll supply you with full details of the planned attack."

"I'll need the information sooner."

Kourani spoke quickly, ignoring him. "Eight days from now I will travel to Vienna. Make sure that your embassy there approves a visa for my travel to the U.S. I will personally deliver and retrieve my passport. Have one of your people write the phone number you want me to use to reach you in pencil on the second-to-last page of my passport. The minute I arrive in New York, I will break away from the group and call."

"What about the information on the first attack?"

"I'll write that now."

Matt slid a legal pad across the table. Kourani removed a pen from his jacket and started writing. "It will take place in Qatar sometime on September seventeenth. A truck loaded with explosives will attack the perimeter of CENTCOM [U.S. armed forces Central Command] headquarters at Doha International Air Base. Two more vehicles will enter through the breach with smaller explosive devices. The operation is being run by two Saudi businessmen who work with the JAFA Trading Company. They've already established an office in Doha. The leader's name is Kahlid al Haznamwi."

"What if the plan changes?"

Kourani slid the pad back. "I assume you'll place these men under immediate surveillance."

"We need to communicate before you arrive in New York on the eighteenth."

"Impossible. When I hand over my passport to your people in Vienna, I will include a slip of paper with a number, which will correspond to a numbered account. If the information I've passed to you is correct, you will wire two million into the account before my arrival in New York."

Matt noted this on the legal pad. "And your wife?"

"I've already made arrangements for my wife and son to visit her family in Toronto."

"You can't move up your arrival in New York?"

"Not without raising suspicion."

Matt's concern showed in his face.

"If you take any kind of preemptive action that puts my family at risk, you can forget about my cooperation," Kourani added.

"You said that already."

"Be smart, Mr. Freed. It's important. Neither one of us wants a war that kills millions of people in retribution for the work of a group of fanatics."

Matt agreed. The Iranian pointed at his watch. "I should go."

"Before you leave, Moshen Kourani, is there anything else you can tell me about the threat to the United States?"

"I told you all I know."

Matt doubted that. "Are you sure?"

"I'm sure," Kourani said, standing and offering his hand. "We both know what you have to do."

Their eyes met for the last time. "Yes."

After Bradley copied Kourani's passport and escorted him downstairs, he returned to find Matt deep in thought.

"How did it go?" the younger man asked him.

Matt answered with another question: "Can you do me a favor and find me a mattress?"

"Sure," Bradley answered.

"I'm sleeping here tonight."

CHAPTER FOUR

September 6–7

N*ow the shit hits the fan*, Matt thought. Flashing before his eyes was an image of someone trying to steer a 747 loaded with passengers through a storm. Him.

I have to be sharp. This is too important. No way I'm going to let bureaucrats five thousand miles away in headquarters tell me how to suck eggs.

Yanking the cell phone from his belt, he typed a text message: "J.J. Out. Stand down." Then took a deep breath.

Before he started answering the dozens of questions that collided in his head, he wanted to make sure that J.J. didn't go after the Iranians alone.

Matt wasn't the most eloquent speaker or dispassionate analyst, but he could think through a problem at lightning speed. He relied on instincts picked up as a teenager running with the wrong crowd.

Native intelligence and tremendous drive had gotten him where he was now. He was one of those anomalies of character, experience, and genes. His father, a plumber, was a fearful, suspicious man who had warned Matt to expect failure and disappointment at every turn. His mother masked huge insecurities with constant chatter that she used to create a false picture of the world.

He had to be real.

Was the man who appeared before me really Kourani?

He didn't know for sure. So Matt carefully lifted the cigarette butts out of the ashtray and bagged them. He did the same with the glass the Iranian had sipped water from. In two or three days, analysts outside DC at NCTS headquarters might provide an answer. Chances were it wouldn't be definitive. Would they be able to lift a clear print? Did they have Kourani's prints on file?

But Matt's gut told him that the man he'd met was in fact a member of the Islamic Revolutionary Guards Corps. Why? Because he'd debriefed so many IRGC members, he could spot them a hundred yards away. The older ones like Kourani were ruthless and fatalistic, traits that manifested themselves physically around the eyes and in the creases of their mouths.

Swimming through rivers of dead countrymen and climbing over mountains of broken bodies and limbs had deadened parts of their souls. They'd lost hope in humanity. Some became unrelenting mercenaries of Allah. Others chose to escape with their families and find a little corner of anonymous peace.

Matt opened his laptop and entered an encryption program. With a copy of Kourani's passport as Fariel Golpaghani before him, he compared twenty pages of entry and exit stamps with ones he read off the computer. He confirmed that the man posing as Golpaghani had entered Romania two weeks ago. There was no evidence, however, that he'd transited through Frankfurt as he claimed.

The solidly built American worked for the better part of an hour without pause, sifting through and identifying the dates and stamps, ignoring the stiffness that crept up his back and the thirst that itched his throat.

There were multiple entrances and exits involving Turkey, Syria, Lebanon, Egypt, France, Great Britain, Afghanistan, and Iraq. The ones that troubled him were a series of trips that began in Afghanistan in late April and included various entries and exits from Uzbekistan and the Russian Federation ending in mid-July.

Why does that bother me? He wasn't sure. He knew the Iranians ran hundreds of sources throughout the Persian Gulf and had contacts among extremists in Central Asia, too.

As the clock drifted past seven, he set out to draft his report. His goal was to warn headquarters of the impending threat and, at the same time, secure an important role for himself in the response. He expected both the NCTS and the CIA to be ruthless and determined. There would be leaders in both agencies who would overplay the threat.

Matt clicked into the format and plugged in the appropriate fields to guarantee his message would be read by NCTS headquarters, Odysseus, and key individuals at the White House and CIA.

He plowed past his incipient hunger and wrote without passion, stating the facts, underlining that the source (Kourani) had not been validated. As he reached the last paragraph, requesting a copy of a photo of Kourani that he knew existed at headquarters, he heard a knock at the door.

"Come in."

It was Bradley, carrying a piece of paper. He seemed jumpier than before. "This just came from J.J."

Included in her message were descriptions of three "Middle Eastern–looking men" who had accompanied Kourani to the embassy. "I believe they're still watching the embassy," she wrote. "I recommend strongly that you stay in place."

"Thanks," Matt said over his shoulder.

"What's going on?"

"Think you can find me a sandwich and a can of soda?"

"What kind of sandwich?"

"Ham, turkey, anything. And that mattress."

Alone with the sound of nearby elevators whirring up and down, Matt began an urgent message to his boss. "Alan: Re the attached report. The threat coupled with the little time I had with Kourani made normal vetting impossible."

He paused. *With General Moshiri gone,* he thought, *we have no reporting or coverage of the IRGC. Given the short amount of time, how do we confirm what Kourani said?*

The options were slim. Surely headquarters would send officers into the field to check all NCTS sources. And the National Security

Agency (NSA) would step up electronic surveillance of Qods Force operatives moving throughout the Middle East.

The question Matt asked himself was, *How do I best utilize my expertise?* The last thing he wanted to do was spend the next two weeks in conference rooms in Athens and Washington jawing about threat assessments and target matrices.

His instincts told him that retracing Kourani's path was the best chance he had of turning up useful clues. So he concluded his urgent message to Alan Beckman: "I need your approval to travel to Afghanistan and possibly Uzbekistan to follow up. I figure a few days in Kabul, then Tashkent. MF."

Matt stood and stretched his arms, confident that his boss would approve. The two men frequently argued about bureaucratic issues, but were usually on the same page when it came to operations and running down leads.

Five minutes later, when Bradley returned with a fold-up army cot, Matt remembered his wife, Liz. Since he was traveling under an alias, he couldn't communicate with her directly. So he returned to the laptop and tapped out a second message to Alan asking him to inform Liz that he was extending his trip by a week.

ALAN WAS SITTING up in bed reading about the death of Brian Epstein when he saw the red light blink on his BlackBerry. As his wife slept soundly, he padded quietly to the bathroom, where he read the message: "Starlite 12:43."

Something from Matt needed immediate attention. Fifteen minutes later, he stood at the door of his downtown office disarming the alarm with "Strawberry Fields Forever" playing in his head.

There were five urgent messages from Matt Freed waiting on his computer. As he read, he used a pencil and yellow legal pad to take notes: "Moshen Kourani. Possible al-Qaeda attack on the 17th. Kabul, Tashkent, U.S. Embassy, Vienna. Five million dollars. Opening session UN General Assembly. New York."

Matt hadn't spelled out the lead he wanted to pursue in

Afghanistan but had cited several recent entry and exit stamps in Kourani's alias passport.

That was enough for Alan, who scratched his beard and sang in a flat voice, "Let me take you down, 'cause I'm going to . . . ," as he opened the safe, found the phone book, and dialed.

"Building 9, Kabul," answered a woman on the other end.

"I'm going secure," he said, pressing a button on the STU-III phone and listening as the encryption aligned into place.

"I have you secure," the woman said.

"This is chief Odysseus base. I need to talk to your jefe."

"Jefe?"

"Boss."

Alan smiled to himself. "Jefe" was an affectation he'd picked up in his last post: Buenos Aires. In his mind's eye he saw its tango bars, soccer stadiums packed with jubilant fans, and an abundant supply of beautiful women in tight pants.

An urgent voice jolted him back. "Alan, this is Burris in Kabul. What's up?" Steve Burris was the CIA deputy station chief. He explained that his boss had been summoned to nearby Islamabad, Pakistan.

"An officer of mine, Matt Freed, will be traveling to your region in the next few days under the name John Paul Morgan. It's urgent. He might need support."

"I've heard he's a good guy, but somewhat of a cowboy. Why Afghanistan?"

"I can't tell you that." He had to protect Matt by keeping the operational circle small.

Next he called the CIA chief in Doha, Qatar—a big, larger-than-life character named Mel McKinsey. They'd trained together many years ago at the Farm.

"Mel, it's Alan."

"Your man Freed better be right about this. Otherwise, I'll give him a huge kick in the butt."

"Mel—"

"You know how goddamn skittish the Qataris are since the attack in 2005. When I tell 'em that Sunni radicals have targeted them again, they're gonna freak out."

"It seems to me—"

Mel cut him off again. "I know. I know. I sound like a whiny asshole."

"It isn't personal, Mel," Alan said.

Mel chuckled. "How come it always feels that way?"

"Because you're sensitive."

"The fuck I am. I'm on my way to Camp Snoopy [Doha International Airport] now. We got the threat assessment and we're acting on it. Guess we can't avoid telling the Qataris. Your guy better be right!"

It was late afternoon in suburban Maryland when Matt's message reached NCTS headquarters. The unit's first director, General Emily Jasper, had just returned from a luncheon meeting at the State Department with visiting Afghan foreign minister Babur Qasim. The acid reflux that had been bothering her for weeks burned the inside of her chest. A young male aide with neat blond hair entered with a mug of chamomile tea. "I thought I asked you to knock."

"It's your tea and an urgent message from the U.S. Embassy, Bucharest."

Reading the name Matt Freed at the bottom, she sat up straight. "Get me General Ramsey in Tampa. And bring me Freed's file."

She was an exceptionally tall woman with a tuft of unruly strawberry blond hair. On the wall behind her was a photo of her shaking hands with the president. Next to it was her prized possession, a picture of her with her husband standing next to the Colombian novelist Gabriel García Márquez, taken when she was serving as military attaché to Bogotá in the early '80s.

She and General Ramsey, who was now the J2 at CENTCOM, had served together in Fort Huachuca before she'd married and mothered kids. Twenty-five years ago they'd played together on a volleyball team that lost to the base champs by two points.

"Paul," she said in a familiar tone when the general came on the line. "Tell your combatant commander that we'll give him up-to-the-minute detailed follow-ups from Bucharest as soon as they come in."

"I just read the reporting."

"What do you think?"

"The attack on Doha doesn't surprise me. We've instructed our commanders there to upgrade security. But the attack on the mid-sized U.S. cities kind of turns my stomach."

"I feel the same way. It's the civilian aspect that gets under the skin."

"I don't like this kind of war."

She said: "If your people in the field pick anything up, I want to know immediately."

"Don't worry. We're taking the threat extremely seriously."

She caught a touch of fear in his voice, but the blinking lights on the phone console pulled her attention. Her aide stuck his head in the door, again, mouthing: "The White House."

She said into the receiver: "Take care, Paul."

Her aide sounded excited: "White House on line two."

"Who?"

He stammered: "N-n-national Security director, Stan Lescher."

"Tell him I'll call back in five minutes."

"But—"

"Get Alan Beckman on the phone. Now!"

"Yes, ma'am."

Sipping from her favorite "Go Blue Devils" mug, she felt more in control. Two minutes later, as she leafed through Matt Freed's personnel file, Alan's deep voice came over the line.

"Good morning, Alan. It's approximately 0600 hours local time, correct?"

"Morning, General. That's right."

"I had a feeling you'd be in your office."

"I'm a light sleeper."

"What with assets being killed in hotels, shoot-outs on highways, and now this news that is sure to send the president's blood pressure through the roof, I'm not surprised. If you were sleeping well, I'd be suspicious."

Alan chuckled good-heartedly. "All in a day's work."

"Tell me about your guy Freed," she said looking at a photo of Matt sneering slightly at the camera. "Do we have a personnel problem here?"

"Not at all, General. He's as solid as a rock."

"I've heard rumors otherwise."

"No. He's sound."

"We're all in deep doo-doo if you're wrong." General Jasper was a deeply religious woman who didn't like to curse.

"Countersurveillance confirmed that there was an Iranian team outside the embassy that may have been there to shoot him. The bigger problem, of course, is the threats to our forces in Qatar and our homeland cities."

"We'll take every precaution. Before the end of the day, I predict Homeland Security will be raising the threat level to Red."

"We have additional sources to task."

"That's why you're in command out there, Alan. I'm counting on your people to confirm this independently. Turn over every rock. Keep me in the loop."

"Yes, ma'am."

"Now I've got some explaining to do to the president." General Jasper hung up, took a deep breath, and reached for the receiver again.

Her aide appeared in the doorway. "General—"

She cut him off. "Get the White House. And find the Iranian ops group chief. I want to see him. Now!" The bureaucratic circle was widening, fast.

MATT LAY ON his back, dreaming that he was flying a 747 down a city street at dusk, coolly navigating rooftops and power lines.

Hearing the slam of a door, he looked up. Simultaneously, stark fluorescent light stabbed his eyes.

"What?" he asked blinking at the shadowy figures in the door. "Bradley, is that you?"

"I'm Steve Danforth," came the raspy voice. "CIA chief here in Bucharest. I've got some questions for you, Freed. You're on my turf."

Matt waited for the fog to lift in his head, then pulled on his pants and walked stiffly to the table. Danforth stood across from it with a scowl on his red face.

"You've set off a fucking firestorm," he growled. "I hope you know that."

Matt took time to get his bearings. "So?"

"An impending attack against CENTCOM forward headquarters in the Persian Gulf. The threat of an even more devastating attack against targets in the U.S.!"

"That's correct."

"You're my guest here, Freed. I would have liked to have seen your reporting before it went out."

Matt shielded his eyes from the glare off Danforth's shaved head. "I don't see your point."

"Have you ever heard of common courtesy?"

"What are you talking about?" He was about to remind Danforth that NCTS had jurisdiction over the CIA in terrorism cases, but decided to button his shirt instead. That's when he noticed the man and woman standing on either side of the CIA chief like bookends.

The woman shook her head. The Hispanic-looking man to the right of Danforth muttered: "He wouldn't even be here if you didn't give your okay."

Matt felt rage building in his stomach.

"I've got a couple of big ones for you, Freed," Danforth started. "Number one, why didn't you focus on where Kourani is staying here in Bucharest? And why the hell didn't you put us in a position where we could have nailed Kourani and his team tonight?"

Matt's mind was distorted by sleep and anger. He answered: "The only threat he presented here was against me."

"Who gives a shit about you?" Danforth growled. "I'm talking about the potential millions who could die as a result of this."

Matt spoke clearly and sharply this time. "We don't want Kourani to think we're planning to act against him. He's a clever man. He'd pick up the slightest insinuation in a second. If he does, we might never hear from him again."

"You should have at least tried to give us an opportunity to enter his hotel room. Have you ever heard of technical operations?"

"And risk tipping off the Iranians, who might grow suspicious and block Kourani from traveling to New York? Wrong."

"You're supposed to establish control," Danforth shot back. "The walk-in doesn't dictate the tenor of the interview."

"With all due respect, sir," Matt interrupted, "it's a little more complicated."

The woman in the black pantsuit *tsked*. The Hispanic man muttered "unprofessional" under his breath. Matt resisted the urge to tell them both to shut up.

Danforth's face kept turning a deeper and deeper shade of red. "I served in Soviet Division for ten years and conducted dozens of debriefings," he spewed. "Your work here is subpar!"

Matt came right back at him. "The Soviet Union disintegrated more than a decade ago. And terrorist walk-ins are a lot more complicated than Soviet defectors."

"You've got some fucking gall."

"I've heard that before. I've also handled dozens of similar cases successfully."

Danforth turned up the volume. "If I were handling this, I'd have Kourani right here where he belongs! I wouldn't let him leave until he told me what he knows."

"Then you would fail and put tens of thousands of lives at risk."

That stunned Danforth momentarily. "All I know is when you operate on someone else's turf, you've got a responsibility to focus on their equities. It's called common-fucking-sense."

Now the woman chimed in: "If you ever return to Bucharest, we'll expect an entire ops plan up front with every *i* dotted and every *t* crossed."

Matt looked at her as though she'd just passed gas.

"In the morning," Danforth added, "I'm going to have to report to the ambassador. He's going to want to know if you're planning any follow-up meetings with the Iranian at this embassy."

"No."

"Thank God for small favors," the woman groaned.

Danforth took a step closer and asked: "What happens next?"

Matt slowly pushed himself up. "You turn out the lights as you leave, and I try to get more sleep."

"You better hope this Iranian is full of shit."

"I doubt it."

Danforth paused at the door for one more retort. "Then, for christsakes, use your head."

CHAPTER FIVE

September 8–9

Liz was sorting the girls' socks when, five hundred miles northwest in Bucharest, the car her husband rode in braked suddenly and skidded to the right, sending his midsection hard into the console between the seats.

She felt a twinge of pain in her left hand and looked down at her wedding band. *Matt,* she thought. *Are you all right?*

He'd told her he'd be home Thursday at the latest, and it was Thursday morning. Fifteen minutes later when the phone rang, she felt a chill at the base of her spine. Alan Beckman's voice on the other end only heightened her anxiety.

Before he got a word out, Liz said: "Alan, tell me he's okay."

"Matt's fine, Liz."

A knot of worry loosened in her chest. "What time's he arriving?"

"I called, Liz, because something came up. He'll be delayed a couple of days. Maybe as much as a week."

"Oh . . . ," she moaned, disappointed. She knew what that meant: Matt couldn't call himself. He was in some kind of danger.

"Can you tell me where he is?"

"I'm sorry, Liz."

She stopped asking questions, because she knew the drill. *Time to focus on family and repeat the mantra: Matt knows what he's doing. He'll be okay.*

• • •

MATT LAY ON the back floor of the Ford sedan listening to Bradley apologize from the front seat: "Damn Romanians all think they're driving in the grand prix."

At least he wasn't riding in the trunk this time. "Just try to get me there in one piece."

They were on their way to the airport. Word this morning from J.J. was that the Iranians had left Bucharest at 10 PM the previous night. Matt had dyed his hair and beard black and was hiding in back just in case.

As Bradley negotiated the traffic, Matt's mind returned to the Eyes Only message he'd received hours earlier from headquarters. NCTS technicians had compared the passport photo Matt faxed with the picture they had on file and found a match. It had been confirmed that the man he'd met with was indeed Moshen Kourani, the deputy director of Qods Force.

Senior analysts at headquarters noted that it was unusual for a man of Kourani's senior grade to participate in an operation. Nevertheless, they'd approved the allocation of 5 million dollars to pay Kourani and told the embassy in Vienna to approve his visa for entry into the continental United States.

Simultaneously, Matt had received approval from Alan Beckman through General Jasper to retrace Kourani's path through Afghanistan and Uzbekistan.

Why Afghanistan? he wondered, anticipating his first stop. Even though it was a predominantly Sunni country, the Iranians had operated there for years as supporters of the Shia Hazara minority. The Hazaras hailed from the mountainous center of Afghanistan and were direct descendants of Genghis Khan and his Mongolian hordes, who had invaded in the thirteenth century.

I'm fishing. I know I am. Could be Kourani was there on other Qods Force business. If so, I'm wasting my time.

Matt was sweating through his cotton shirt by the time Bradley slowed to a stop.

Bradley said, "I forgot to ask you if you need funds."

"I've got ten thousand on me. Thanks."

At the terminal, he paid with a credit card in the name John Paul Morgan: Turkish Airlines to Istanbul, Emirates Airlines to Dubai, then, after a three-hour layover, Ariana Afghan Airlines to Kabul.

Interesting, he thought, *how the Iranians first ID'd me in Kabul.*

His last visit to Afghanistan had ended in late 2002, roughly a year after the Taliban were driven from power with the help of small teams of CIA and U.S. Army Special Forces supported by U.S. air power. Since then, the Bush administration had let an opportunity to help redevelop the country slip away. The regrouped Taliban had established a stronghold along the southern border with Pakistan, which the United States and NATO were now trying to displace.

Matt felt eyes on him as he leaned over to retie his shoes. Across the waiting area near the entrance of the duty-free shop, he saw two Middle Eastern men in dark suits. His body tensed for a second and then, when he realized he was on the other side of Security, relaxed. If the two were part of the team that had been sent to kill him, there was little they could do now.

Twelve hours later—10 PM local time—he finally deplaned in Kabul. The highlights of his day included fresh baklava in Atatürk International Airport and the serene beauty of the Persian Gulf at twenty-five thousand feet.

A cool breeze off Afghanistan's Shomali Plains welcomed him as he emerged from the terminal and flagged down a cab. "Heetal Plaza Hotel in Wazir Akbar Khan," he told the driver in Farsi, which was close enough to Dari for the driver to understand.

When Matt had left Kabul in late 2002, the city lay in shambles from two decades of war. Judging from what he could make out through the gauzy streetlight, it hadn't changed much—ghostly ruins, piles of rubble and refuse. Uniformed soldiers with AK-47s stood guard at traffic roundabouts. Jersey barriers and sandbags blocked access to some streets.

He woke at 5:45 AM with the memory of Danforth floating through his head. *Stupid second-guesser,* he groused as he left the hotel. *I wonder what Danforth thinks now that the confirmation of Kourani's identity has increased the possibility that the threat is real.*

His Nike-clad feet took him past his favorite Indian restaurant and through the smoky haze that hung over the city—the result of garbage burned in the streets. Past it, shrouded in bilious white clouds, were the timeless peaks of the Hindu Kush. They reminded him that Alexander the Great had visited before him, along with the British Empire, the Soviet Union, and Genghis Khan.

Two hours later, after a breakfast of fresh yogurt, eggs, figs, green tea, and nan, he watched from the backseat of a taxi as shopkeepers lifted the aluminum doors that protected their wares. The morning rush of cars, white SUVs, motorcycles, bikes, and carts pulled by oxen, horses, and people lurched forward past roadside vendors who sold everything from balloons and pomegranates to mobile phones.

Matt paid the serious-looking driver in dollars when they arrived at the Jameh-yi Fatemieh Mosque. The old brick building housed a Shia place of worship used mainly by Hazara tribesmen. It was also gossip central for any information about Iranians passing through Kabul. *The mullah is the best chance I have of finding out why Kourani was here.*

Leaving his shoes on the stairs, Matt climbed to a landing where an old man swept with a handmade broom. "I would like to speak to Sheikh Hadi Zadeh," he said in Farsi. Matt had met the mullah in early 2002 through his son, Tariq.

The old man held up his hand, disappeared around a corner, and returned a minute later with an even older smallish man with flat Mongol features and a sparse gray mustache and beard. He wore *shalwar kameez*—dark pajama pants and a brown tunic down to his knees.

"We haven't seen the sheikh in over a month," the old man groaned.

"And his son, Tariq?"

The old man shrugged so that his round head was nearly swallowed by his shoulders.

"I'm a friend of Sheikh Hadi Zadeh. His son worked as a translator on my team back in 2002."

The old man looked up sideways over wild strands of eyebrow. "A month ago Sheikh Zadeh traveled to Khost on behalf of some Hazaras who had been unjustly arrested by the local authorities," he said with sadness. "They were accused of doing bad business with some Pashtuns. When the sheikh went to see the district commissioner, the two men argued. The district commissioner got so angry that he slapped the sheikh, a mullah. The sheikh's guard raised his rifle and shot the district commissioner on the spot. The local authorities put them both in jail."

"Unfortunate," Matt replied. It wasn't unusual in Afghanistan for a dispute over honor to be settled with guns.

The elderly Hazara nodded. "We went to the U.S. Embassy. We told the Americans that the sheikh had helped them during the war. They said this was an internal Afghan matter and they couldn't interfere. We have sent word to Dr. Karim Khalili, who is one of our vice presidents. But the district commissioner is related to a very powerful Pashtun clan."

"Do you know where Sheikh Zadeh is being held?" Matt asked. "No."

"Was he transported outside of Khost?"

"We don't know that, either. Some people say he's in Pul-e-Charkhi."

Pul-e-Charkhi was the biggest prison in the country, located approximately forty minutes east of Kabul.

"And Tariq?"

"He went looking for his father about a month ago. We haven't seen him since."

Matt was fond of Tariq. The two of them had passed several evenings together in a Kabul safe house back in 2002 listening to the Kaboul Ensemble on the radio and discussing the future of Afghanistan, the global economy, and the films of Angelina Jolie.

•   •   •

APPROACHING THE U.S. Embassy, Matt found the street blocked by a military checkpoint. So he paid the driver in dollars, and dialed his cell phone.

"I'd like to speak to Steve Burris."

"This is him."

"I'm John Paul Morgan. I believe you're expecting me."

"Where are you, Johnny boy?"

"Outside the embassy."

"I expected a heads-up. Your timing sucks."

"I didn't have time to call ahead."

"I'll call the front gate and have them let you in."

Security was tight. First, U.S. marines at the barricade, then more U.S. soldiers at the front gate. Gaining entrance to the modern four-story structure, Matt saw a short, balding man with the build of a weightlifter waiting impatiently at Post One. Beside him stood a younger, taller man with glasses and red hair.

"You Morgan?" asked the human fire hydrant.

"Yes, I am."

"I'm the deputy here," Burris said in a big voice that echoed through the lobby. "I saw your threat reporting out of Bucharest. What'd you want?"

Before Matt had a chance to answer, Burris turned to his red-haired assistant and added: "Let's hope he isn't one of those god-damn terror tourists who keep wasting our time."

Not likely, Matt thought, leaning closer. "Is there somewhere we can talk?"

"I'm up to my ass in alligators. Tell me briefly why you're here."

"There's a certain mullah, a Hazara, who I believe might be able to supply me with details about the walk-in's background and activities."

"You know where this mullah is at the moment?"

"He was arrested in Khost about a month ago during an altercation with the district commissioner."

"So where the fuck is he?"

"That's what I need to find out."

Burris grunted, hands on his hips. "If you think I've got time to look for a friggin' mullah, you're nuts. I'm dealing with attacks all over the country. Over six thousand tons of opium harvested last year alone. I've got a congressional oversight committee descending on me in two days. Don't take it personally, Morgan, if I tell you I've got no time to hold your hand!"

"I'm not asking for your time, Burris. I'm simply telling you why I'm here."

"I leave with the ambassador to Jalalabad in two hours. Why don't you sit and relax until I get back."

"I got a deadline."

The stout man's jaw tightened. Then, turning on his heels, he barked, "Follow me." Up an elevator to the third floor, down a lobby, they entered a warren of offices, stopping at the desk of an army colonel with dark hair.

"Lieutenant Colonel Russo," the human fireplug said, "this man, John Paul Morgan, is a colleague. Needs help finding a prisoner."

The lean lieutenant colonel seemed perplexed. "Sir?"

"Go with him; protect his ass; keep me informed."

Matt sipped black coffee and listened as Lieutenant Colonel Russo worked the phones. Matt's Dari was good enough to ascertain what he'd suspected from the start: the Afghan government bureaucracy was a mess, with records scattered all over the country.

Lieutenant Colonel Russo offered a more detailed explanation: "The prisons used to be under the Interior Ministry. Then they were shifted to Justice. No one wants responsibility for them. They've got tens of thousands of common prisoners tossed in with members of the Taliban and al-Qaeda. Sounds like a fertile recruiting ground, don't you think?"

Matt didn't have time to consider that now. "Can you get me into Pul-e-Charkhi?" he asked.

Russo made a face. "Foulest goddamn place I've ever been in my life."

"Can you get me inside?"

"Ikbal Bakshi, the warden, is a friend. Two months ago the attaché's office donated soccer balls and uniforms for his club's team."

"I'm in a hurry. Let's go."

An hour later, with loaded Glocks stashed in their belts, Matt and Lieutenant Colonel Russo rode in a jeep that bounced around a wading pool–sized pothole. Russo, at the wheel, hung a right through a huge field strewn with refuse. "Rumor has it that thousands of prisoners are buried here," he said.

"Nice place to end up."

A long, crumbling yellowish structure peeked through the mist. It featured a circular watchtower that looked as if it had been borrowed from a '40s-era Soviet airport. Pul-e-Charkhi prison had been the scene of recent riots and prison breaks. Somewhere in this vast structure lived terrorists from the Philippines, Chechnya, Pakistan, Yemen, and Russia, along with several American soldiers of fortune convicted of torture.

As they approached, Matt wondered: *Am I wasting my time? Is there anyone else I know in Kabul who might have had contact with Kourani?* The answer: unlikely.

They parked the Cherokee outside the huge cast-iron gate and waded through a succession of Tajik guards, all armed with AK-47s. A man with a short black beard and hazel eyes waved them in.

Water and sewage dripped from the ceiling of the long, dark corridor. Russo held his nose all the way to the warden's office on the second floor.

The chief wasn't in, but an aide by the name of Samad was. He led them through more fetid corridors to a cell packed with angry Taliban prisoners.

"Sheikh Zadeh is a Hazara," Matt said. "This can't be the right place."

But Samad wouldn't be deterred.

Seeing Matt's Western features and GORE-TEX vest, the Taliban prisoners started spitting through the bars. "We're going to kill you! We hate all Americans!"

Armed guards used long metal poles to beat their way through the screaming men. Minutes later they emerged from the darkness holding an old man with a long snow-white beard that fell to his chest.

"Sheikh Zadeh!" Samad declared.

"No, Samad, this is the wrong man."

"You said Sheikh Zadeh. Are you not Sheikh Zadeh?"

The white-haired man nodded.

"There must be another Sheikh Zadeh," Matt said. "Because the one I'm looking for is a Hazara."

The prisoners shouted more insults. Samad topped them with a loud "*Hmph!*" delivered with the shaking of his finger in Matt's face: "This is the only Sheikh Zadeh. There is no other, sir. The man you're looking for doesn't exist."

He spoke proudly of upcoming renovations and pending reforms as he escorted them downstairs through a courtyard where women gathered around fire pits cooking rice, lentils, and scraps of meat. Some had children by their sides.

"You have children living here?" Matt asked.

"Some are born here," Samad answered. "Some choose to be with their mothers."

It was cold for early September. Matt watched his breath turn into a stiff white mist as he scolded himself for wasting time on a rumor that seemed to lead nowhere. Among the motley mix of faces in the courtyard (Tajiks, Hazaras, Pashtuns, Arabs), he spotted a familiar one with broad Mongol features. He craned his neck for a better look. "Tariq!"

The short, solidly built young man lifted his head and shouted, "Agha Matt, khali vaght-i-nadidametun." (Mr. Matt, so much time since I have seen you.)

The two men hugged and kissed.

"It's so good to see you," Matt exclaimed in English.

"Since I last saw you, God has given me a wife and two children. He rewards and punishes with the same hand."

"How come they're holding you here?"

The young man glanced quickly at Samad, then down at the ground. "I came looking for my father. Because I'm Hazara, I was treated badly by some of the guards. I fought back."

"He insulted prison authorities," Samad added in Dari.

"I want this man released immediately," Matt ordered, reaching into his pocket.

"There are proper legal channels!"

The American counted out ten new hundred-dollar bills. "Send the paperwork to my colleague here, Lieutenant Colonel Russo at the American Embassy."

The money quickly disappeared into Samad's pocket. "As you wish."

MATT SHOWED TARIQ a picture of Kourani when they met two hours later at his hotel. "You ever see this man around the mosque?"

Tariq nodded. "Several months ago, maybe. He was with another man. Another Iranian. They talked to my father."

"Did your father tell you what they wanted?"

"I think they were looking for someone."

"Who?"

"I don't know."

"Think, Tariq."

"My father doesn't tell me everything."

Matt returned the photo to his pocket. "Where's your father now?"

Tariq's eyes brightened. "My sources tell me he's still being held at the prison in Khost."

Khost was in one of the more dangerous area of the country, the site of continual raids by the Taliban from the border of Pakistan.

Matt thought for a second: *I might be able to wrangle a helicopter ride down, but getting permission to fly back with a mullah could take a while. And I can't afford to wait.*

He turned to Tariq. "If I arrange a ride on a helicopter down, can you organize a convoy to get us out?"

"The roads are full of Taliban," the young Afghan answered.

"We'll need armed men."

An hour and a half later, Matt was back in Lieutenant Colonel Russo's office trying to hitch a ride on a resupply copter when

Burris walked in. The human fireplug, who had just returned from Jalalabad, was in a foul mood.

"What does he want now?" Burris growled at Russo.

The lean lieutenant colonel seemed amused. "A bird to take him to Khost."

Burris looked at Matt like he was crazy. "Not gonna happen."

"I have an Afghan traveling with me who may be able to—"

Burris cut him off: "What's his name?"

"He's the son of a mullah."

"What the fuck do you need him for?"

"So he can help me find his father."

"For what?"

Matt didn't like being bullied. "This is my case. I know what I'm doing."

They were nose-to-nose now. The stout man cut into Matt with razor-sharp eyes. "Just stay on the fucking reservation," he said wearily. "This whole place is going to shit."

"I don't need advice from you," Matt added.

"Nothing crazy. You got it?"

"Take a couple of Midols and get off your feet."

The fireplug almost grinned. He grabbed the redheaded aide, who stuck his head in. "Tim, get Rambo here a satellite phone, long gun, Glock, vest, whatever other gear he needs. Make sure he signs a receipt."

"Yes, sir," Tim replied. "The ambassador wants to see you in his office."

"I'll be right there." Burris turned back to Matt: "Contact me as soon as you get to Khost, whatever time, day or night. I don't sleep. I can't guarantee a lift out immediately, and don't break my chops with twenty fucking calls a day. You might get stuck down there a week. And don't lose my goddamn satellite phone. Understand?"

There was a touch of hostility in everything he said. But Matt didn't care. "I read you loud and clear."

"Have fun."

Back at his hotel, Matt slammed a magazine into the Glock and tested the satellite phone that Tim had given him, lifting the cover to twenty degrees to serve as an antenna. Inside the backpack he found a second battery, two more 9mm magazines for the pistol, and a couple of maps.

After a dinner of lamb kebab and couscous, Tariq called. "I have three cars with nine Hazara men," he reported. "One of them speaks Pushtu. But the drive takes sixteen hours."

Matt could only imagine the roads. "Have them leave tonight," he instructed. "I want them there ready to take us out."

"Yes."

"We'll meet here at six tomorrow morning," Matt said. "The flight takes about an hour and a half."

"Have you secured my father's release?" the young man asked.

"I'm working on it."

THE MOMENT MAGGIE and her sisters alighted from the green school bus, Liz saw that her oldest daughter wasn't her bubbly, confident self. "What's wrong?" she asked.

"My stomach hurts," the eight-year-old complained.

Liz decided it was probably the sweets the kids traded at school. "How many times have I told you to eat your lunch before you have dessert?"

"It's not that."

Three hours later, when Liz put pasta and meatballs on the table, Maggie threw up. "Crawl in bed, honey. I'll clean this up."

She sat the other two in front of *101 Dalmatians*, then went to Maggie's room to take her temperature. A hundred and one. *Great time to catch the flu*, she thought.

"It hurts all over," Maggie groaned, holding her stomach.

Liz watched her swallow Pepto-Bismol and children's aspirin, then said, "Try to get some sleep."

Twenty minutes later, when Liz checked in again, Maggie pinpointed a sharp pain between her right hip and belly button.

Liz hugged her. "Don't worry, honey. It's going to be okay."

Back in the living room, she called Sally Keaton, the embassy nurse, left a message on her cell phone, then dialed the Beckmans.

Alan answered.

"Alan, it's Liz. Is Celia there?"

"Sure. Just a sec."

Alan's wife was a quiet, bookish woman with short gray hair. She understood the situation right away.

"You've called Sally?" Celia asked.

"She's not picking up her cell."

"I'll be there in ten minutes to watch Samantha and Nadia while you take Maggie to the hospital. You want Alan to drive?"

"I can manage that. Thanks."

Maggie's face had a strange green tint; she couldn't stand. So Liz and Celia carried her to the backseat of the Corolla, where they laid her down.

"Stay the night if you need to," Celia said. "I'll take the girls to school."

They hugged like sisters. The Mellision General Hospital was only twelve minutes away.

The clerk behind the counter looked up from his book. "The doctor will be here in a few minutes," he said in Greek. "Take a seat."

Liz had worked a part-time job at University of Virginia Medical Center when she was in college. She'd seen the horrors of the ER firsthand.

Amid the bright lights, she screamed in English: "My daughter needs a doctor!" She didn't care that people looked at her like she was crazy. She ran down the corridor and grabbed the first nurse she could find.

The Greek doctor with the large bristly black mustache calmly took Maggie's temperature, then pressed his fingers into her stomach.

The young girl cried out in pain. "Mom!"

Pulling Liz into the hallway, the doctor spoke in perfect English: "It appears your daughter has appendicitis. You were very wise to bring her in."

With her rising blood pressure turning her skin hot, she remembered Matt and wished he were there. Nurses scurried around Maggie, removing her clothes, taking blood, swabbing her stomach with iodine.

Maggie started to cry. "Are they going to hurt me, Mommy? Am I going to die?"

Summoning all her courage, Liz looked her daughter straight in the eye. "You'll be fine, sweetheart. I promise. I won't leave your side."

CHAPTER SIX

September 10

Even though he was exhausted from a long day of travel, Matt kept waking up every forty minutes to check the clock. At 4 AM he showered, dressed, and went down to the lobby, where he asked the clerk at the front desk for a pot of tea.

Matt didn't spend much time on introspection. But that didn't mean he couldn't appreciate subtleties of beauty, color, sound, and art. He was sitting in a leather armchair admiring the colorful paintings and South Asian décor when he dozed off.

The next thing that floated into his consciousness was an awareness of sitting with Liz and his dad in the backseat of a cab that negotiated the streets of DC. His father issued a steady stream of complaints about Matt—his sloppy thinking, his lack of discipline, his inability to complete a job to his dad's satisfaction. When Liz called Matt's father "a bully," the old man ordered the driver to stop.

Matt watched silently as his father walked away with a cane.

"You should have said something," Liz groaned.

My dad uses negativity as a crutch, Matt thought. *It helps him explain his own failures.*

His silence was hard to justify, complicated by feelings of love, frustration, and rage. Early on, he'd made a subconscious decision to push past doubts about himself or explanations.

Was this a reaction to his father?

Yes, in the sense that he'd oriented himself toward action. No, because Matt had adapted his dad's bullheadedness into a blind dedication of his own.

But doubts lingered. Doubts planted by his dad. Woven tighter by his mother, who said the two were "like two sides of a rough coin."

Matt believed he was a force for good. He viewed his life in the context of a simple proposition: individuals require a political order that allows their dreams and ambitions to breathe life into the greater whole. His job was to protect that order from those who wanted to create chaos as a means for acquiring power for themselves.

It was this clarity that allowed him to do his job. And to some extent it was his rage at his parents that propelled him forward.

Matt remembered that his father had wanted to be a navy pilot and failed. "A bum eye" had eliminated him. "All because that little Cowans kid blindsided me with a stick when I was fighting his older brother," his father explained. "That's all it took."

That's when the clerk with the bushy black hair arrived with a tray of tea.

One last phrase echoed from his father: "One stupid thing like that, and you're sunk."

More negative crap. I've got to keep moving. Can't let it slow me down.

"Sir, do you want it here or in your room?" the clerk asked.

Matt quickly checked his watch: 5:15. *Does it make sense for me to travel all the way to Khost? Would I be considering going there if Hadi Zadeh wasn't Tariq's father? Maybe I should check with Alan. Screw that. One father was enough.*

He looked up at the clerk and said, "I'll take it here. Thanks."

A THOUSAND MILES east in Athens, Liz stood outside the lime green recovery room of Mellision General Hospital listening to the Greek doctor. "Invasive bacteria penetrated the wall of the appendix. . . . The tiny tubelike organ has been removed. . . . There's danger of infection. . . . Your daughter is resting now. She's on antibiotics."

Liz's mind had been shredded by sleeplessness and worry. "Please tell me Maggie's all right," she said bluntly.

"Yes," Dr. Angelopolous answered. "She's asleep. I'll ask the nurse to prepare a bed for you in a nearby room."

"Thank you . . ." She couldn't get the rest of the words out before her eyes teared up and a tremendous knot of fear, relief, and rage burst and spilled forth. "Ohhh," she moaned. "Oh, doctor. I'm sorry. I'm . . . I'm angry, I think. Angry at my husband."

"You need to rest."

She started to ramble. "If he were here, if I could see his face, everything would be clear. Because I read his thoughts, if that makes sense. And knowing what he's thinking makes me feel better."

"The greatest danger has passed," the doctor purred, squeezing her arm.

"Yes." Wiping her tears, she remembered Maggie's pained face. "He doesn't even know."

The doctor had other things to attend to.

"What has to happen before he pays attention?"

He patted her on the elbow. "You'll have to excuse me."

She felt cold standing there in the naked fluorescent light, fighting against the feeling of abandonment, reminding herself that Matt was serving his country in an important way. But even that seemed trivial at a time like this.

Determined to derail that train of thought, she fished a cell phone out of her purse and called Celia, who reported that Samantha and Nadia were finishing breakfast and would soon be off to school.

"Hi, Mommy," Nadia's three-year-old voice bubbled. "How's Maggie's tummy?"

"Much, much better."

"Mrs. Beckman gave us Frosted Flakes."

Liz felt something clutch in her chest and experienced a moment of panic, which passed. Life was precious; it could end any second. The girls and Matt were her world.

"I can't tell you how much I appreciate your help," she told Celia when the older woman got back on the line.

"I'll stay as long as you need me," Celia replied.

"Can you ask your husband to tell Matt? Please tell him I love him, and that Maggie's okay now."

"Of course."

A COOL WIND pulled at their hair and clothes as Matt and Tariq helped the U.S. soldiers carry boxes of gear, ammunition, MREs, and water into the back of the CH-47D Chinook.

It's a risk I have to take, Tariq thought, *for a chance to see my father.*

The young Hazara was spiritually exhausted from the endless internecine fighting. Warlord against warlord, ethnic group against ethnic group, each trying to gain an advantage so they could put the others down.

Americans were now targets of the largely Pushtun Taliban, because the Americans had committed themselves to trying to establish a political order that amalgamated the interests of the various tribes. The Taliban, with the help of their fundamentalist Islamic allies in Pakistan, were waging a guerrilla war.

Some of Tariq's friends called the Americans "children" and "naïve." He wondered how long it would take for them to lose patience with his country and leave.

"You guys are OGA, right?" one of the soldiers asked Tariq and Matt as they lifted the last boxes from the truck.

Matt nodded. OGA stood for "other government agency," or civilian intelligence.

"Strap on your six-shooter," the soldier shouted. "And when you hear dogs bark, duck."

Tariq aped Matt as he buckled into the seats along the fuselage as the dual engines fired up. The Afghan clutched an AK-47 with a folding stock between his knees; Matt braced a sleek new M4. The big green bird lifted off the ground, then lurched forward over a *wadi* (a dry riverbed).

"Here we go!"

Tariq would have preferred a day of reading Rumi poetry under the shade of a pomegranate tree.

The painful noise ended when a copilot tossed them a couple of packs of earplugs and Tariq stuck his in. Glimpsing mud-colored Kabul out the back door, he sighed.

The city had once been a lush oasis of gardens and tree-covered hillsides. A frown cut deep into the Afghan's face.

"What's wrong?" Matt asked.

"No more trees!" Tariq shouted over the racket.

"Why?"

"The Russians cut the trees. The Afghans burned the trees for fuel. The Taliban burned them because they didn't believe in the beautification of Kabul."

Matt nodded. "We'll plant some more!"

A THOUSAND MILES west, a sleek white Iran Air DC-10 touched down on the north-south runway of Tehran's Mehrabad International Airport. Carefully eyeballing the passengers as they entered the terminal were two men in dark gray suits with Iran Air Security badges pinned on their lapels. Recognizing a weary Moshen Kourani and his four associates, they stepped forward and introduced themselves.

"Welcome home, Agha Kourani."

"It's good to be back on sacred ground."

As the men from Security led the way through customs and immigration, Kourani took out his cell and made a call.

"Ali, it's Kourani. God willing, we'll get the next one."

"What went wrong?"

"I think maybe they saw my men. Some of them weren't so discrete."

"The general is more concerned about this matter in Iraq."

"Tell him it's under control. My officer will see the source in two days. We should know everything then."

"He has immediate concerns."

"Tomorrow I'll answer everything."

"I'm sorry. He wants to see you now."

A black 500-series Mercedes stood waiting at the curb. Within minutes it was whisking him to IRGC headquarters for a meeting with Major General Yahya Rahim Safavi.

Kourani sat on the tan leather seat fingering jade prayer beads and repeating "Subhan Allah" and "Alhamdulillah" thirty-three times each.

Past the first ridge, Matt looked out over miles and miles of more mountains and inhospitable terrain and tried to imagine what was going on in Kourani's head.

He played with two suppositions. In the first, the Iranian was telling the truth. Matt constructed a man exhausted by the religious rigidity of the mullahs headquartered in Qum. This version of Kourani genuinely feared a Shia-Sunni war and cared for his people and, especially, his family. He believed a better, more secure future awaited them in the United States.

The second Kourani was a religious zealot acting as a wily operator trying to outwit the Great Satan, hoping that one day Iran would dominate the Persian Gulf and spread its influence across the globe.

Sheikh Zadeh will help fill in the blanks, he hoped.

After two hours, the CH-47D started to descend into torrents of dust thrown up by the tandem rotors. A line of twenty soldiers filed past as they stepped out the back. Immediately both Matt and Tariq were blinded with sand. The American grabbed the Hazara by his jacket and pulled him toward a Humvee parked seventy yards away.

Tight curls of dust swirled over rugged, hard, grayish brown terrain. They could have been on the moon.

"Welcome to Forward Operating Base Salerno," announced a female sergeant who appeared from behind the truck in combat uniform and goggles. "You must be Mr. Morgan."

"Correct."

She was almost six feet tall with a strong jaw and auburn hair pulled under a Kevlar helmet. Matt could read her blood type (A) on a thin plastic band that stretched around the bottom.

"This gentleman is Tariq, my translator."

"Good to meet you, Tariq. I'm Sergeant Flynn from Beaver, Oklahoma. Home of the nastiest dust storms in America. That's why this little fuss the chopper is kicking up doesn't bother me a bit."

Tariq smiled. He didn't have a clue what she was talking about.

"You ever see the inside of a tornado, Tariq? You ever been sucked up and taken to the wizard of Oz?"

"Oz?"

Behind them the helicopter took off with a roar and banked over the first fold of mountains. "Hear you're a couple of crazy dudes," the sergeant shouted at Matt.

"What?"

"We've had several TICs around the area of the prison. Reports of enemy in the vicinity now."

"TICs?"

"Troops in contact. You want a cup of hot java before we depart?"

Under normal circumstances Matt would have spent a few minutes trading barbs with her, but not now. "We'd better proceed right away."

She pointed to a patch on her shoulder. "I'm from Civil Affairs. We'll wait for our escort."

Matt didn't want to attract attention. "Why take two vehicles when one will do fine?"

"General order number one: Don't move anywhere without two vehicles, long guns, communications."

They'd just finished loading their gear when a Humvee pulled up with an African American corporal named Randal behind the wheel, one soldier manning the 50-caliber machine gun in the turret, and three others below. Flynn did a radio check; then both vehicles took off past a series of mud houses, hole-in-the-wall-type shops, hills, patches of woods.

"This is town," Sergeant Flynn said as she braked for a large Jinga truck that was trying to turn around. The brightly painted truck backed into a commercial lot, then screamed off in first gear, leaving behind a trail of black smoke.

"You been to this prison before?" Matt shouted over the engine.

"Ten days ago. First time. Met the new prison commander. Khurram. Speaks a little English."

Matt took that as a good sign. "What's the general layout?" he asked.

She held up three fingers. "Building One houses administration. Two is for prisoners. Three is the armory."

Five minutes later she slowed to a stop on a graded strip of land in front of a walled compound crowned with razor wire. Tariq jumped out and ran to the other side of the lot, where nine Afghan men lounged around three parked SUVs.

"Who are they?" Flynn asked.

"My men, Hazaras," Matt answered. "They drove all night."

"Tell 'em to stay alert. Them hills back there are filled with Taliban caves."

An AH-64 Apache helicopter flew past on its way to reload with missiles. Tariq conferred with the guards at the gate, then returned. "They won't let us bring our weapons into the prison," he said.

Matt, Sergeant Flynn, and Tariq shed their guns and ammo, then started for the gate. Corporal Randal and the U.S. Army escort waited with the Hazaras.

Flynn led the way down a concrete hallway and into a small office.

"Where's Khurram?" she asked the nervous-looking male receptionist.

"Prayer."

"When do you expect him back?"

"Five minutes," he answered, pointing to his Soviet-style watch.

An old poster for the movie *Grease* clung to the wall. Sergeant Flynn stood before it, hands on her hips. "What do you make of that, Morgan?" she asked.

"Decent movie; liked the stage show better."

"Whatever happened to Olivia Newton-John?"

"*Xanadu*," Matt answered.

She was about to say "Right" when a loud thud shook the building. She uttered "What the fuck" instead.

It was barely out of her mouth when the walls shuddered again from what sounded like a strong explosion inside the building. The crack of automatic gunfire followed.

"The Taliban," Matt said.

"Or a riot."

The male receptionist crawled under his desk.

"Now what?" Sergeant Flynn asked.

Matt grabbed her by the arm. "Let's go back to the vehicles and get our weapons."

They passed a lone guard at the gate, and another three crouched at the far corner of the compound firing old M1 carbines.

"They're attacking from the far side!" Tariq yelled, pointing at the rocky hills beyond the walls. An explosion rocked the corner of the wall where the guards were firing and threw Flynn to the ground.

Matt helped her up. She said: "Mules kick harder than that!"

Grabbing their weapons, Matt, Corporal Randal, and the other Americans took positions behind a burned-out vehicle that stood near the far wall. The Hazaras hated the Taliban and were already on their bellies returning fire.

Flynn crouched fifty feet behind them near the Humvee, calling the forward base. "Salerno One-Four, this is Flynn. We're at the prison. Looks like a sizable attack."

Training her binoculars on the hills, she spotted flashes from the muzzles of at least a dozen different weapons. Men in dark Punjabi clothing and black turbans ran toward a small hole that had been blasted in the wall.

"We've taken up position at the northwest with nine armed locals. We're not at immediate risk."

"Stay in place," the voice on the radio squawked back. "QRF [quick reaction force] en route."

I've got to get the mullah out of there before he's killed, Matt thought as several more rocket-propelled grenade rounds (RPGs) pounded the compound wall.

Behind his position near the burned-out truck, Corporal Randal took out two Taliban with his specially outfitted M4. Nearby, Tariq spoke excitedly with a young Hazara with a big smile and very thin beard who pointed to the hills and gestured wildly.

"What's he want?" Matt asked.

"To climb around above them."

Before Matt had a chance to offer an opinion, the young Hazara let out a shout and he and his comrades scurried up into the hills, looking for cover.

"Let's go," Tariq shouted running inside the prison. Matt followed with his M4 ready, hard on the heels of Tariq, who stopped at each corner. Security personnel inside had taken up positions and were returning fire.

Down the first corridor, back to reception. The room looked empty and was quiet except for the *clack clack clack* of gunfire that echoed off its walls. They heard screams coming from farther inside.

"Check this out."

Matt pointed to two Afghans cowering in the warden's office. One of them was the rail-thin receptionist they'd met before.

"We need access to the prisoners," Matt said to him in Farsi.

The other Afghan produced a large key, which he used to open a steel door that led to a large courtyard. Pandemonium greeted them on the other side—panic, cordite, and dust. Guards rushed by to reinforce the west wall. Others pushed past, hoping to find refuge outside.

Matt grabbed one of the retreating men and shouted: "Who's in charge?"

As he opened his mouth to answer, an explosion rocked the courtyard, causing the ground they were standing on to bounce like a trampoline. Matt lost his footing when a hot piece of shrapnel pinged off the metal door and skimmed his forehead.

"Fuck!"

With his ears ringing, he got to his feet. Someone shouted in Dari, "Escape! Escape!" His face was obscured by dust.

Matt and Tariq ran with their heads low, diagonally across the

courtyard. Entering a dark corridor on the other side, they were hit
by a thick smell. Eyes glared at them from left and right. Hundreds
of men packed twenty or thirty to a cell rushed forward and thrust
their arms through the bars, screaming to be released.

Tariq leaned on Matt for support as rage and desperation rever-
berated off the walls. "Friendly or Taliban?" Matt shouted.

Just then two wild-eyed guards backed around a corner and
crashed into him. One of them pointed a pistol at Matt's head.

"He's an American!" Tariq screamed at the top of his lungs.
"Don't shoot!"

A guard with silver teeth smiled and patted Matt on the shoulder.
"My bro-ther. My bro-ther. Kan-sas City." Seconds later a mortar
hit the roof with a terrible shattering of metal and concrete.

The corridor quickly filled with dust as prisoners on both sides
pleaded for help from Allah. Matt wiped away a thick clot of bloody
mud that obstructed his nostrils. "Where's the Hazara mullah?" he
asked one of the guards.

The silver-toothed man led the way toward a hallway that angled
sharply to the right.

"Here!" the guard shouted. "Over here!"

The strange sight took a minute to register: three men seated
calmly on the floor of their dark cell praying amid the violence and
panic. Seeing his son, Tariq's father put down his beads and walked
to the bars. Father and son grasped hands.

"Open the cell," Matt ordered the guard.

He mumbled something about having to go get a key.

Matt barked: "*Zud bash!*"

IN HOT, sticky Athens, Alan Beckman adjusted the vents on the
window air conditioner while he waited for the nurse to bring Liz
to the phone. That's when his Lebanese American aide Bashir
rushed in with an urgent message from General Jasper.

"What's she want?"

"Something about returning to headquarters."

Last thing Beckman wanted to do today was fly to Washington. "Ask her to hold on."

Alan called it "circling the wagons"—the tendency of headquarters to call senior officers together whenever there was a crisis. He was ready to argue strenuously that he was needed in the field supporting officers and sources who were trying to validate the Kourani warning and identify the threat.

A very sleepy-sounding woman came on the line. "Liz, is that you?"

It was the Greek nurse telling him that Mrs. Freed was still resting.

Alan said, "Please tell Mrs. Freed I called."

General Jasper came across clear and in command. She wanted Alan on the next flight back to Washington and was ready to dispatch a plane to Kabul to fetch Matt Freed, too.

"He's not in Kabul," Beckman said.

"Is he with you?"

"No, he went into eastern Afghanistan looking for a Shia mullah who he thinks made contact with Kourani."

"For what purpose?"

"He doesn't know yet."

"I hope he's not going to cause problems for Kourani. Last thing we want to do is tip off the Iranians."

"Freed's a professional. He understands the stakes."

"Alan, we need to conduct a soup-to-nuts threat assessment. The White House wants all contingencies covered. It would be advantageous to have Freed here."

"Yes, General, but—"

"Tell him this takes precedence. If he can spare a day and a half, we'll whisk him right back."

"I don't know if I agree."

"I rely on your judgment, Alan. To paraphrase one of my heroes, General George S. Patton: If everybody is thinking alike, somebody isn't thinking."

"I appreciate that, General."

Alan Beckman did try Matt's satellite phone several times—twice from the office, once from home as he packed his bag. Matt didn't answer. So Alan kissed Celia good-bye and headed for the airport. "I hope to be back tomorrow," he told her.

"Godspeed."

CHAPTER SEVEN

September 10–12

Matt inched forward along the concrete wall with Tariq, Mullah Hadi Zadeh (Tariq's father), and the guard on his heels. Reverberating in their ears were the sounds of chaos: explosions, gunfire, screams, guards running for cover, prisoners denouncing America, and others begging for mercy.

Nice of the Taliban to attack now, he thought. *Is it a coincidence, or did someone in the prison tell them they had a chance to kill some Americans?*

M4 ready, Matt peeked around the corner to view the courtyard. What he saw wasn't good. Black-turbaned men with long beards, Kalashnikovs, and RPGs had taken up positions behind trees and overturned barrels and appeared to be in control. A half dozen gathered around an archway that led to a smaller building at the opposite end.

Matt pulled the trembling guard closer. "What's that?" he asked in Dari.

"The armory."

A volley of bullets tore at the concrete around them, sending up a cloud of dust. The guard started to run. Matt grabbed him by the tunic. "I'll protect you if you show us the way out!"

The guard led them through a maze of hallways. He used a big key to open a metal door that led to the kitchen. They discovered seven men cowering in a pantry.

"We won't hurt you," Matt told them in Dari. "Help us get out."

An older man with one eye pointed to a rusty door behind a pile of crates. But it was locked and no one had the key.

Matt ripped the crates away and tried to kick open the door. It wouldn't budge.

"We'd better get out of here," Tariq warned. "We could be trapped."

OUTSIDE, SERGEANT FLYNN had set up a command post on the west side of the parking lot behind the Humvee. "The Taliban have control of the prison. I need the QRF!" she shouted into the radio.

Most of the fighting was taking place to her right in the hills above the prison. The Hazaras had taken up position behind a large outcropping of rock that looked like the head of a bull. From their vantage they had a clear view through the hole in the wall the Taliban had blasted and into a piece of the courtyard. With carefully placed shots, they picked off five of the enemy.

It was personal for them. As Shias, they were avenging terrible abuse directed at them during the Sunni Taliban regime, including massacres in Bamiyan and Mazar-e Sharif.

"No, sir, I can't account for the civilian who entered the prison, sir," Sergeant Flynn explained over the radio to a major back at Forward Base Salerno. "Nor do I think it's prudent to send my men in after him."

The major agreed. "If he's toasted, it's his own damn fault."

Flynn's heart jumped at the first barrage from the 50-caliber machine gun. Turning, she spotted six Humvees speeding toward her, guns wailing. Each carried a crew of three and six additional grunts.

Within seconds, a first lieutenant covered in camouflage was in her face.

"We have a group of friendlies at two o'clock flanking the enemy," Flynn explained, pointing to the hills.

"Who the fuck are they? Where?"

"Hazaras," she said handing him a pair of binoculars and directing him to the bull's-head rock.

"What the hell's that?"

THE HALF-DOZEN Taliban Matt spotted outside the armory used an RPG to blow the steel door off its hinges, leaving five feet of rubble on each side. They planned to kill the guards, free the prisoners, and loot the armory. But with the roar of the 50-caliber machine guns closing in, their leader directed his men to lay C-4 explosives among the mortars, ammo, and RPGs piled in the armory.

Three men with long black beards worked quickly, using a non-electrical fuse with detcord and blasting caps. They grabbed an armful of RPGs each, then lit the fuse and fled.

MATT WAS STANDING in the kitchen, trying to pry the outside door open with a crowbar, when the blast went off. It lifted him off his feet and threw him against some wooden shelves. His ears ringing, his face numb, he got to his feet and went at the door with added fervor. With more secondary explosions reverberating behind him and dust filling his throat, he finally got the damn thing open.

"Hump! Hump! Let's go!"

He helped the mullah to his feet, then found Tariq, dazed, walking in circles, coughing blood. They squeezed through, past two terrified goats tied to a post. Flames shooting up from the roof, debris flying everywhere, they ran.

"Cover your heads!"

Into the fresh air, they moved along the east wall to the entrance that Matt and Tariq had used before. Out the front gate, Matt directed them toward the Humvee, where Corporal Randal shouted: "The uglies are escaping at the other end. I'll cover this side of the wall with the Hazaras. Get the friggin' 50-calibers over there!!!"

Helmeted Americans in full battle gear ran past, firing M4s. Matt slumped against the vehicle, wet with sweat and blood that ran down the side of his head and soaked his shirt. Secondary explosions rocked the prison, followed by shouts that echoed through the hills.

He wished the machine guns would stop roaring in his head. Then he became aware of Tariq hunched on the ground next to him, hyperventilating. Blood oozed from a wound in his shoulder. His father, the mullah, crouched beside him and spoke softly in his ear.

The buzz in his ears made it impossible for Matt to hear what the mullah was saying. But he marveled at the transformation in Tariq's face.

"Nice work."

"What?" Matt asked into the sun.

Sergeant Flynn cast a shadow over him. She pointed at the prison behind her. "I said: Nice work."

"Anytime."

She coughed and spat on the ground. "My CO is gonna put my ass in chains. He also wants to know if you knew the attack was going to take place before you arrived."

Matt half-laughed. "Tell him I left my crystal ball in Kabul."

"I bet half the damn prisoners are dead. On the positive side, we're hammering the bejesus out of the enemy. So far, we've counted twenty-one Taliban dead."

Matt gasped for breath and felt throbbing pain on the right side of his chest. Grabbing his pack, he walked to the east side of the lot, found a boulder, and used a compass to find the southern sky. Removing the satellite phone, he pointed the cover south. He waited until the little screen indicated that he'd reached a satellite; then he dialed a number.

"Burris," he said. "This is Morgan. Take down this report."

HALFWAY ACROSS THE globe, Alan Beckman watched as gray hangars and rows of military aircraft whizzed by. The Gulfstream V he sat in had just touched down at Andrews Air Force Base outside of Washington. As they taxied, he reviewed the report he would soon be delivering to his boss.

First, he'd tell General Jasper how he'd dispatched his people to check their sources across the Middle East. Their mission: to uncover any lead that might confirm or shed light on the al-Qaeda attack forecast by Kourani. He would emphasize that the chance of his people coming up with anything meaningful was slim. Al-Qaeda was extremely secretive, fragmented into cells. None of NCTS's sources went deep.

Second, he'd tell her that the Qataris had been thoroughly briefed about the impending attack on Camp Snoopy in Doha. Surveillance on the JAFA Trading Company had been established. He and his lieutenants had drawn up a plan to take down the terrorists the night of September 16.

A young NCTS officer greeted Beckman on the tarmac and led him to a black Ford sedan. As soon as Alan settled into the backseat, the young officer handed him a manila envelope. "For you, sir."

It was an Eyes Only report from Burris in Kabul implying that Matt's presence at the prison in Khost had provoked a Taliban attack, which resulted in the destruction of the prison and at least a hundred casualties.

"Holy shit!"

TWENTY MILES NORTHEAST, the tall general with strawberry blond hair reread the same report, took a deep breath, then looked up at her executive aide, Shelly Mauser—a woman with short, spiky black hair and an aggressive manner. "Where's Freed now?"

"Still in Khost as far as we can tell. Suffered some minor injuries. Burris expects him back in Kabul within the next two days."

For the last three days General Jasper had been running nonstop. Teleconferences with the State Department, CIA, Homeland Security, and Defense Department, even a briefing of the president in the Oval Office. The morning had started with a long examination of Kourani, including his background and probable motives.

Jasper and her advisers had learned: (1) The CIA had been able to confirm that Kourani was deputy director of the Qods Force. (2) The unsettled state of internal Iranian government politics at the present time heightened the believability of Kourani's offer. (3) Reports from Qatar indicated that Kourani's warning about a pending attack on Doha International Air Base were accurate.

Next on her agenda was a meeting with Homeland Security about defensive measures that needed to be taken in a dozen mid-sized U.S. cities against a possible terrorist attack.

Ever since the report from Afghanistan had arrived this morning, her top aides (including Shelly) had been urging her to call Freed home.

"It's clear that Kourani is walking a tightrope internally," Shelly explained. "Freed poses a risk."

"Maybe it's a risk we need to take."

"Say he does something that raises suspicion within the Iranian government and Kourani gets cold feet. If Kourani doesn't reappear and we're unable to close the loop on the threat, the White House will be apoplectic. Three thousand American casualties were unacceptable on 9/11. Imagine millions now."

Shelly had a way of hammering the obvious that made General Jasper's hair stand on end. "Let's try to think creatively."

"It's possible we'll know more when we hit the terrorists in Qatar," Shelly continued. "That's on the sixteenth."

The general looked at the September calendar, which had been hastily taped to the wall. Today was September 10. Eid al-Fitr began at sundown the eighteenth. September 6, 7, 8, and 9 had already been crossed out with red pen. "We have eight days," she said before another aide interrupted them.

"It's Dr. Stalworth."

Another task to check off her list. She reached for the receiver and simultaneously located an e-mail on her desk. "Doctor," she said, "we've got an eight-year-old dependent daughter at Odysseus base who just had an emergency appendectomy. Get your regional medical officer to Athens tomorrow. I want a report on that girl's status."

"Yes, ma'am."

"Thanks."

• • •

MATT'S THIGHS WOULDN'T stop shaking as he entered the medical unit of Forward Operating Base Salerno. Through the pre-fab window he saw the red sun setting beyond the mountains.

"Mr. Morgan?"

Beyond the mountains are more mountains, he thought looking up into a beam of sunlight that glanced off the medic's shaved head.

"Your Afghan friend was hit by shrapnel. Left a nasty gash on his shoulder and fractured his collarbone. He won't be dancing for a couple of days."

Matt had a contusion on the right side of his chest, along with lacerations on his forehead, torso, and arms. He asked, "Where's the rest of my gear?"

Instead of answering, the bald-headed medic reached into his pocket and produced a plastic vial, which he shook like a maraca. "Ibuprofen. You'll thank me in the morning."

Matt found Tariq and his father alone in a twenty-bed room. He listened as the moon-faced mullah prayed softly to a gentle, forgiving Allah until his son fell asleep. Outside in the hall, the mullah asked if Matt had money to provide the other Hazaras with food and accommodations.

Freed had forgotten them. "Where are they now?"

"Waiting at the gate."

Standing unsteadily in plastic slippers and a hospital gown, Matt did his best to thank the nine men for their courage. In exchange for three hundred dollars they promised to return at dawn.

In the ward, a medical officer brought food on trays. Matt listened to the Shia mullah on the opposite cot talk quietly about his projects to help the poor.

"This work is necessary to bring us closer to holiness and Allah," Sheikh Zadeh explained.

Matt's own father, when he was alive, would sometimes talk with compassion, too. But he also had a dark, paranoid side that para-lyzed him.

"This country needs more people like you," Matt said, hoping that a good night's sleep would clear his brain.

The mullah lowered his head to remind the American he was a humble man. Then he borrowed a small carpet from the waiting room and prayed.

SEATED ACROSS FROM General Emily Jasper at the conference table were Alan Beckman and NCTS's chief of Iranian operations, Stanley Volpe, who held a doctorate in Middle Eastern studies from Johns Hopkins University. Jasper's executive assistant, Shelly Mauser, sat attentively by her side.

Volpe spoke in a careful, colorless voice. "We've reviewed the exits and entry stamps in Kourani's passport and all reported activities at those locations."

"Good."

"We start with an assassination of a Mujahideen al-Khalq member in Turkey four years ago."

"Asad Zandi?" Alan asked.

Volpe nodded. "Kourani directed that operation."

Zandi had been a fervent critic of the Islamic regime. Alan had recruited Zandi as a source even though he'd participated in the student takeover of the U.S. Embassy in Tehran in '79.

Volpe continued: "A killing of a Saudi diplomat in Bangkok eighteen months ago; a failed attack on the Israeli ambassador in Cyprus seven months ago."

"All directed by Kourani?"

"Yes," Volpe answered. "There's a pattern here, General. This guy appears on the ground for a week or two before an attack, then gets out before it goes down."

"You're saying those attacks are linked to travel on the passport copied by Odysseus base officer Freed?" Shelly asked.

"Precisely," Volpe answered. "And I would expect Mr. Kourani has other documents, which we're unable to trace, that probably lead to other undisclosed activities."

"Basically, you're saying he has a lot of blood on his hands," General Jasper concluded.

"Let's just say we'd better have our lawyers ready if we're going to give him sanctuary in the U.S."

Jasper looked at Beckman and rubbed her knuckles. "If he's in a position to save hundreds of thousands of our countrymen, we'll pay that price. Won't we?"

They all agreed. "Yes."

She was ready to move on. "Is there anything else I need to know about Kourani?"

"On his last trip into Uzbekistan, he entered the country with a second Iranian, a man named Amin Kasemloo."

The name Amin Kasemloo rang a bell. Alan Beckman sat up.

Volpe adjusted his wire-rimmed glasses and continued. "We received HUMINT [human intelligence] reporting that Kasemloo died during the trip. Apparently he was involved in some sort of traffic accident in Tashkent."

"That came from us," Alan interjected. "Freed got that from a source he was running."

"Tell us more."

Beckman couldn't. "I'll find out from Freed."

Volpe, who appeared pleased with himself, had more. "The interesting part is that Kasemloo went in as a tourist, but after his death the Iranians produced a diplomatic passport. They went to the trouble of flying in an Iranian Air Force transport plane to transport the body."

Alan suddenly remembered. "General Moshiri," he blurted out.

"What?"

"General Moshiri was the source of that information. He's the one who reported it to Freed."

"So?"

"General Moshiri is the man who was assassinated in Oman six days ago."

"And?"

"There could be a connection."

Volpe folded his hands on the table. "Can you explain what that is?"

Alan shook his head. Shelly frowned and said, "We need answers. ASAP!"

Beckman wanted to reach across the table and slap her, but grinned instead. He didn't need her or anyone else telling him how to do his job.

General Jasper turned to Volpe. "Get somebody out to Tashkent. Work with the Agency to run this information down."

Beckman cut in. "Matt Freed's on his way. He's already got a visa."

General Jasper looked impatient. "I thought he was still in Khost."

"No, he's on his way back to Kabul."

"When's the last time you talked to him?" Shelly asked.

"Yesterday."

"Before or after he destroyed the prison?" she jabbed back.

Beckman held his ground. "Knowing him the way I do, I'm sure he'll arrive in Uzbekistan forthwith."

"Call the CIA station," Jasper ordered. "Get them on this."

"But what about Freed?"

"Call him back. We can't waste time!"

MATT WOKE UP early the morning of the eleventh to the sound of male voices swooping in his head. It was the first prayer of the day, Fajr. "In the name of Allah, the beneficent, the merciful. By the name of Allah and his sacred progeny . . ." The morning sky hung thick and gray.

When he opened his eyes again, he saw the sun. Across from him sat the mullah pulling a brown tunic over Tariq's chest. His head felt like it was filled with Styrofoam and his body ached. The constant bouncing of the Nissan Pathfinder they were riding in didn't help.

I dreamed again about flying a plane. He remembered banking through puffy white clouds. *Strange.*

They were second in a convoy of three vehicles packed with

guns, headed northwest on Highway 157 at twenty miles an hour. Destination: Kabul.

Tariq, looking tense, said: "This road is constantly under attack."

Matt tightened his grip on the M4 and willed himself to ask the questions that needed to be asked.

"Sheikh Zadeh, you once lived in Hamburg, is that correct?"

The bearded cleric peered at him through playful Mongol eyes. "That was thirty-five, forty years ago, my friend. The Beatles played across the street. I was busy studying and paid no attention."

"I understand you were a student at the Islamic Center."

"I was."

"You remember Ayatollah Beheshti?"

"Indeed."

"How about a man by the name of Kourani?"

The mullah furrowed his brow in concentration. "Not an unpopular name . . . There *was* a Kourani!" He smiled and held up four fingers. "Daughters! All four. How can Allah do that to a man?"

Matt remembered how blessed he was to have three daughters of his own. "Was there another Kourani who would have been close to Ayatollah Beheshti?"

"Beheshti. Beheshti . . ." The mullah rubbed his round forehead like a lamp. "I vaguely recall another Kourani. Serious, very devout."

"Might he have been a mullah? With three sons?"

Zadeh smiled. "If he was, he would have been a more fortunate man than the first."

Sheikh Zadeh spoke about Beheshti's time in Hamburg before he became a major figure in the Iranian Revolution. But he couldn't remember the other Kourani.

Matt produced the passport photo of Moshen Kourani he'd been carrying in his pocket. "This is one of his sons."

Zadeh's eyes widened. "This man I know. But I don't believe his name is Kourani."

"Maybe he called himself Fariel Golpaghani."

"I believe he did."

"Did he ask for your help in finding someone?"

"He came to see me two months ago with a heavier man. They identified themselves as officials of the Iranian government. They were looking for an Uzbek by the name of Juma Khuseinov."

"Were you able to help them?"

"I found out that Khuseinov had been an associate of people who had used chemicals to kill dogs. Bad people. Terrorists."

"Did the Iranians find him?"

"I don't know."

"Did they tell you why they were looking for him?"

"No."

Before nightfall, the vehicles pulled over, and bedrolls were laid on the ground. As the wind kicked up, Matt hiked to the top of a knoll, where he set up the satellite phone.

"Burris, I need to see you as soon as I get to Kabul."

"You're in a shitload of trouble, Freed. I need to see you, too."

PEACOCKS SHRIEKED FROM the house next door when Matt arrived at Burris's front gate. Tariq, in the lead car, asked Matt if he wanted him to wait.

"Take your father to the mosque," Matt answered. "My friend will drive me to the airport. Please contact me through Mr. Steve Burris at the embassy if you or your father learn anything else about Kourani."

"Agha Matt, yes. We'll be forever in your debt."

Light had just started to tint the sky over the linden trees when Burris shuffled out in a blue robe. "Tell me this isn't a nightmare," the bald man groaned. "You look like shit."

"Nice seeing you, too, Burris."

In the kitchen, as a houseboy boiled water for coffee, the deputy CIA station chief started firing questions about the attack on the prison in Khost. Matt cut him off: "I'll write up a full report when I catch my breath."

"If you don't want your head handed to you, you'd better do it now."

"I've got something more important."

"Look, Morgan, or whatever the hell you're calling yourself—"

Matt raised his voice. "Juma Khuseinov."

"What?"

"Juma Khuseinov. Tell me what you know."

The deputy CIA station chief shook his head. "I can't."

Matt leaned in close enough to smell his foul breath. "I'm leaving for Uzbekistan in two hours. I don't have time to play cat-and-mouse."

Burris looked like he'd just been forced to swallow a rat. "Catch your plane, Morgan. Get the hell out of here. Leave me alone."

"You gonna make me go through channels and put thousands of people at risk?"

"Tell me why I shouldn't."

" 'Cause you give two shits about helping your country. Because underneath the gruff veneer, you're a stand-up guy."

Burris tried to squelch a grin. "Khuseinov's a full-time scumbag, part-time arms dealer, and narco-terrorist."

"What's this about him and experiments killing dogs?"

"He got some training from Midhat Mursi, a chemical and biological expert who ran a terrorist training camp outside of Jalalabad before the war."

"Any idea where Khuseinov is now?"

"Last rumor we picked up, he was trying to get his hands on a biological weapon. We lost track of him near the Uzbek border in early July."

"What kind specifically?"

"Could be a dirty handkerchief. The guy's a bottom-feeder."

"You hear anything about him working with the Iranians?"

"Where'd you get that?"

"My grandmother. Why's it matter? Do you think he's al-Qaeda?"

The deputy CIA station chief sneered. "I'd call him more of a freelancer. An opportunist."

"Do me a favor, Burris. Pull everything you've got on Khuseinov and forward it to Alan Beckman at Odysseus base in Athens."

"As long as you promise to leave me off your Christmas card list."

"Here's hoping we never cross paths again. Vaya con dios."

FROM KABUL INTERNATIONAL Airport, Matt called Alan Beckman in Washington. It was 7:45 AM in Kabul, but 11:15 PM the previous day in Alan's hotel room in Silver Spring, Maryland. "The general wants you back at headquarters," the head of NCTS's Odysseus group announced.

"Tell her this is too important," Matt responded as his flight was called. "Tell her that Kourani was in Afghanistan looking for Juma Khuseinov, who's been trying to get his hand on a biological weapon. Tell her that Khuseinov was last seen near the Uzbek border in July. Kourani was also in Uzbekistan in July."

"Juma Khuseinov? When did you learn this?"

"No time to explain. My flight is boarding. I'll contact you as soon as I arrive in Tashkent."

"Wait, Matt. I'd rather you get to the Kabul embassy now and file a report."

"I can't."

"We've got a CIA station in Tashkent we can task."

"Explain to General Jasper why it's critical that I get to Uzbekistan as soon as possible."

"Dammit, Matt, you're not listening!"

"My flight's boarding, boss. I'll call you when I land."

CHAPTER EIGHT

September 12

Moshen Kourani gazed out the window of the silver 500-series Mercedes as it sped through middle-class streets lined with high concrete walls and fig trees. The sparkling city of Tehran lay behind him.

The moment the car stopped at a rusted iron gate, his heart filled with nostalgia. He remembered his brothers, Abbas and Hamid, and saw himself chasing them across the gravel drive. Bushy-haired Abbas was laughing, effortlessly juggling a soccer ball. One second the ball was on his toe; next it was on his head, his chest, and down his foot again. *"Moshen! Moshen, hurry! You run like a girl."*

The driver interrupted him by turning and asking if he should wait.

Kourani ran a hand over the leather seat and said: "No. Go get yourself something to eat. I'll call."

"Thank you, sir."

A young man opened the gate before Kourani could use his key. He looked down at it on the ring with the head of a bull and thought: *I've had this key for decades.* Then he heard the crunch of the gardener's steps on the gravel.

Darius was an old man now, with bowed legs and stooped shoulders. Moshen pictured him thirty-five years earlier when he used an ax to cut down the cherry tree in back, his muscles rippling, his spine strong and straight.

He found his mother in the kitchen making tea, almost as if she'd been expecting him. They hugged and kissed. "I'm so glad you've been visiting me more regularly these past few months."

The lines of her face spoke of hardship and sorrow. They were almost like a book. The deep creases around her mouth had appeared when Hamid died in Afghanistan. The deep circles under her eyes spoke of her husband's sudden death. She seemed lonelier than before.

"Tell Abbas he needs to visit me more often," she moaned.

Moshen loved to tease her. "That's because Abbas has always been your favorite, Mother."

She gave it right back to him: "No, Hamid was my favorite, Moshen."

"He was my favorite, too."

She smiled, and for a moment he remembered her when she was young and full of hope and didn't dress in black.

"Why do the Americans and Israelis threaten us like they do? Why are we cursed?"

He took her hand and held it. "Mother, the world is complex. Allah tests us continually. He asks us to understand, even when others can't. He asks us to act, when others, even those we love, will not understand those acts."

"You should have been a philosopher, Moshen, not a soldier."

This was the opening he was looking for. "Mother, Abbas and I need to do something for our country."

She sighed heavily. "I tell you: follow your own heart, not the will of other men."

Her face creased with worry, she squeezed his forearm. "My son, a man from the power authority came here the other day to inspect the house. Maybe I'm just being an old woman, but I was suspicious."

"What did he want?"

"Darius said he just looked around."

After his mother went to bed, Moshen returned to the little yellow room he had slept in as a child. He locked the door, moved the bed away from the window, and used a screwdriver on his pocket-knife to remove a piece of floor. From a compartment underneath, he extracted a small gym bag. Inside was the black book with the addresses he kept to himself. Soon he would burn it.

He returned the piece of wood, put back the bed, then unlocked the door. *I might never see this room again,* he said to himself. It seemed crowded with memories frozen in a mystifying stillness. He sighed, then looked at his watch.

Six days before the start of Eid al-Fitr, he thought. *Everything's on schedule.* Then gently shut the door.

A STRONG WIND almost knocked Matt off his feet as he stepped onto the tarmac of Tashkent International Airport. As the engines of the Uzbekistan Airways DC-10 whined down, he pushed himself toward the modern terminal.

What am I looking for? Matt asked himself as enormous runways and dilapidated 1950s-vintage Soviet-style buildings filled the periphery. *Certainly a clearer idea of what Kourani was doing in this part of the world in July. Did he join up with Juma Khuseinov? Was he using him as a source into al-Qaeda? Or was he recruiting him for something else?*

The dangerous ambiguity of the mission would have repelled most people. Not Matt.

He smiled to himself as grim-faced Uzbek security officials in stiff brown uniforms watched him from the door. He enjoyed the speed of running his own operation, relying on luck and instinct, not having to stop and get approval from headquarters at every turn.

Equally dour Immigration officers sat in glass booths, moving at a snail's pace despite the long lines. After thumbing through Matt's passport, examining former entry and exit stamps, and checking his photo, a man with enormous jowls waved him through, past signs hawking Marlboro cigarettes, Beefeater gin, and various brands of lingerie. The tall, blond, sharp-featured models looked hungry and raw.

I'd better succeed.

Matt flashed back to a group of aggressive dancers he'd met in a nightclub in 2002, sweating and kicking through "At the Copa," then inviting Matt and his men back to their rooms. Matt, out of deference to Liz, hadn't gone. But his colleagues had come back with stories of sexual acts they'd never seen before.

After plucking his bag off an ancient conveyor belt, he entered a large hall crowded with stout people awaiting incoming flights, calling out names in a mix of languages. Most men wore shiny worn suits; women sported black and navy skirts down to their knees. Amid this time warp stood a woman in her forties in a sharp Burberry raincoat with her hair pulled back, minimal makeup.

"Mr. Morgan, I'm Rachel Stack-Heinz," she said with cool confidence.

Two eager-looking young men reached out for Matt's bags. She stopped them politely in perfect Russian and the men moved on.

Matt followed the click of her high heels through the melee at the front door, to a silver Nissan Patrol. Without a word, she popped open the back and pointed to a place where he should deposit his things.

Two sharp turns later, they were on the main road. Tall Soviet-style apartment blocks rose in the background. Turbaned shepherds marshaling sheep passed on the right. Rachel said: "I'm the station chief here, Morgan."

"I'm glad," he responded, sensing he'd like her. She had a wide face with high cheekbones and a strong chin that made her face somewhat severe. Dark brown eyes that danced with ironic humor and smarts softened the effect.

In most places beside Uzbekistan she would be considered tall. Here she seemed a slightly older, more sophisticated version of the attractive young women he saw waiting at bus stops and pushing baby strollers. When they reached forty, they seemed to balloon in all directions and lose interest in how they looked.

"Your friend Kourani has been a busy boy," she started in slightly accented English.

Matt guessed she was German by birth.

Rachel drove with one hand and checked her cell phone messages as she talked. "We find that he's been principal planner and chief operative on the ground in almost a dozen attacks in the last several years. What was he like?"

"Tightly focused, very much in control. Late forties, I'd say. Intriguing."

"I'm sure," she said, lifting an eyebrow as they whizzed by a massive equestrian statue of Amir Tamur outside. Tamur, also known as Tamerlane, had conquered much of western and central Asia during the fourteenth century. "I get the impression he's a hands-on manager."

"I'm thinking of signing him up to conduct some leadership seminars when he defects."

She smiled. "Stranger things have happened. But right now Washington's freaking out."

An unsettled feeling returned to his stomach and remained through the smell of beef Stroganoff they encountered as they entered her neatly kept English Tudor–style house. "My husband does the cooking. He's a professor of Russian lit."

The man offering the vodka was younger looking than his wife, with a weathered Western face, leather vest, and cowboy boots. Definitely not what Matt had expected. "Have a shot," he boomed. "Wakes up the palate."

With his missus inside "freshening up," the professor said he hailed from Bishop, California, and had played two seasons of varsity football at Berkeley before he ruined his ankles. "Figured I'd settle down in San Francisco. Never imagined I'd end up at the end of the earth."

If he hadn't been traveling as John Paul Morgan, Matt would have been inclined to share, too. He'd have told him, for instance, that he played defensive back for Quantico High School and the name on his birth certificate was Matthew Mattaponi Freed. This would have led to the story of how his parents met at a shad fishing competition on the Mattaponi River, where his mother, an Irish girl from upstate New York, had won first prize.

Rachel returned in black slacks and a cotton top, looking fresh and fit and bearing the latest intel on Kourani. Her husband muttered something about being "a kept man" and returned to the kitchen with a wink.

"Seems Kourani entered under the name Fariel Golpaghani on July fourteenth with a colleague named Kasemloo, who died mysteriously and was returned to the Iranian Embassy in a steel box," she said. "We have it on good authority that the box was welded shut before it returned to Tehran."

"Welded shut?"

"Yes. People were paid off."

"You have any idea what they did here?"

"They stayed at the Bumi Hotel downtown."

"That's not what I meant."

They were both type double-A personalities. "I'm telling you that we can start there," Rachel said.

"I assume that you've checked on any mysterious deaths or disappearances during their stay."

"Thank you. I know how to do my job."

Matt thought it was a good bet that the Iranians had come to Uzbekistan for some sort of acquisition. After the collapse of the Soviet Union, the Qods Force had used Tashkent as a base for setting up front companies.

Rachel slipped a Segovia CD in the stereo and took a sip of Pinot Grigio. "Not a heck of a lot has been going on since the end of the Soviet-Afghan War. LUKOIL, the Russian energy giant, has been developing the Kandym, Khauzak, and Shady gas fields in the south. Another Russian company, Gazprom, is working the Ustyurt plateau, which borders the Aral Sea in the northwest. The Uzbeks have been coaxing the Russians to bring in transport aircraft and exploit the Aktau deposits. They have reserves of over forty-five hundred tons of uranium."

Matt paused before he tossed the cashews in his mouth. "Uranium?"

"All these southern former Soviet countries are struggling, but more natural resources are being discovered all the time."

Something in the back of his mind clicked in place. "You ever hear of a Juma Khuseinov?"

"Narco-terrorist. Arms smuggler. Why?"

"Kourani was looking for him in Afghanistan."

"Do you know why?"

"Burris in Kabul picked up a rumor having to do with the acquisition of a biological weapon. He lost track of him entering Uzbekistan in early July."

Rachel stood, pulled the band out of her hair, and shook it out so that it brushed her shoulders. "Kourani and Kasemloo arrived on the fourteenth."

"The three Ks. What do you think? You have a picture of Juma Khuseinov on file?"

"I'll get one from Internal Security."

"It could be useful."

She continued thinking out loud. "Soviet bioweapon programs ended nearly two decades ago. The government of Uzbekistan has nothing like that. I would know."

As soon as her husband appeared, they changed the subject. Over light jazz and candlelight, Matt listened to the Heinzes talk proudly about their adopted son, who was in Boston participating in a fencing meet. "He's just shy of sixteen but is already being recruited by the Ivy Leagues," the husband bragged.

For the first time in days, Matt allowed himself to think about the girls. He wanted very much to call Liz, but knew he couldn't without possibly compromising their safety and his.

So he refilled his plate and drank more Pinot Grigio and discussed favorite Russian authors with his hosts, then the mullahs in Iran. "Middle Eastern Nazis," Professor Heinz called them.

Matt agreed. He'd been raised a Presbyterian and had always been leery about organized religion, especially men who advocated violence in the name of God.

KOURANI ENJOYED the freedom of driving his own Mercedes. And the swooping, soaring voice of Ustad Nusrat Fateh Ali Khan on the CD player sent shivers up his spine. His colleagues wouldn't have been pleased if they found him listening to *qawaali*—Sufi devotional music—but he didn't give a damn about that now.

He'd traveled through this bleak, flat land many times before. To his right passed the great salt lake where the Shah's secret police had thrown the bodies of their political opponents so they dissolved and left no trace.

He admired the beauty in the pink and yellow striations of rock. As the last piece of *sohan* (pistachio brittle) melted in his mouth, the undulating domes and minarets of Qom faded behind him. One of these was the gold-domed shrine of Fatima, the Infallible One—sister of Imam Ali bin Musa Al-Ridha, the eighth Imam, and daughter of the seventh Imam, Musa al-Kadhim.

It looks like they're dancing. The thought pleased him.

Instead of continuing on the paved road, Kourani turned off into a parking lot outside a huge cemetery. He passed a sign that read Behest-e-Zahra (Paradise of Zahra) and entered past barefoot children hawking shriveled eggplants and prayer beads. Fountains spraying enormous quantities of fresh water into the air framed the main boulevard. The cemetery was divided into lots. One housed common folk, another martyrs of the revolution, another martyrs of the war with Iraq.

He passed the famous Fountain of Blood—a multilayered cement structure with a spout in the middle from which oozed a thin, red liquid that fell in thin ripples—which designated the area set aside for martyrs, and found the grave marked with his brother Hamid's name. He sat in the white plastic chair used by his mother every week and waited for a familiar sadness to come over him. He found it comforting.

Life felt cruel and brief, with so little time for love, friendship, joy, and laughter—all things he associated with Hamid. He remembered how his brother had dreamed of opening a record store and marrying a blond girl with long legs. A tear rolled down his cheek, which surprised him because he hadn't cried in years.

"Salaam aleikum," said the soft voice above him.

He looked up into dark, compassionate eyes. They belonged to a young mullah wearing a black turban. "Wa-aleikum es-salaam," Kourani responded.

The mullah crouched beside him. "My two older brothers are buried here as well," he said. "God's path can be difficult. We will be rewarded."

The older man nodded. "Yes."

"The leader wanted me to check on you." The mullah spoke quickly in a hushed voice. "His schedule is very demanding and there are many conflicts and problems. You must know there are those who question your intentions and . . . your loyalty."

Kourani's mouth turned grim. "Those who question me could not walk in my shoes from here back to the parking lot."

"Don't get angry, my brother."

"I make no apologies. I'm prepared for God's judgment."

"We all must submit to God's will."

Kourani's mouth trembled as he fought a mix of emotion—anger, fear, sadness. He said: "Pass on my regards to the rahbar [the leader] and tell him that I walk hand in hand with the Prophet wherever he leads."

"The best of men are but men at best."

"Salaam."

CHAPTER NINE

September 13

Matt woke early the next morning to the chatter of birds and immediately started scolding himself. *I need to make faster progress. Today's September 13.*

Tomorrow morning Kourani was scheduled to arrive in Vienna to pick up his U.S. visa, four and a half days before the planned attack on the United States.

Matt sat silent and frustrated all through the drive to the Bumi Hotel, thinking: *What have I really learned? Maybe the trip to Afghanistan was a waste of time. I traveled all the way to Khost for what? To find out that Kourani was looking for Juma Khuseinov? How significant is that?*

Not very, according to Alan Beckman, whom Matt had spoken to before breakfast. Matt's boss seemed more concerned about the attack on the prison in Khost.

Kourani could have been looking for Khuseinov for a whole lot of reasons unrelated to the warning he delivered in Bucharest. Maybe I'm being bullheaded. Maybe I'm all wrong.

He pictured his mother folding the laundry, muttering: "The acorn sure don't fall far from the tree."

Matt reminded himself not to think irrationally as a disappointed-looking Rachel Stack-Heinz pulled in front of the hotel. "You sure you want to do this?" she asked.

It was unusually warm for a September in Tashkent. Everything felt slightly off. He said, "Yes."

"Let me handle the manager. He's a friend."

She didn't know Matt well enough to tell if he was hung over, depressed, or just not a morning person. But she wasn't impressed.

The manager of the Bumi was a thickset man of fifty with Mongol blood. Matt tried to follow Rachel's Russian as she patiently explained what she wanted. His year and a half of Russian conversation and literature at the University of Virginia helped.

The manager led them to an office that had been turned into a storage closet. Mumbling under his breath, he tore through handwritten ledgers and stacks of photocopies. A tattooed waitress with a red bow in her hair curtsied and served lemon tea.

Since everything was written in Cyrillic, Matt wasn't much help. Instead, he busied himself stacking boxes that had already been looked through under a Pirelli calendar with nude pictures of Naomi Campbell. His mind had wandered back to Tariq and Mullah Zadeh when he saw a smile of recognition spread across Rachel's face.

"I think I got it."

"What?"

"Guest records of July fourteenth." She pointed to two hastily written names in the ledger: Kasemloo and Fariel Golpaghani.

The manager hurried out to make copies and returned with a broad-faced young woman with yellow streaks in her hair. "Vasha remembers the men who rented the car."

"How many men?" Rachel asked in Russian.

"Two."

Rachel showed her the picture of Juma Khuseinov. "Was this one of the men?"

The girl shook her head.

Then Matt held up a photo of Kourani.

"I think so," the young woman answered in Russian.

"What kind of car was it?"

She twisted her face into a strange smile, then threw up her hands.

"Do you remember the name of the company?"

Vaska looked down at her faded black Adidas. "It's the only one that delivers. ABTA."

"ABTA. Good."

The manager rewarded her with a pat on the rump. "Now describe the two men and tell them what you saw in their room."

She shook her head. "I don't snoop through the guests' things."

"Don't lie to me!" He spanked her hard enough to make her jump.

"Plastic gloves, a CD player, money from Germany, and some Andrea Bocelli CDs. I like the way he sings."

"You sure about the plastic gloves?" Rachel asked.

"Yes."

The woman in the tight red skirt and pink sweater behind the counter at ABTA Car Rental refused to help. So Rachel used her cell phone to speed-dial someone in state security. She handed the cell to the tight-lipped woman, who was soon nodding vigorously and saying: "Da, panimayu. Da, znayu."

She returned the phone to Rachel with a sneer. "I couldn't show you the records without official approval."

"Of course."

She led them into an inner office, where she logged onto an ancient Wang computer. Perplexed, she got up quickly and wiggled past Matt to a file cabinet.

"I remember clearly," she explained in Russian. "A Mr. Kasemloo rented two vehicles. One of them had to be recovered. It had engine trouble in Muynoq. We had to send two men to retrieve it."

She handed the paperwork to Rachel. "The Russian never asked for a replacement vehicle, a reimbursement, or a refund. The engine had blown a piston while it was stuck in the sand."

Rachel translated everything for Matt, who asked: "Stuck in the sand? Where?"

The CIA chief turned back to the female manager, who explained: "Mr. Kasemloo rented two four-wheel-drive vehicles because he was doing agricultural research of some type."

"Where exactly?"

The manager used a long red fingernail to trace the route on a map to the far western part of the country and a city on the Aral Sea.

"Thank you," Rachel said, pulling Matt outside and explaining that the Iranians must have been chasing someone because there was nothing in Muynoq and nobody went there.

Matt said, "I'll go alone."

"You can't."

"Why not?"

"The Uzbeks are very sensitive, because the whole area was poisoned by the Soviets."

"I'm going anyway," Matt said.

Immediately she was on the phone telling someone named Phil to meet her at the airport in twenty minutes with a satellite phone and two hazmat suits.

"You coming with me?" Matt asked.

"Muynoq is lovely this time of year," she answered snidely. "You're in for a treat."

GENERAL JASPER GREW increasingly uneasy as the big man sweating through his U.S. Customs uniform pointed to the long line of container trucks waiting to leave the port. "We're trying to find a way to move this stuff faster," he shouted to her, Shelly, and the other VIPs from NCTS who stood near the VACIS (vehicle and cargo inspection system) unit. It was a big stainless steel contraption that looked like a scaled-down tollbooth.

Customs agent Bob Acosta explained that before a truck could be released, he had to get an okay from the trailer nearby, where technicians studied gamma images on a computer monitor. If the cargo in a particular container didn't match the declared manifest, a physical inspection had to take place.

"We move over six hundred thousand containers a year. Rank number one in roll-on/roll-off cargo on the East Coast."

General Jasper had been briefed many times on the numbers and advanced technology, but given the threat identified by Kourani, she insisted on seeing the current detection capability firsthand. It was the job of her agency to identify terrorists and neutralize them before they attacked U.S. assets. FBI, Homeland Security, and local law enforcement were responsible for the defense of the United States.

Acosta explained that the slow crawl at the Seagirt Marine Terminal in Baltimore had started two days before with the announcement of Code Red. Since then, everything that left the port was carefully scanned with gamma rays and Geiger counters. Similar inspections were taking place at all local airports.

Next, General Jasper and her aides listened as Barbara Collins of the Maryland Port Administration Safety Department briefly reviewed the differences between chemical and biological weapons. The gist was that bioweapons were more difficult to trace and manufacture in a fine, easily dispersible form. On the other hand, a college-level-chemistry graduate could improvise an effective chemical weapon.

"I'm here to actually see the difference between the real and the theoretical," the general said, adjusting her sunglasses. "Show me what we have in terms of detection."

"We're making big strides on the chemical side with advanced X-ray analysis, gas chromatography, and even acoustic wave sensors."

"What about biological?"

"Presently we have no silver bullet," Barbara Collins explained. "We regularly use handheld polymerase chain reaction devices, PCRs, which are the same kind that were used by the UN inspectors in Iraq. They monitor the air at regular intervals but can only begin to detect an agent once it's been deployed."

"You have those in operation here?"

"Correct."

"But if a sealed biological agent passed through right now, you'd have virtually no way of knowing?"

"I'm aware that DOD [Department of Defense] is developing higher-efficiency collectors, but those also deal with agents once they've been deployed."

"That doesn't answer my question."

"There's a lot of R&D going into dry detection technologies. For example, optical standoff like LIDAR [light detection and ranging] that fuses radar signals with an intelligent warning algorithm."

"But you have nothing in place."

"Unfortunately biological detection technologies are in a much less mature stage of development than chemical detectors."

"That's what I was afraid of," General Jasper said, wiping beads of sweat off the bridge of her freckled nose. Then to Shelly: "Let's go."

MATT SHIELDED HIMSELF from the glare off the two-engine Cessna as Rachel Stack-Heinz issued last-minute instructions to her second-in-command. "Phil, run the names of everyone staying at the Bumi when Kasemloo and Kourani, aka Fariel Golpaghani, were there. Ask Yuri for the names of guests in other major hotels on and around July fourteenth. And check their flights."

Matt's father had been a Phil, too. He imagined his dad's face, worn and suspicious, gazing back. He had once told his son to "keep your eyes wide open and expect the worst."

What would he make of this?

Rachel's Phil stood at medium height with reflector shades, short blond hair, and a light brown beard. "You can't be serious, Rachel," he protested. "There's gonna be hundreds."

Nothing seemed to upset her poise. "I'm talking about visitors with foreign passports, Russians especially, and Germans, French, Pakistanis, North Koreans."

"That's better," Phil answered. "Foreigners we can manage."

She said: "Use your judgment."

As Matt counted the days he'd been away from his family, Phil's mind explored possible avenues of pursuit.

"If we go to Washington with this, the process could drag on for weeks."

Rachel patted her deputy on the arm. "That's why I suggested you call Yuri first."

Phil had arrived with gear—a satellite phone, two Glock pistols with three magazines each, and two hazmat suits packed in briefcases.

Matt popped his open and found a funny-looking breathing apparatus, a plastic decon suit, plastic bags, swabs, and test tubes. Turning to Rachel, he asked: "What's up with these?"

"Normally I don't go near the border with Kazakhstan without a Geiger counter. Northern Uzbekistan has the highest rate of still-born deaths in the world." The Cessna engines fired up, drowning out the rest of her explanation.

Her attention turned to an Uzbek man with enormous ears. Matt watched as she handed him an envelope, then joined her as she walked to the plane.

"That takes care of getting you through Customs," Rachel shouted in his ear.

"I like your style."

Her almond-shaped eyes were defensive. "I hope you're up for a new adventure."

"Always."

"We should be on the ground in Muynoq before dusk."

Rachel passed the first hour reading *The Bookseller of Kabul* while Matt dozed off. Again he dreamed of flying a commercial airliner low over a city at night, skillfully avoiding tops of trees, buildings, and power lines. When he realized the tremendous chance he was taking, he woke with a start.

Never panic! Get a grip! He scolded himself, remembering that he'd seen panic turn people into brutal, unthinking animals—a crowd of peasant protesters in Bolivia trampling their own children; U.S. marines stationed in Guam clawing each other as they tried to escape a burning movie theater.

Rachel, half asleep on the other side of the aisle, smiled enigmatically through half-open eyes. Reaching over, he helped her pull the red blanket up to her chin. Below he saw endless harsh brown terrain with scarcely a tree, road, or other sign of life.

Why it made him think of football camp at Quantico High School in Virginia he didn't know. As clear as if it happened yesterday, he pictured his mother in the kitchen peeling onions and chatting with his sister. Through the pass-through he saw his dad pissed off, staring at the TV.

The memory was vivid. Sixteen years old, he stood staring down at his cleats and muddy pants.

His mother stopped him. "Don't go in there."

"I want to tell Dad about the game on Friday."

"He's busy, honey."

"It's a night game against the Crusaders."

"He'll be tired. Leave him alone."

The feeling of aloneness, of anger and failure, penetrated his heart and sank into his bones. It bothered him that his mother protected his father even though she admitted that he'd let her down.

"How come Dad never comes to my games?" he'd asked his mother.

"Because he knows he'll feel bad if you lose."

No matter what Matt did or how he approached his parents, it seemed like he was wrong—all through junior high when he was constantly in trouble for vandalizing soda machines, setting off fire extinguishers at school, cutting class, staying out till all hours of the night with his friends, getting drunk on cheap wine; when he played football instead of basketball, the sport his parents liked best; when he took the summer job at the local nursery and earned ten bucks an hour instead of working for his dad for nothing.

He'd been made to feel like he was a bad kid. Other parents warned their sons and daughters to stay away from him. Yes, he'd done stupid things when he was drunk, like the time he knocked on the front door of his girlfriend's house at 2 AM and her father chased him away with a shotgun. One New Year's Eve he'd drunk so much he blacked out for a day and was found sleeping by the Rapidan River.

It was one of the few times he got his dad's attention. Matt remembered him standing over him in bed with the scar across his nose and his full head of hair brushed back, saying: "You've done it this time."

"Done what?"

"Proved that you're a dumb-ass with two strikes against you," his father explained. "Add a third, and you'll end up like me."

"What does that mean?"

"It means I was young once, too, and thought I was something."

"I *am* something."

"Something about as smart as a brick."

"You watch."

"I *am* watching. That's the problem." He was a good-looking man despite a broken tooth that showed when he smiled. "Could be I know how it ends up."

Matt had found himself stuck in a conundrum with no place to put his frustration. He excused his mother for drinking and being neurotic. "Everything scares me no end," she told him in a rare quiet moment. "Your father was the best-looking, smoothest talking man I ever met. I thought he had the tiger by the tail."

"I'll protect you."

"You worry me, Matt," she said before returning to the constant chatter about neighbors, TV shows, the weather, the latest Hollywood scandal, the price of milk, et cetera, that kept her fears at bay.

He couldn't wait to get out of Quantico and didn't like looking back. But a part of him had never left. Beneath the tough, highly trained exterior hid a boy who'd been programmed to expect failure.

For some reason he peeked out whenever Matt was flying, looking out at the passing clouds. His father had dreamed of becoming a pilot. *Must be some connection*, Matt thought.

He couldn't deal with that boy now. *The stakes are too high to question myself or lose focus.* So he did something he couldn't remember doing since his grandmother got sick. He prayed.

"Please, God, help me. Keep me strong. Help me stop this attack."

In the depths of his soul Matt still hoped that once he showed people he was a good person, worthy of their praise, the voice of his father in his head, all the negative imprinting he carried, would fade away.

Out of the corner of his eye he saw something that made him blink and look again. It was a freighter parked in the sand. *Strange.* Then he spied a large fishing trawler, then another. He counted eighteen or twenty like gravestones.

"Where's the water?" he asked, straining his neck to the right. The Aral Sea was still a good forty to fifty miles away.

One of the Uzbek pilots pointed to a large, sail-shaped steel structure that marked the former harbor. "Monument to the Great War," he shouted sarcastically in Russian.

Her dark eyes peeking over the top of the blanket, Rachel explained: "The Aral Sea was once the world's fourth-largest inland body of water. Now something like sixty to seventy percent of it is gone. The Soviets built two large canals to try to irrigate the desert and grow rice and cotton. This destroyed Muynoq, which was once a thriving fishing port, and has produced an ecological disaster. Something like twenty out of twenty-four species of fish have disappeared. There's been a thirtyfold increase in cases of chronic bronchitis, typhoid, and cancer."

"Nice."

The Cessna banked over dilapidated shacks and abandoned concrete buildings. Muynoq appeared to be in the last throes of death.

ALAN BECKMAN'S MIND was numb from a day and a half of endless meetings at the National Security Council, State Department, CIA, and Pentagon. Most had been a rehash of the same questions and arguments. Is Kourani who he says he is? What are his motives? Is the threat real? What are the likely targets? How can we best defend ourselves? Have any other sources confirmed the potential attack from al-Qaeda?

Alan had patiently answered each question. Yes, Kourani is the number-two man in Qods Force. He expressed concern about the possible outbreak of a Middle East war and the welfare of his family. Based on what we've uncovered so far in Qatar, we believe he's telling us the truth. Kourani warned of an attack against midsized

U.S. cities. Special FBI teams have been deployed; local authorities have been put on the highest alert; the most sophisticated tracking devices have been deployed and are operational 24/7. No, we have been unable to confirm the attack from other sources, but it fits the pattern of attacks that we know al-Qaeda has been planning.

And he had listened in horror as experts at NCTS explained the destructive potential of various nuclear, chemical, and biological agents, including sarin, ricin, dirty bombs, anthrax, brucellosis, glanders, tularemia, and melioidosis, as well as viral agents like smallpox, ebola virus, and Bolivian hemorrhagic fever. He learned that a rocket loaded with a hundred kilograms of anthrax spores could kill as many as 3 million people under the right atmospheric conditions.

Based on the fact that the Iraqis during Saddam Hussein's rule had produced and stockpiled twelve tons of weaponized anthrax, intel gleaned from raided al-Qaeda camps in Afghanistan and Pakistan, and Kourani's possible association with Juma Khuseinov, NCTS analysts concluded that anthrax was a potential weapon. Alan Beckman agreed.

All he wanted to do now was get back to Athens and make sure his people were getting the support they needed.

As he packed his briefcase, Jasper's executive assistant, Shelly, appeared at the door and said: "The general wants to see you."

"Fine, but I need to leave for Andrews in half an hour."

General Jasper wanted to get out of the office, too. It was 10:35 PM; her back was killing her; her husband was in bed suffering from bronchitis; and their daughter, who had just started her first semester at Johns Hopkins Medical School, needed help. But National Security Council Director Stan Lescher had strongly urged that she meet with someone from Human Rights International first.

Tamara Hall, a short African American member of the White House public relations staff, was sitting next to a tall Norwegian representative from HRI named Oluf Brunner when Beckman and Jasper entered the oak-paneled conference room.

Brunner, who spoke with a thick accent, cut right to the chase. "Our representatives in Afghanistan drove to Khost and filed a very troubling report about what happened at the prison."

"We appreciate your sharing this information with us," General Jasper said smoothly, "before you release it to the press."

"Our reps interviewed three surviving prison officials," Brunner continued. "So far they've accounted for one hundred and forty prisoners dead."

"That many?" Jasper looked concerned.

Alan sensed where this was going and cut in. "Did the guards tell you that it was the Taliban that blew up the armory?"

"They did," twenty-four-year-old Tamara Hall interjected, "but I'm afraid it's a little more complicated."

"Why?"

Everyone stopped when Shelly entered, quickly crossed to General Jasper at the head of the table, and without so much as an "excuse me" whispered in her ear. She'd just received a flash report from NSA about an electronic intercept out of Bahrain that referenced an upcoming al-Qaeda attack.

"We get one a week," Jasper whispered back. "Why's this one different?"

"I don't know."

"Find out."

Shelly left the same way she entered, and all eyes turned to Brunner, whose large ears had turned a deep shade of red.

"General, as you know, we take these things very seriously," the Norwegian said, raising his voice. "I'm not here to make charges, simply to share what we've discovered."

"We appreciate that."

"Our people were extremely thorough. They asked the guards: How do you account for so many prisoners locked in their cells? Didn't anyone think to let the prisoners out so they wouldn't die in such a horrendous fashion? And the guards answered: We thought of letting them out, but were ordered not to by an American official."

General Jasper folded her hands in front of her. "Which American official was that?"

"The same one who released Mullah Zadeh. A large, dark-haired man in civilian clothing who arrived with a translator, directed resistance against the Taliban, and disappeared shortly after the arrival of U.S. military forces."

Alan Beckman couldn't remain quiet. "Aren't you presuming that this American knew the Taliban assault on the prison was going to take place?"

"That's a good question," Jasper added.

Oluf Brunner's voice turned deeper and more authoritative. "Like I said before, I'm not here to make charges. We will simply release a preliminary report, and later follow up."

General Jasper turned to young Tamara Hall. "I assume you've read the report."

"That's correct."

"If I may be blunt, how does it characterize the American's actions?"

Brunner quickly answered: "Clever in a sinister way."

Beckman didn't like Brunner's judgmental tone. "What does that mean?"

"We let the facts speak for themselves."

Alan was hot. "What facts?"

Brunner squared his shoulders. "This American official allows a Taliban attack on the prison to take place, which kills almost all the Taliban prisoners, then calls in the U.S. military to destroy the attackers. From your standpoint, I think, it's a perfect operation. Yes?"

CHAPTER TEN

September 13

The man at the wheel of the '82 Lada Samara with the mouth full of silver teeth provided a constant stream of commentary in Russian as he negotiated the abandoned, dust-filled streets of Muynoq. The surrounding sky had turned an eerie shade of orange gray. Somewhere through the thick gloom the sun was setting. "That's where the engineers used to go to gamble, drink, and meet young girls," the driver said pointing to a gray cement structure.

The satellite phone burped. Rachel answered and passed the receiver to Matt. "For you."

It was Alan Beckman calling from Washington. "This isn't a good time," Matt explained. "I'm not alone." He didn't know who the driver might be working for and how much English he understood.

"Just one question: Did you order the guards at the prison in Khost to keep the prisoners locked in?" Alan asked.

"Absolutely not."

"Do you think the presence of you and the Hazaras somehow spurred the Taliban to attack?"

"Come on, Alan. How would I know that?"

"We're just trying to understand the sequence."

"I'll call back later."

It pissed Matt off no end that headquarters seemed more concerned about Taliban casualties in Khost than his mission.

Rachel read the annoyance on his face. "You okay?" she asked. "More bureaucratic crap."

Outside the window, everything looked broken down and deserted. A few unhealthy-looking people seemed to walk in slow motion with their heads staring at their feet. Matt watched two kids haul a cart filled with large vats.

"Water," Rachel explained. "The only so-called safe supply is from thirty wells scattered throughout the town."

As Matt steamed, the big-bellied driver drove with one hand and used his other to help put over a joke. "Grandpa, is it true that in 1986 there was an accident at Chernobyl Nuclear Power Plant?"

His voice deepened into his chest: " 'Yes. Oh, yes, grandson.' And he patted the boy's head."

"Grandpa, is it true that there were absolutely no consequences?"

" 'Yes. Absolutely.' And he patted his grandson's second head. And the two of them strolled off together, wagging their tails."

They stopped in what looked like the lobby of a former hotel for a meal of stew, rice, Coca-Cola, and old apples for dessert. "Don't drop your food on the floor," the driver warned them. "Two cats have already died." Rachel called ahead to the local police commander, who promised to wait for them to arrive.

The silver-mouthed driver had a joke about policemen, too. "Do you know why our policemen always travel in threes? One knows how to read. One knows how to write. And the other is there to keep an eye on the two smart ones."

It was pitch black when the battered sedan pulled in front of a white concrete structure illuminated by sodium lights. An overweight man in a wrinkled uniform waited outside smoking a cigarette. He escorted them in, past wooden desks and stacks of ledgers, with a 9mm Makarov pistol on his hip. Matt didn't see a single computer.

They entered an office with big stuffed chairs and a taller, thinner man in a blue suit who stood and offered his hand. He asked for a series of documents that Rachel didn't have. She showed him her diplomatic ID instead.

"Is this all?" he asked sharply.

"I can call someone at the Ministry of Interior if necessary."

He held up his hand and smiled with a row of broken teeth. "How can I help?"

Even with the dental problems, he struck Matt as vain. Rachel asked the commander about the vehicle that had broken down on July 14.

The dark-haired Russian raised a thin eyebrow. He knew all about it, he said, and had even filed a report with Internal Security headquarters in Tashkent.

"Why file a report on a broken-down vehicle?"

"Because it was involved in smuggling," the police commander said.

"What kind of smuggling?" Matt asked. His Russian was coming back.

The commander answered: "I don't know. But the vehicle crossed the dried-out lake and entered Vozrozhdeniye."

At the mention of Vozrozhdeniye, Rachel sat up.

"The tire tracks were clear when we saw them." He paused to light another Camel Light, which Matt guessed was either seized contraband or fake. "The witness took us there."

"Who?"

The commander blew a stream of smoke at the ceiling and continued: "We learned from this man that an open truck traveled with wooden boards to allow these men to traverse several sectors with soft sand."

"These men were Iranians?"

"Three Iranians, one Russian."

"Do you know their names?"

"No."

"Could one of them have been Juma Khuseinov?"

The commander looked confused. "He's an Uzbek. Why would he be involved in this?"

"We think he might have met with some Iranians in Kabul."

"All I know is that it took them five hours to cross. They paid this local man to wait with the two vehicles while four men went in on foot."

"This happened when they got to Vozrozhdeniye?"

"Yes."

Rachel turned to Matt and explained in English: "The island isn't an island anymore because the water has receded so much."

The commander nodded like he understood, then continued: "They were gone a full day and came out carrying loaded back-packs and several large nylon bags. One of the men with them was Russian. He paid the local man well to keep his mouth shut, be-cause he said they had recovered heroin that had been sealed and buried."

"Did the local man believe him?"

"Yefim didn't know. It's true that we have a lot of heroin and opium that is being smuggled out from Afghanistan."

"Can you have this man, Yefim, take us back to the island?" Matt asked.

The commander choked on the cigarette smoke. "Why in the name of God would you want to do that?"

"Because—" Matt stopped.

"I can call Internal Security if we need permission," Rachel added.

"Vozrozhdeniye is sealed off. No one can get in."

Rachel called Internal Security to try to make arrangements. Twenty minutes later as they exited the building, she shook her head. "I was afraid of this," she said to Matt.

"Afraid of what?"

"Vozrozhdeniye, aka Rebirth Island—which translated in English means 'Place of Darkness'—was the primary testing site for the So-viet Union's Biopreparat during the '80s and early '90s. Tens of thousands of rabbits, guinea pigs, and monkeys were imported and died horrible deaths."

"What did they test?"

"Weapons-grade anthrax, plague, tularemia, Bolivian hemorrhagic fever, smallpox, glanders. Everything. When the Soviet Union col-lapsed, the island was evacuated. Seven years ago we sent teams in with the support of the Uzbeks and Kazakhs to clean it up. When they drilled in some of the pits, they found live anthrax spores. We imported tons of bleach to kill what was found. Then our teams left. We know they didn't get everything."

"Doesn't sound good."

"Precisely why I brought the chemical suits."

"Understood."

When Rachel frowned, she looked more vulnerable. "But there are two problems. First, U.S. government regulations only allow MASINT [Measurement and Signature Intelligence] specialists with Level C gear on the island. By the time we ask permission from Washington, a team gets assembled, they get visas and travel, we're looking at three, maybe four days."

"We don't have that kind of time," Matt said. "Besides, I recommend we don't set off more alarm bells until we have something concrete."

"Agreed. I won't send back anything until we have hard information."

He liked her even more. "What's the second problem?" Matt asked. "You said there are two."

Rachel took a deep breath as they stepped into the thick darkness. "The Uzbeks didn't give us permission. It's going to take me a day or two to reach the right people."

"I'll go in alone," Matt said.

"Bad idea."

Back in the car, Matt offered the big-bellied driver fifty dollars if he could take them to a man named Yefim. The driver asked Rachel to explain who this man was. He listened, then held two fingers up to Matt's face. "Two!"

"Two what?"

"Two hundred."

Matt counted out the money. Then he and Rachel watched as the driver ambled over to the uniformed policeman, who was smoking another cigarette under the sodium lamp. The two big men entered the station together.

"I'm not liking your friend Kourani," Rachel muttered softly in the backseat.

"Neither am I."

Five minutes later, when the driver emerged, the streetlight gleamed off the silver in his mouth.

"I think we're in business," Matt said.

"Vozrozhdeniye," Rachel shivered. "Death . . ."

ALAN BECKMAN'S MIND twisted in turmoil as the Gulfstream tore through the sky over the Atlantic at Mach .85. He tossed aside the half-eaten turkey sandwich and did what he thought any other self-respecting man would do under the circumstances: he composed his resignation. Fully satisfied with its disgusted tone and language, he rehearsed the words he would use to break the news to Celia, imagining her arguments and countering them.

Forty minutes into the point-counterpoint in his head, Beckman realized that he had no intention of resigning. So he sat back and started to review the tumultuous events of the last twelve hours.

At the center of them stood several exchanges with Matt, one from the U.S. Embassy in Tashkent, and a second, briefer one from Muynoq. In both, Matt answered questions about the prison attack in Khost and the particulars of his search.

Matt emphasized two things: first, the discovery that Kourani had been trying to make contact with Juma Khuseinov, a known terrorist who might have been trying to get his hands on a biological weapon. But Matt supplied no evidence that Kourani actually met with Khuseinov, and NCTS files characterized the Uzbek as "a highly unreliable low-level criminal."

Matt's second point referred to the man who had accompanied Kourani to Tashkent and apparently died during the trip: Amin Kasemloo. Alan reported that neither the CIA, the FBI, nor the NSA had ever heard his name before.

Matt pressed his boss with more demands. "Tell them to look harder. Maybe he was using an alias."

Alan tried to explain that Washington was preoccupied with defending the country against the upcoming attack.

"Tell them that Kasemloo could be critical!"

"I will." Matt could be a pain in the ass.

After both conversations, Alan reported back to Shelly and General Jasper, whose faith in Freed seemed to dissolve by the second. As it did, the questions directed at Alan became more aggressive and, to Alan's mind, ludicrous.

"Was Freed armed when he went into the prison?"

"I believe so. Yes."

"Why?"

"SOP." (Standard operating procedure.)

"Then he knew about the Taliban attack."

"No. He was told that there was ongoing combat in the area."

"But still he went."

"He was looking for the mullah. Why would he go into the prison if he knew it was going to be attacked?"

"That's a question that begs to be answered."

"Like I said, Freed went to the prison for a specific purpose. He knew there was danger, but his interest in the mullah superseded that."

"Why did he want the mullah?"

"Because Mullah Zadeh's son had seen Kourani with the mullah at his mosque several months ago."

Shelly said: "It sounds weak."

She had a way of getting under Alan's skin. "Look," he explained, "this is how intel collection works. You follow a lead and see where it takes you. You're looking at a process of inferences and deductions. It's never a straight line from point A to point B."

"Spare us the lecture."

General Jasper cleared her throat. "Do we know if he personally killed or injured any of the prisoners?"

"I can't imagine why he would."

"We're getting eviscerated, Alan. We have to be thorough. Don't you see?"

He understood that General Jasper, the rest of the intelligence community, and the White House seemed more concerned about the release of the Human Rights International report than finding out more about Kourani and his activities. Their anxiety had crested with a front-page story in this morning's *Washington Post:* "Human Rights Officials Point to Suspicious Activity of U.S. Intel Officer in Afghan Prison Uprising."

Forty thousand feet over the Atlantic, Alan was still smarting from a dressing-down he'd received from Shelly, who accused him of "losing control of his staff" and "plunging the government into chaos."

After hearing her call him "incompetent" and "dangerous," he'd stormed out of NCTS headquarters and hailed a cab to Andrews Air Force Base. From there he'd telephoned General Jasper, who indicated that the controversy seemed to be blowing over.

She said: "I think we're safe."

They both agreed that maybe the best thing for him to do "under the circumstances" was to return to Athens.

He couldn't get there soon enough.

CHAPTER ELEVEN

September 14

Rachel pulled down the checked scarf she had wrapped across her mouth and ordered the driver to slow down.

Yefim was a small fifty-five-year-old Uzbek with nerve damage to half his face. One eye had yellowed and looked like it didn't work.

"Not so fast!" she shouted over the jeep's engine.

Finally the words got through, and he eased up on the accelerator so the jeep didn't bounce and lurch as violently.

"Good!" she said to Matt. "Now I won't get sick."

The sun pummeled the barren landscape as it scaled the pale blue sky. More rusted trawlers passed outside like monuments to a different era. Hard plastic cases and backpacks bounced in back as the jeep jumped a slight embankment and landed on hard-packed sand.

They followed a dirt road west along what used to be the coastline. Matt spent the time remembering chemical suit drills he had participated in during the First Gulf War.

Twice they had to stop and lay down planks so that the jeep could pass over areas of loose sand. Then they got stuck and dug and pushed for almost an hour.

By the time the jeep moved again, they were covered with sweat.

"Fun, isn't it?" Rachel asked, unbuttoning the top of her khaki shirt and fanning herself. Matt tried not to imagine the texture of her skin.

Her face reminded him a little of an eagle's—sharp dark eyes; always alert, ready to face the next challenge.

Another fifteen minutes and he made out blue-green water to their right. "That's the land bridge," Rachel shouted. "Appeared two years ago during a full moon and has been growing wider ever since."

Yefim hung a wide right and stopped at a gate connected to a barbed-wire fence. Signs in Russian, French, and English warned all trespassers to stay out or risk death by contamination.

The tiny wooden guardhouse was empty. Yefim used a pocket-knife to pick the lock.

"This was all controlled by Soviets," Yefim said on the other side. They passed over a huge expanse of gray silt that clung to the island. "Uzbeks were never allowed to enter."

Inhaling the mix of salt and chemicals that rose from what was left of the lake and looking out at the desolation, Matt found it hard to imagine that the planet they were on sustained the lives of 6.5 billion people.

After forty minutes more of slowly negotiating mounds of silt, they arrived on the rockier older land of Vozrozhdeniye Island. Immediately Yefim pulled over and looked behind him. He wore dirty jeans and a camouflage scarf around his neck.

"What do you see?" Rachel asked in Russian.

He pointed to a little cloud of dust miles behind them that disappeared behind a ridge. Directing his half-frozen face at a plateau several hundred yards east, he spoke in Uzbek.

"Yefim says that first they went through the buildings farther north. And ended up digging over there," Rachel translated.

Matt said: "I think we should retrace their steps."

"Agreed."

They followed an unused asphalt road that snaked north. "The headquarters and barracks run by the Red Army's Fifteenth Directorate housed up to eight hundred scientists during peak test periods, from April through August," Rachel explained.

"When was it shut down?"

"Nineteen eighty-eight," she answered with a frown. "Slurries of anthrax spores and other pathogens were trucked in from Sverdlovsk and Irkutsk for decontamination and burial. They mixed anthrax spores with bleach in 250-liter stainless steel containers, then buried them in pits."

"Is it safe?"

"That depends on how carefully you think they handled the pathogens. Remember, this was at a time when the Soviet Union was coming apart."

"Good thing we brought the suits."

"These were special strains developed for military purposes, so they'd been rendered resistant to multiple antibiotics and environmental stresses."

Matt nodded. "I thought we cleaned it up."

"The Defense Department sent in a group of specialists five years back as part of the CTR [Cooperative Threat Reduction] Program. They spent millions dismantling the equipment and soaked the soil with a special solution. According to their report, no viable pathogens remain on the surface. But some, including anthrax, form spores that can live in the soil for a hundred years."

"IS THERE AN art more beautiful, more divine, more eternal than martyrdom?" the black-suited man at his elbow asked over the gentle gurgle of waterfall that stood at the center of the modern red and gold lobby.

"None that I know of," Kourani answered carefully. Although the man with the terrible nose claimed to be a Persian businessman living in nearby Baden, Kourani couldn't be sure he wasn't a spy sent by the president or the Ministry of Intelligence and Security (MOIS). As a member of the Qods Force, he had reason to be suspicious of both.

As the two men approached the mirrored elevator "The Blue Danube" waltz played in Moshen Kourani's head, which was entirely appropriate given the fact that he was in Vienna, staying at the Marriott Hotel.

Conveniently, the same building housed the U.S. Consulate.

Leave it to the Americans to erect a building with a Mississippi riverboat façade smack in the center of Vienna's elegant Ringstrasse, Kourani thought to himself.

A mere glance at the disgusted expression on the man on his left—the aviator glasses, the short beard, the guarded, weary eyes—and he imagined he could read his whole life. They'd arrived together on the Lufthansa flight from Istanbul. Kourani knew at the first whiff of the man's lime cologne that he couldn't trust him.

"Go and wake your luck," the businessman said peeling off and heading for the front door.

"You, too."

Kourani had hoped to spend the two days before the arrival of the rest of the Iranian delegation quietly, taking care of last-minute details and preparing himself for the challenge ahead. His eyes followed the so-called businessman out the revolving door past a young American couple who seemed to watch him from near the concierge desk. *Walls have mice and mice have ears.*

Alone in the elevator, Kourani filled his mind with remembrances of the sights and sounds of the Stadtpark across the street. He'd captured many images on his digital camera and hoped to send them back to his mother—the Opera House, St. Stephen's Cathedral, the flower clock, and, especially, the gilded bronze monument to Johann Strauss II. The lithe blond girls flirting with their boyfriends as the sounds of schoolchildren playing violins drifted overhead amused him. His brother Hamid would have considered this place paradise.

Part of Kourani wished he could, too. But he wasn't a dreamer like Hamid had been. And everywhere he looked, he saw traps.

THEY RUMBLED PAST a primitive landing strip covered with withered brown grass and approached the half-dozen tumbledown barracks that had once served as the scientific headquarters for the Soviet Biopreparat. There were no birds in sight, only an occasional lizard. Warm winds swirling off the desert steppes provided a slight respite from the heat.

There wasn't much to look at, either—broken mesh monkey cages with rusting locks, stacks of empty yellowed notebooks with the logo of the Fifteenth Directorate on the cover, an old incinerator, a graveyard filled with headstones with illegible names, damaged porcelain and stainless steel canisters. Everything was covered with reddish dust.

"Nothing but ghosts," Rachel said.

The Uzbek guide, Yefim, explained that the Iranians had seemed disappointed, too.

"Did they take anything away with them?" Rachel asked.

"Not from here."

Circling back south, Yefim parked near the plateau and scanned the landscape to the south. Rachel used her binoculars as Matt drank bottled water.

"See anything?" Matt asked.

"I think we're good." Rachel hoisted on a backpack. Matt picked up his and both plastic cases. Yefim noted that the Iranians had carried cases, too.

When the Uzbek told Rachel he'd wait by the jeep, she scolded him in Russian.

"Do you think he'll stay?" Matt asked as they started picking their way up the slope, around rocks and dried shrubs.

"I told him if he left, I'd hunt him down and kill him."

Fifteen minutes later, when they reached the top, they were greeted by a thick, sour smell that turned their stomachs.

"A rotting animal," Rachel groaned.

Matt spotted a series of pits ten feet in diameter that had been disguised with dead shrubs. "Someone dug here," he said. "Look."

"I'd say recently."

"Seems like."

Around the first pit lay a dozen dead rodents with long black hair in various stages of putrefaction. As Matt bent down to get a closer look, Rachel shouted: "Back away! Don't touch."

"I wasn't planning to," Matt countered. "Let's move back and suit up."

Rachel apologized: "Germs and diseases creep me out."

Five hundred feet away, near the edge of the plateau, they dropped their gear. Matt watched the lean, fit woman struggle with her suit. It reminded him of a scene from *Barbarella*.

Matt stuffed some plastic bags from the cases in his pocket. Together they sweated profusely back to the pits. When they were within thirty feet, Rachel stopped him.

"I'd better call in a MAZINT team."

"There's no time."

Matt counted the decomposing bodies of twenty-seven rodents. There were dozens more in the shrubs.

"Use the bags," Rachel said, looking for a suitable stick.

Twice he tried using sticks to push the bodies into a plastic bag, and twice the rotted bodies broke. When he reached down to scoop one with hand, Rachel shouted: "Don't! There's a proper way to do this. I saw a shovel in the jeep."

"That's not gonna happen," Matt said through the suit. The breeze had stopped. The barren plateau offered no respite from the sun. He was about to kneel again when he heard a muffled shot.

"What was that?" Rachel asked.

Three more shots cracked in the distance.

"Was Yefim armed?" Matt asked.

"I don't think so."

"You wait here," Matt said backing away from the pit. "I'll get our weapons."

As a spurt of automatic weapons fire echoed up from the roadway below, Matt removed his mask. Fear leaped from Rachel's dark eyes. She said: "We were followed."

"I'll find out."

Hurrying to the lip of the plateau, Matt saw Yefim on the ground, bleeding from his chest. Two men were searching the interior of the jeep. When one of them turned to face the plateau, Matt ducked.

Grabbing the backpacks, weapons, and satellite phone, he scrambled back to Rachel.

"What's the situation?" she asked, pulling off her mask.

"Get your deputy on the phone. Tell him we'll need help getting out."

"He's in Tashkent. He'll have to call a helicopter."

Matt slammed a clip into the Glock and said: "Wait here." He picked his way along the ridge of the plateau south to get a better view. Breathing hard, sweat pouring off his body in the plastic suit, he took in the situation at a glance. Two SUVs had parked around a large outcropping of rock to the south. Four men in civilian clothes armed with shotguns and rifles were starting to scale the slope.

"Fuck."

He didn't say anything to Rachel when he returned to find her fumbling with the satellite phone. "I'm still trying to get a signal," she said.

"We don't have time for that now," Matt answered, stuffing his and Rachel's masks into his backpack. "Follow me."

He traced a wide arc around the pits and continued north toward the barracks, stopping every fifty yards or so for Rachel to catch up. She started pulling off her yellow suit. "Don't," he said. "Not yet."

"What happened?"

"Yefim's down. A group of men followed us."

"How many?"

"I saw four in two SUVs."

She clenched her mouth and fist. "What are we gonna do?"

"Put some more distance between us, then call Phil."

Her mouth started trembling. "I'll call him now."

That's when Matt remembered. "I forgot the rats!"

"Mr. Kourani?" the sweet voice asked.

He lifted his eyes from the article on British football. "Yes."

"Follow me, please." She was a short blond woman with a pleasing face. White blouse, tight blue skirt, black heels. "My name is Pam Lassiter," she said as she closed the door behind her.

They had entered a small rectangular office with spectacular photos of Western vistas on the walls.

"Are these yours?" Kourani asked, pointing at two sunsets over dramatic outcroppings of rock.

"Yes, they are. I took them in New Mexico and Utah. Those on the other wall are of Half Dome in Yosemite."

"Brilliant," Kourani said. "I love the American West."

"Me, too. Thanks." She hadn't expected him to be so charming.

"You're a talented woman. Why are you wasting your time here?"

"I consider it a privilege to serve my country."

He appreciated her intelligence, too. "Very good answer."

Kourani handed over his diplomatic passport issued in the name of Fariel Golpaghani and explained that he was traveling to New York City as the fifth member of the Iranian government delegation to the United Nations General Assembly.

"I will be handling refugee issues," he said.

Pam Lassiter, who was really a CIA case officer, played along. "Mr. Morgan informed us that we should be expecting you."

"I was hoping Mr. Freed might be here today," Kourani said deliberately using the NCTS operative's real name.

"He's on leave with his family."

Kourani doubted this was true. His agents had lost Freed four days ago in Kabul. What he had been doing there wasn't clear.

"Mr. Morgan sends his best and plans to meet you in New York," the sunny-faced CIA agent continued.

"Yes," Kourani said, folding his hands on his lap. "I look forward to that."

Pam Lassiter went about her business, guiding Kourani through the appropriate forms and showing him where to sign.

"Is there any message you want me to forward to Mr. Morgan?" she asked at the end.

"Tell him I'll call him on the eighteenth when I arrive in New York."

"I certainly will."

He removed a small notebook from his inside pocket, wrote something in it, ripped out a sheet, and handed it to Lassiter. "One other matter," he said with a slight grin. "Mr. Freed and I made a financial arrangement. In order to complete the transaction, he must wire that amount into this account."

Pam stared at the numbers. The first was 2.5 million. The second was a numbered account in the Geneva International Bank.

Headquarters had told her that the Iranian would request only 2 million up front. But since the whole 5 million had been approved, she decided not to quibble.

Kourani took this as a good sign and changed the subject: "When will my visa be ready?"

"You can pick it up here tomorrow morning after eleven."

"I'll be here tomorrow at noon," Kourani said. "Please confirm with my friend Mr. Freed that the transfer will have taken place by the seventeenth. That way I won't have any problem calling him when I arrive in New York."

"I will."

He wanted to make sure. "I assume everything's in order."

Pam had been instructed to project calm confidence. She answered: "Everything's in order, Mr. Kourani."

"Thank you," the Iranian said extending his hand.

"It's been a pleasure."

CHAPTER TWELVE

September 14–15

A lan Beckman sat at his desk, looking at the yellowish brown smog that hung over the Parthenon, and let his mind drift. Since his return to Athens he'd been trying to assimilate shards of intelligence and rumor that had been picked up by NCTS, CIA, FBI, NSA, and military intelligence officers across the globe. Some had monitored the movements of known MOIS and Qods Force officers in and out of Tehran. Others had talked to sources with ties to al-Qaeda units in the Persian Gulf. Others had liaisoned with Saudi, Israeli, and Jordanian intelligence. Specially designed NSA computer programs had sifted through tens of thousands of monitored cell phone calls and e-mail messages in and out of Iraq and Iran.

For no apparent reason, a quote he'd read somewhere lodged in his head: "When we can't defend our beliefs with words, we resort to violence."

It didn't seem to belong, so he chased it away. Maybe it had to do with the jet lag that twisted his brain or the fact that he'd recently turned fifty-three. Whatever the reason, philosophical ideas like these had started to interrupt his thinking at the strangest times.

What he wanted his mind to do was sift through the maze of fragments and discern a significant pattern or anomaly. He tried. Nothing.

So he willed his brain to try again. And again it came up blank.

By the time Beckman summoned his Lebanese American assistant, powerful lights made the Parthenon glow in the murky night sky. He marveled again at the monument to Athena, daughter of Zeus, and the fact that the architectural wonder had been constructed without the use of mortar or cement.

"Bashir, you've looked through the same intelligence," Alan said as he plucked two Mythos lagers from the fridge under his bookshelf and turned off the computer. "What do you think?"

The burly man with the bad right leg lowered his thick body into a chair. "The bottom line, boss, is we're vulnerable as shit."

Alan stroked his gray beard and smiled. "You don't believe in foreplay, do you?"

"Not at a time like this."

"You didn't find anything, did you?"

"Not really."

"Me either. And, by the way, I pity your wife."

The swarthy-skinned man pressed on. "I don't like the position we're in, waiting in the burning building for lover-boy Kourani to come in and save us."

"What have we learned about him?"

"We know he's been active lately eliminating opponents of the regime. In terms of personal data, we've got more on his brother who died in Mazar-e Sharif."

"Other members of his family?"

"He told Freed his family was relocating with relatives in Toronto. But the Canadians and CIA and FBI officers working there haven't found a trail."

This sounded wrong to Alan. "How many Persians can there be in Toronto?"

The barrel-chested Bashir downed the beer in two long gulps. "It's his family, Alan. This Greek beer tastes like piss."

"So?"

"He deliberately gave us the wrong city."

"Then he lied."

"Would you trust us to leave them alone? You have to look at this through his lens."

Beckman felt his brain growing tired and wanted to shift gears. "Let's focus a minute on probabilities."

Bashir rubbed the thick black stubble that covered his face. "Everything he's told us about Doha checks out. The Qataris have everything in place for the sixteenth. I've arranged for our jet to fly you in."

"Anything from our sources in Iraq?"

"The usual rumors, but nothing we can substantiate."

"So how seriously should we be taking the threat to the mainland U.S.?"

Bashir, who had family in the DC area and friends in Dearborn, Michigan, groaned: "The problem's always the same. We know a lot in some areas and too fucking little in others. We know that various elements of al-Qaeda have been trying to get their hands on a nuclear device or biological weapon for years. According to the CIA, the probability of them eventually getting their hands on one is fair to high."

"But the probability of their delivering one to the United States and detonating decreases."

"I don't like our odds."

Alan Beckman popped the caps off two more beers, then shifted gears again. "I keep going back to Kourani and the Iranians."

"Alan, wait."

Beckman barreled ahead: "Over the last six months we see a lot of activity on their part going in and out of Uzbekistan. Let's assume this was in response to a threat they picked up from their source in al-Qaeda. Why Uzbekistan? According to our threat assessment people, it's the perfect place to buy WMD components."

MATT WAITED FOR the sun to go down, then crept forward with the ripe orange moon lighting the way. Water bottle in one hand, Glock in the other, plastic bags stuffed in the pocket of his hazmat suit, he picked his way past boulders and low shrubs. *Expect the un-expected*, he said to himself, listening to the breeze hiss over the rough landscape, his heart thumping in his chest.

Then: *Son-of-a-bitch Kourani. What the hell was he digging up? Why?*

Rachel crouched behind a clump of boulders clutching a loaded Glock, two extra clips of ammo, and the satellite phone. An hour ago they'd reached the CIA station in Tashkent. Her deputy, Phil, had contacted CENTCOM headquarters in Tampa, Florida, which was preparing to deploy a Special Forces team from northern Kyrgyzstan to attempt a helicopter rescue at sunup.

The moon had started rising before dark, so Matt knew that its illuminated side marked west. He lifted the mask so he could pick up the fetid scent and followed it to the nearest pit. With the help of a water bottle, he pushed three rats into a plastic bag, sealed it, then double-bagged it per Rachel's instructions. He was starting to fill a third when he heard the crunch of loose rock and froze.

Out of the corner of his left eye he saw the beam of a flashlight wash the edge of the plateau, north to south. *Trouble.* He ducked low to the sand, and as he did, the plastic suit squeaked. The flashlight went out.

Two men, possibly three, whispered in what sounded like Russian. He sensed them moving in his direction and considered taking off the suit and burying it, but decided he didn't have time.

Instead, he carefully undid the ankles, rolled the legs up past his knees, and jogged in a low crouch along the outline of the pit, across an outcropping of rock that spread like an open hand and continued a couple of hundred yards west.

With the moon glowing behind him, he dropped behind some shrubs and waited. Five minutes passed with no voices, nothing.

Turning left, he located the Big Dipper, then Cassiopeia, then Polaris in between the two. He ran with the moon rising on his left. One hundred yards, two, three. He pushed himself. Four and counting. He made a diagonal line now, straight toward Cassiopeia, which marked north and formed a zigzag in the sky.

Over a slight undulation, he stopped and hit the ground. Two silhouettes—no, three—stood in contrast to the mottled gray horizon. He waited, breathing hard, wondering if he'd been seen.

A bald-headed man with a pistol; another with an AK-47; a third flanking farther west. They'd spotted Rachel hidden by the tooth-shaped boulder and were slowly closing in on three sides.

Matt picked up a palm-sized rock and heaved it toward the ridge.

"Da!" the man closest to the ridge grunted, turning, readying his AK-47, and taking three steps east.

Matt hugged the sand, his heart pounding, and crawled close enough to see thin stripes in the man's white shirt. *Now!* Rising, he squeezed the trigger. Sparks flew. Bullets sprayed across the thick silhouette. The big man crumpled at the knees and went down shouting: "Yebat!"

Confused, the other two Russians opened fire on Rachel. She shot back. Bullets ricocheted off rock. Matt pounced, circling around the second man and surprising him with a volley to the side of his head. *Two!*

The man farthest from the ridge turned and sprayed a torrent of bullets that ripped past. Matt dove for cover, adrenaline pounding.

Before Matt could decide what to do next, Rachel seized the distraction and rose above the rock, firing at the third man only ten yards away. For a moment, they faced each other, bursts of light marking the barrels of their guns. Rachel spun violently to her left and simultaneously nailed the short man twice in the chest. Matt watched him fall backward, then realized that Rachel was now shooting at him.

"Rachel!" Matt shouted. "Rachel, it's me! Don't shoot!"

A minute of eerie silence dragged by, then Rachel's voice echoed back: "Matt, I've been hit."

ALAN BECKMAN LOOKED down at the half-eaten feta cheeseburger, then up at the clock. 11:25 PM. Out his window, the stripped-down Parthenon shone dull gold in its spotlights.

Back in 499 BC, the greatest threat to Athens came from Persians armed with arrows and spears. The Athenians hadn't conceived of bioweapons and dirty bombs. But men's minds had spun out generation after generation of increasingly deadly weapons ever since.

In his darkest moments, Alan wondered if the destructive potential of advanced technology now made it impossible for rational societies to defend themselves. He also wondered if the speed with which reams of data could be collected and transferred now overwhelmed the human mind's ability to process them.

He was considering the twin ironies when Bashir returned from the john. "Let's go back to Moshiri's death."

"You talking about the general who was offed in Oman?"

"Freed's contact. Correct."

Bashir popped two Dexedrine tablets. "You suggesting something funny was going on?"

"You think the Iranians killed him?"

"Of course they killed him. Who else?"

Alan didn't have time to take offense. He was trying to push a line of thinking through his mind, shredded by exhaustion and a half-dozen beers. *What had General Moshiri been telling Matt the last couple of months? He was telling him the conflict within the Iranian government was heating up. The mullahs were battling the president. Qods Force had started conspiring against the Ministry of Intelligence and Security.*

His thickly built aide started to push himself up from the chair. "How about I fix us some coffee?"

"So somebody in the government shut Moshiri down. Why now?"

"Kourani told Freed it was probably Tabatabai, chief of MOIS Special Operations."

"Maybe not."

"Maybe I don't follow."

Beckman didn't bother with a direct answer. He said: "Two days later Kourani showed up in Romania."

Bashir scratched his head. "I don't see the connection."

Alan didn't see a clear one either: "It's there, hiding."

"Maybe."

Alan's facial muscles tightened when the phone rang. The clock read 11:43 PM in Athens, which meant 4:43 PM in Washington, DC.

"Alan, Shelly," the serious voice said on the other end. "I'm going secure."

While the encryption program was locking in, Alan's mind wandered to a scene from the movie *The Lives of Others* he'd watched with Celia just a few days ago—before the whole mess had started—then back to Moshiri. "Pull up all of Matt's reports on Moshiri," he said to his aide.

Bashir stood as General Jasper's airy voice came over the line. "Alan, good evening. Where's Freed?"

"Still in Uzbekistan. When I spoke to him early this morning, he and the station chief were on their way to Rebirth Island. I expect they'll spend the night in Muynoq."

Following a pause, the general's voice returned with more steel. "Call him, Alan, as soon as we're finished."

"I will."

"Tell him I want him back at headquarters as soon as possible."

"Why?"

"First, we need to prep him for his meeting with Kourani on the eighteenth. Second, this Khost problem isn't going away."

"But—"

"The White House has questions."

"General, it's critical to retrace Kourani's path."

"Do you realize what day it is, Alan? We don't have time."

Alan suddenly felt like he was twelve years old. "Yes, General."

"Here's our thinking: Kourani's either telling the truth, meaning he'll deliver on the threat when he meets Freed in New York, or he isn't. If Kourani has a real tip for us, we deploy on the eighteenth. We're as well prepared here as we can be, which isn't optimal. We can't correct that now. If Kourani doesn't deliver on the threat, it's simple: we rescind our offer of money and asylum."

Alan sensed his career slipping down the drain. He wanted to reassert himself, but didn't know how. "I'll call Freed now."

"Please do. And tell him that the transfer of the two and a half million to a numbered account in Switzerland has been completed."

"I thought the amount was two million."

"So did I."

"BREATHE DEEPLY," MATT whispered into Rachel's half-opened eyes, his hands sticky with blood. "You're doing fine." He'd stopped the bleeding from her shoulder and was using his shirt to apply pressure to a second gunshot wound above her knee.

"Phil," she moaned. "Call Phil." The tramadol Matt had given her had numbed the pain. But it, together with the loss of blood, was affecting her brain.

"I called him already."

"What did he say?"

"He said a Special Operations team was being deployed from Manas Air Base in Kyrgyzstan."

"When?"

"Soon. Don't worry." He didn't want to tell her to close her eyes and sleep, because that would increase the likelihood of her body's going into shock. "You never told me how you met your husband."

"I took his Russian novels class at Stanford. Brad introduced me to Dostoyevsky. It changed my life."

The bleeding wouldn't stop, so Matt removed his belt and, using it as a tourniquet, tightened it halfway up her thigh.

Rachel began to shiver. "I'm cold."

Removing his undershirt, he covered her. Warm air cleaved to his skin.

"What's your favorite," she asked. "*Crime and Punishment* or *The Gambler*?"

"I'm partial to *The Brothers Karamazov*."

"I love Alyosha, but think I'm more like Vanya, the rationalist, tormented by the senseless suffering in the world. What about you?"

Her forehead felt hot. "I don't know. I started off like Ivan, but I'm evolving."

"I hope so."

Matt tried to do two things at once: attend to her wounds and listen for remaining men with his Glock and the captured AK-47 ready. He'd seen two SUVs late in the afternoon, so there could've been another carload of guys hunting them.

"I wish I could have some oranges."

He finished dressing the wound in her shoulder with gauze bandages and tape.

"I love oranges."

Hearing a rustle, he clamped a hand over her mouth. Nothing—just the rattle of dried leaves moved by the warm breeze. He loosened the belt he'd used to staunch the bleeding from her thigh. The blood seemed to have stopped. *Thank God.*

He applied antiseptic wipes, then covered the jagged entry hole with the rest of the gauze. The adhesive tape ripped easily with his teeth.

Pleased with his work, he removed his hand from her mouth. Rachel's face appeared pale and shrunken in the faint light cast by the moon, which had receded high into the night sky.

"Phil?" Rachel asked, trying to push herself up.

"He's not here," Matt whispered. "We'll be home soon."

Hearing a muffled sound in the distance, he lifted the captured AK-47 to his shoulder and adjusted the day/night vision scope. He scanned slowly east to west. Nothing.

"Phil, am I bothering you? Phil, are you on the phone?"

RACHEL'S DEPUTY WAS actually five hundred and fifty miles southwest in the U.S. Embassy in Tashkent looking at a flash report he'd just received from the CIA station in Moscow. He underlined the sentences: "Amin Kasemloo landed at Sheremetyevo International Airport in Moscow on an Uzbekistan Airways flight from Tashkent on July 8. Observed leaving the Iranian Consulate in the company of a Russian by the name of Oleg Urakov. Urakov is a former bioengineer from the Soviet Biopreparat."

Phil had started punching out a reply when a young African American officer, Beatrice, appeared in the doorway. "Phil, you on the phone?"

He held up a hand and continued typing: "Need an immediate trace put on Oleg Urakov. Check his residence, etc. Arrange to have him arrested if necessary. This is of EXTREME IMPORTANCE!!! TIME IS OF THE ESSENCE. Phil Heller, Tashkent."

Phil prided himself on being a realist. He understood that a majority of people inside most organizations were a waste of time—crippled by fears, self-doubts, and cynicism. In his previous job in the European Division of Operations he'd kept a list of thirty-five officers out of hundreds deployed throughout the department whom he could count on to get things done. He hoped that someone in the Moscow office would now step up.

Pushing "Send," he looked up at Beatrice's cornrows. "What?"

"I got a confirmation from CENTCOM."

Fear and excitement clashed in his eyes. "When?"

"They're looking at a window of two to four hours depending on weather and flying conditions."

"They can't move any faster?"

Beatrice shook her head and watched the excitement drain from his face.

Despite his mixed feelings about Rachel as a boss, Phil was proud she'd had the guts to go to Rebirth Island. Now he felt a huge responsibility for getting her out. "Any chance we can get a local military helicopter? I'll fly there myself."

"Not without pissing off the Uzbeks, who are going to want to know what we were doing on Vozrozhdeniye."

"Anything further from Morgan?"

"Negative."

Gritting his teeth hard, he said: "Drive out to the airport and wait. Make sure the ambulance and emergency team are there and don't leave. Take money. Pay off anyone you need to. As soon as the helicopter touches down, call me. I'm waiting for an answer from Moscow. I'll hold down the fort."

CHAPTER THIRTEEN

September 15

Tariq gazed up at the ceiling's peeling yellow paint and thought about Matt Freed. The proverb his grandfather repeated many times echoed in his head: "A real friend is one who takes the hand of his friend in times of distress and helplessness."

With the smell of charcoal hanging in the air, he reviewed his troubled life: the exiles to Pakistan and Uzbekistan, the long trek to Bamiyan during the civil war, his struggle to finish his education, his sister's marriage to a Turkish merchant at fifteen, the almost daily harassment by Tajiks, Uzbeks, and Pushtuns for being a Hazara "peasant," the beating by Pakistani border guards that made it difficult to see out of his left eye.

It had been friendship, even more than family, that had pulled him through. Maybe Freed didn't understand his country; maybe it was dangerous to "mix" with Westerners as his father warned. But the truth was that Matt had rescued him and his father from jail.

The previous night, Tariq had stayed up late serving green tea, biscuits, and pomegranates to his father and an Iranian mullah visiting from Mashhad. He'd heard them talk in hushed tones about the suicide attack at Zainabia Mosque in the city of Sialkot in eastern Pakistan. Thirty Shia worshippers had died and more than fifty were badly injured when a man entered the mosque and opened a briefcase during Friday prayers. The explosion left a two-foot-wide crater in the concrete floor.

"This is the work of either Sipah-e-Sahaba or al-Qaeda," Tariq heard the Iranian cleric say, referring to two extremist Sunni terrorist organizations. "They're trying to ignite a holy war."

Later, Tariq heard Mullah Yazdi talk about his work with Ayatollah Beheshti, who led the Islamic Center in Hamburg in the '6os, when Tariq's father was there, and mention the name Kourani.

The young Hazara brushed his thick black hair and carefully pulled a brown tunic over his pants. His collarbone no longer bothered him, but the wound in his shoulder still hurt. Pushing open the door to the tiny office upstairs, he found his father with his white beard in a book.

"Good morning, Father."

The old man looked up with eyes that had seen everything.

"God is great."

"Have you asked Mullah Yazdi what he knows about this man Kourani?"

Mullah Hadi Zadeh scrunched his mouth and brow. "Mullah Yazdi is a very devout man."

"You mean he hates the Americans."

"He doesn't hate them, my son. He feels that his people have been humiliated, damaged, ignored, rejected, abused."

"So do all the Persians. And they're arrogant, too."

The old man grinned as he lifted his round body. "Don't stop a donkey that isn't yours."

Tariq reminded him: "You made a promise."

The mullah opened his mouth to say something and stopped. "We're beset with so many problems, Tariq. Do we need this, too?"

Tariq raised his voice. "You told me yourself: repay those who are kind."

The mullah sighed. "I will speak to him, Tariq. You are right."

•   •   •

GENERAL JASPER DOWNED two Tylenol with the Diet Coke and held her head. *How can this be possible? With all the billions we've spent on security* . . .

She'd spent most of the day at Homeland Security going over readiness and probabilities. Analysts there had prepared a threat matrix designed to pinpoint likely targets of the al-Qaeda attack. But any way you looked at it, the parameter of "midsized U.S. cities" remained large.

After eliminating the top five population centers—New York, Los Angeles, Chicago, Houston, and Phoenix—thirty-eight cities remained with populations ranging between 1.5 million (Philadephia; San Antonio; Dallas; San Jose) and 400,000 (Kansas City, Missouri; Cleveland; Virginia Beach; Omaha; Miami).

The logistics of covering thirty-eight cities spread from coast to coast proved extremely challenging, to say the least. Local medical teams and law enforcement had been placed on 24/7 Red Alert. FBI special response and biohazard teams had been stationed in five "important" midsized cities spread out by region. Deploy points included Washington, DC; Detroit; Jacksonville, Florida; Seattle; and San Diego.

The hope was that Kourani would supply detailed information on the eighteenth and steps could immediately be taken to prevent any attack. Once a bioweapon like anthrax actually deployed, the prognosis wasn't good.

Analysts projected that a successful bio or chemical attack on three cities simultaneously could result in as many as half a million casualties before it could be contained.

Half a million casualties! That's the entire population of Boston. General Jasper couldn't get the number out of her head. She wasn't one to rely on luck or prayer.

"Half a million," she repeated to Shelly, who arrived with that evening's intelligence summary.

"Staggering."

"I can't imagine."

"I don't want to."

General Jasper lifted her throbbing head and walked to the window. "How can we be so unprepared?"

THE BEAT OF Matt's heart pulsed in his head. When he concentrated, he heard drums. A progression of power chords. A cowbell marking the backbeat. A man sang:

B-B-B-Baby, you ain't seen nothin' yet.
Here's something that you're never gonna forget.

Bachman-Turner Overdrive. One of my favorite bands. He spun with the others and kicked up his legs as lights smiled past his shoulder.

Then he heard a rotor and the rasp of a sliding metal door. A man in a camouflage looked down at him and scratched his chin. "Are you all right, sir? Can you hear me?"

Nothing seemed to come out. But Matt could identify the Tennessee accent in the second voice, which said: "Once we get some fluids in him he'll be fine."

In what seemed to him like the blink of an eye, Matt lay in bed with stiff white sheets tucked around his chest. When he sat up, a nurse with Mongol features put down a magazine with Paris Hilton on the cover.

"Where am I?" he asked in Russian.

She made a clicking sound with her tongue and left.

Matt looked around. Putty brown walls, a loudly ticking clock, tubes connected to his arms that led to hanging bottles labeled "Glucose" and "5% Saline." A minute later, blond-haired Phil appeared. "Welcome," he said, smiling broadly. "You made it."

"Where?"

"Tashkent. You're suffering from severe dehydration."

It came back in a rush: the bone-wrenching roar of the helicopter, blinding lights, tracers burning through the dark, men with strange helmets screaming in his ears. Two soldiers had helped him into the helicopter—then he'd blacked out.

"Rachel?" Matt asked.

"They're working on her leg now. She's gonna be fine."

As he thought back to the orange landscape, tightness and fatigue returned to his arms and thighs.

"We were lucky," Matt said.

"No, you went fucking commando."

He remembered the three men shot and killed. "You recover the bodies?"

"What bodies?"

"Bastards who killed our guide and tried to snuff us."

Phil looked like he'd slept in his clothes. "The rescue team was only tasked with lifting you out. Uzbek authorities are on the island now."

Matt pointed to the clock on the wall that read 3:15 and asked: "What day is it?"

"The afternoon of the fifteenth."

"Shit."

Phil explained that a contamination team had scrubbed down the helicopter and observed Matt and Rachel for hours before moving them to the hospital.

The moon-faced nurse reentered with a tray of toast, yogurt, and tea. "Get that in your stomach, then we'll talk."

Twenty minutes later, with disinfectant from the freshly swabbed hallway burning their eyes, Phil said: "Kasemloo flew here from Moscow on July eighth. Accompanying him was a Russian by the name of Oleg Urakov, a bioengineer who used to work for Soviet Biopreparat. He currently runs a consulting firm out of St. Petersburg."

A chill ran up Matt's spine. "Where's Oleg now?"

"Our people tracked his passport back to Moscow. They believe he checked into the Buteyko Clinic in Moscow under an alias. We're trying to confirm that now."

"Buteyko. I've heard of that."

"It's a breathing method used to treat a range of diseases."

"The Russian's ill?"

"If he's who we think he is, he's very sick. A nurse there said he was suffering from advanced lung cancer."

Matt remembered something. "The rats," he said. "I put them in Rachel's backpack."

"Yes."

"Where are they?"

"The contamination team's got 'em. If you were planning on keeping 'em as pets, they died."

"They need to be sent back to NCTS headquarters for testing. Can you make sure they go out in the next pouch?"

Phil folded his arms across his chest. "I got a better suggestion. You can take them yourself."

"Sorry, Phil. I'm on my way to Moscow."

Phil reached for an e-mail printout in his jacket pocket. "Your boss wants you back at headquarters ASAP."

"Can't." Reading the message felt like a kick to the head.

"Not what you had planned?" Phil asked.

There's no fucking way they're calling me back. Why? So I can get called on the carpet, when I should be tracking down this Oleg guy? Matt stood and grabbed Phil by the arm. "Lead me to the closest secure phone."

THE MEETING BETWEEN the Hazara mullah and the Iranian mullah had gone well so far. They sat at a small table under a conifer tree as peacocks wandered the grounds. Men from the mosque served kofta (meatballs) and bonjan (spicy eggplant) salad.

"I worry that the many challenges we face are making us rigid," Mullah Zadeh, Tariq's father, said.

They'd spent most of the hour discussing Pakistan and its support of the resurging student movement (the Taliban), which now controlled three provinces in southern Afghanistan.

"Praise be to Allah and His Messenger. In the name of God, the Compassionate, the Merciful. Allah has promised us victory and he will give us victory," Mullah Yazdi said.

"The Pakistanis want to make us their colony."

The Iranian mullah with the wart on his nose almost choked on a leek. "Maybe it is blasphemy to say this, but the American infidels will never let that happen."

This was the opening that Mullah Hadi Zadeh had been waiting for. "Yes. The Americans can be useful."

"It used to be that if Afghanistan was mentioned, no one would recognize the name or where it was. But today, and for Allah is all praise, everybody knows it as the land where the crusaders have tried to take a stand."

"You know, my brother, it was an American who saved me from jail."

The Iranian leaned across the table and poured himself more green tea.

The short, round Hazara mullah skillfully steered the conversation to recollections of the Islamic Center in Hamburg. Both men had been pupils of the great Ayatollah Beheshti. Beheshti had been Yazdi's spiritual mentor.

"Deceit is not an honorable trait between men like us," Hadi Zadeh began. "So I ask you not to be offended if I make myself transparent."

"All praise to the Wise One."

"My brother, I have nothing to hide. The American who saved me, the infidel, as you call him, asked me for information about a man named Kourani who was also at the Hamburg Center in the early sixties. I told him truthfully that I don't remember much about the man, except that he had three sons. I also gave him my word that I would help him. Now in the spirit of friendship and compassion, I turn to you."

When the Iranian stood, Hadi Zadeh feared he would leave. But pulling at the beard that curled around his long nose, he slowly circled a tree as a peacock screeched nearby. Minutes later he stopped and looked down at Hadi with a tenderness the Hazara mullah found surprising.

"I have asked the great Allah to temper my anger with reason.

The Great One has answered because you are a good man and a friend. Your heart is pure."

Hadi Zadeh clasped his hands and bowed. "Allah is great. He speaks the truth."

Mullah Yazdi pointed a short, crooked finger at Mullah Hadi Zadeh's round face. "You said something earlier that the Compassionate One asks me to visit again. The infidels can be useful. This is how a wise man speaks."

"My presence with you today is proof of that, my brother."

Mullah Yazdi reached under his white robe and removed a cloth pouch. Opening it, he took out a photo. Turning the picture over, he wrote something on the back.

"I don't have to tell you all the ways the infidels have caused me to suffer. With their friend, the devil Shah, they tore apart my family, tortured me, threw me in jail, inflicted unspeakable acts of humiliation. But they have never broken my spirit, thanks to the strength of the great Allah."

"Praise to Allah."

"Allah is great in ways that surprise me every day. And he is compassionate and clever beyond comprehension. That's why he brought us here today." With a trembling hand, the Iranian passed the photo to Mullah Hadi Zadeh. "This is my son, Nazad. He is nineteen years old this month. His mother couldn't understand the constant travel my work required. She sought refuge with her sister, who lives in France. They are part of a group of Iranian exiles who live outside of Paris. The smaller boy standing next to Nazad is Javed Mohammed, the son of Hamid Kourani, who was martyred by the Taliban in Mazar-e Sharif."

"Praise to Allah," Mullah Zadeh said looking at the photo of the two boys with their bikes.

"Javed is the grandson of Mullah Kourani. He also lives with his mother, who is a widow. I hear that he's an odd boy, who loves birds and wants to study them in the United States. Maybe your American friend can help him. Maybe, in return, Javed knows something about his grandfather, Mullah Kourani."

"Praise to Allah."

"Praise to the Compassionate One. He works in surprising ways."

"The Great One's work will be done."

"THIS IS ASS-BACKWARD, Alan!" Matt shouted into the secure phone from an office on the ground floor of the hospital.

Alan counted to ten before he answered: "Calm down, Matt. You and I get it. Others don't."

"Okay, Moses, which commandment is that?"

"Eleven. Thou shalt not leave pandemonium in thy wake."

"Maybe I've lost my sense of humor."

"Everyone's on edge. We've got to keep our heads."

"I need your support."

"The point is that General Jasper has got her skirt all ruffled about the riot in Khost and the need to violate Uzbek airspace with the search and rescue."

"It wasn't a riot! Why do they keep calling it that? It was a friggin' attack."

"What did I just say?"

"I was there, Alan. I was the one who was shot at."

"I know that."

"Who the heck is briefing the general?" Matt asked. "They've got their priorities up their butts."

"The long and short is: Jasper wants you in her office tomorrow."

Matt swallowed hard. "That's not going to happen."

"Listen, Matt."

"Tell her I'm delirious from the medication. Tell her I'm in traction up to my neck. Buy me time."

Alan loved that his deputy's spirit hadn't been dampened. "I'm passing on orders. I can't force your hand."

"What's that mean?"

"It means I delivered the message and I'm on my way to Qatar. I'll meet you in New York on the eighteenth."

"Have fun."

"Anything you want me to tell headquarters?"

"Tell them my wounds are infected and my fever's up and down. I'll be back in Washington as soon as I'm healthy enough to travel."

Alan smiled to himself. "Stay in touch with HQ while I'm gone."

Matt pictured the four shining faces of his wife and girls back home. "How are Liz and the kids?"

"Good. Your mother-in-law arrives today."

"My mother-in-law?" Matt knew that meant Liz was feeling stressed.

"You have anything you want me to say?"

Matt's voice started to wobble. "Tell them I love them with all my heart and miss them. Tell Liz to be strong. Tell her that I know what I'm doing, and that I'm doing what has to be done."

TARIQ HAD BEEN waiting an hour in the windowless room at the U.S. Embassy when the door flew open and a short, muscular man burst in.

"Burris," the American said, extending a hand. "What can I do for you?"

Tariq struggled not to be overwhelmed by Burris's spiky energy. A part of him wanted to blurt out "Sorry" and leave. Instead, he took a deep breath and plunged in, relating the story he'd rehearsed in the cab. It started with his days working with Matt as a translator, covered the rescue of his father in Khost and Matt's interest in a man named Kourani, who studied at the Islamic Center of Hamburg in the sixties.

It annoyed him that instead of listening, the American scrolled through messages on his cellular phone. It disrupted him even further when Burris excused himself and left the room.

A thin, redheaded man who had come in behind the shorter American smiled. "Please be patient. He's a busy man."

Tariq wanted to like the Americans. But a part of him argued that their arrogance would make it impossible for them to ever understand the Afghan perspective.

Five uneasy minutes elapsed before Burris returned. "An emergency message from Washington," he explained. "Where were we?"

Tariq cut to the chase. "I need you to show this picture to my friend Mr. Morgan."

Burris scrunched his forehead into a question mark as he studied the color photo of Javed Mohammed and Nazad. "Who am I looking at here?"

"The boy on the right, Javed Mohammed, is the grandson of a certain Shia mullah who Mr. Morgan asked for information about. The boy's eighteen and lives in France, outside of Paris. His name is printed on the back."

Burris turned the photo over. "Mr. Morgan doesn't work for us."

Tariq couldn't suppress a grunt of astonishment. "He told me he's employed by the U.S. government."

"We're not in the same branch."

"But you work together?"

"Yes and no."

With his square body and his feet planted apart, the American with the weightlifter's body represented an impediment. Tariq's brain worked hard to think of a way around him. "Mr. Morgan asked me to find this information and bring it to you as fast as I could."

Burris raised an eyebrow. "How do I know you're not working for the enemy?"

Tariq stumbled for words. "Because . . . your people . . . know me."
"We do?"

"I was employed by you Americans as a translator. I recently traveled with Mr. Morgan to Khost."

"Why should I believe you?"

Tariq answered straight into the American's eyes. "Mr. Morgan assured me that you would be able to communicate important news to him."

The human fireplug snatched back the photo from his aide. "And this is important? Why?"

Tariq didn't hesitate. "Mr. Morgan will understand."

"I don't have time."

"I'll inform Mr. Morgan you said that when I speak to him next time."

Burris stuck out his chin. "Why are you bothering me with this if you know how to reach him on your own?"

The anger Tariq felt trembled down his legs. "It's a matter of technology, sir. It's something you have and we Afghans lack. You like to remind us that we live in the seventeenth century. And in some respects, that's correct. Mr. Morgan told me that this matter was of urgency to him. He didn't tell me why. That's your business. I've come here today out of respect for Mr. Morgan and the great favor he did for me and my father."

Burris was moved enough to address Tariq as a fellow human being. "Okay, Tariq. I hope you understand that I have to ask these questions."

"I don't pretend to understand you Americans. I'm simply here to help my friend."

"Morgan's an unusual fellow," Burris said nodding back to the redhead, who stood like a statue. "What do you think?"

The redhead spoke with a warm, friendly voice. "We should thank Tariq for his assistance and do as he says."

Burris still wasn't convinced. He waved the photo in Tariq's face. "You sure about this?"

"The tragedy of my country is the product of distrust. What was once one people has fragmented into tribes that hate one another. I assumed you Americans were strong because you are united. *United* States. Maybe that's an illusion."

Burris smiled without showing his teeth. "I didn't ask for a goddamn lecture."

"A friend to my friend is a friend to me."

"I'll make sure he gets this."

Tariq nodded. "Please send Mr. Morgan my best."

CHAPTER FOURTEEN

September 15–16

Moshen Kourani studied his reflection in the mirror and tried to look pleased. "Everything's going according to plan," he said out loud. But anger and doubt still swirled like a desert twister through his head.

Eleven hours ago he'd returned to the American Consulate to retrieve his passport and visa. On the next-to-the-last page written in pencil was a telephone number put there per Kourani's instructions to Freed when they'd met in Bucharest. It was the number Kourani would use to reach Matthew Freed when he arrived in New York City on the eighteenth.

The Iranian with the close-cropped black and silver beard moved quickly in underwear and socks. Item by item, he laid his documents on the dresser: diplomatic passport under the name Fariel Golpaghani; Iranian government ID, driver's license, and credit cards all issued to the same name; photos of his nephews, mother, father, and brothers.

With his heart racing, he stopped, took six deep breaths, and uttered a prayer he'd learned from his father:

O Lord! Bless the companions of Muhammad. Enlarge for them the gardens of Your paradise. Protect them thereby from the cunning of Satan. Assist them in those righteous things wherein they beg of Your assistance. Induce them, thereby, to hope largely from You. To covet what is with You. To give up blaming others about that which lies in the hands of Your creatures, in order that You may recall them to long for You and fear You. Restrain them from desiring worldly prosperity. Make them prepare for what is after death. Facilitate for them every pain that may come upon them on the day when the soul leaves the body. Secure them from that wherein may occur a trial of their terrors, from torment of the Fire and eternal continuance therein. Remove them to the peace of the resting place of those who guard against evil.

More at ease with himself, he sat at the desk and composed a letter to his wife, Sanaz. This proved difficult, because of the unexpected emotions that flooded back. What had started out promisingly twenty-eight years ago after a chance meeting at a friend's house on the mountain slopes of Londoil had yielded two painful miscarriages, years of separation during the war, and an estrangement two years ago when Sanaz moved into an apartment with her sister outside of Tehran.

They'd disagreed on many things. Most important, Sanaz had never understood what she called Moshen's "blind" dedication to the revolution.

For his part, Kourani hadn't been able to accept her trust in feelings and intuition. How could a woman sense the shape of the future? How could she know what people hid in their hearts? Wasn't this blasphemy?

The more he'd pushed her away, the more desperate she'd become. He'd never forget the disgust he felt the night she collapsed on the bathroom floor and begged like a dog to be listened to and treated like a human being.

Now that he looked back, maybe he'd judged her too harshly. She didn't understand that Islam was a form of mental submission that grew from an awareness of the reality behind existence. It transcended one's vision of one's surroundings and the narrow confines of time.

He wished he could take back the insults he had spit in her face. Words like *temptress, idiot, witch*.

The best he could do was ask for her forgiveness and promise to provide her with comfort in the next life.

Hearing two quick raps on the door, he wiped a tear from his eye and answered it with a glance at the clock. 1:44 AM. His aide, Jamshad, was several minutes early. Kourani held a finger to his lips and escorted Jamshad to the bathroom, where he turned on the shower. "In order to accomplish the task before us we need to be resolute."

"Yes, master."

"There are enemies all around us," he said into Jamshad's ear as the room filled with steam.

Since arriving in Vienna, the deputy director of Qods Force had taken strict precautions. He knew the Americans were following him everywhere and suspected that his phones were tapped.

Rail-thin Jamshad whispered in a raspy voice. "The remainder of the delegation has arrived."

This was welcome news to Kourani. "So the Iranian ambassador is here with the foreign minister?"

"And two security agents."

"Of course." Kourani smiled, knowing that he feared the agents of MOIS even more than the Americans.

"Your brother has also arrived," his younger aide added.

"Abbas. You've seen him?"

Jamshad nodded. "I picked him up at the airport."

"How does he look?"

"Perfect."

Drafting his only surviving brother for this dangerous mission had been difficult for Kourani. But in his role as warrior for Iran's religious leaders, he reminded himself that obedience to the reality of the Qur'an—the foundation of all creation—was not a passive servitude but an active movement. *This a chance for both of us to become martyrs for the sake of all mankind.*

"Is Abbas ready?"

"He walks in the footsteps of the Most Noble Messenger."

"O thou shrouded in thy mantle, arise and warn," Kourani quoted from the Sura as he handed Jamshad the electronic key. "Give me another fifteen minutes. Then show him in."

Jamshad bowed awkwardly; he didn't know what to say. "I pray for your success, master. Allah is great."

"Yes, Allah is great. Thank you, Jamshad, for everything. Now go."

TEN MINUTES LATER, Moshen Kourani stood facing his younger brother, Abbas. "Remarkable," he uttered over and over as his eyes passed from his hair down to his eyebrows, nose, and chin to the little belly pushing out the gray silk shirt.

"The sacrifice has been great," Abbas said. "No more bastani-e gol-e bolbol [Persian ice cream flavored with saffron, rose water, and chunks of heavy cream], shirini nokhodchi [clover-shaped chickpea cookies], or bamiehs [oval-shaped dough deep-fried and covered with a syrup]."

By losing ten pounds, growing a close-cropped beard, and clipping his hair, Abbas had transformed himself into a near duplicate of his brother. There were subtle differences of course. Abbas's face was still puffier around the cheeks and eyes. The eyes themselves were somewhat narrower and darker. Abbas was a half-inch shorter than his brother and more thickly muscled through the thighs and chest.

"It is time for us to surrender, Abbas," Moshen said.

The younger man nodded. Then they held hands, knelt together, and prayed.

GENERAL JASPER DREAMED she was riding in a helicopter descending through clouds and mist. The landscape below was covered with forms that looked like sleeping cows. *Of course*, she thought, *it's going to rain.*

But the mist carried with it a sadness that grew thicker and clung to her skin. An owl hooted in the distance, summoning her to look closer. The shapes came into focus not as cows, but as human bodies—thousands of them huddled together, men, women, and children, dead, their faces contorted with pain.

Hearing the "Hoo" again, she sat up in bed. The clock read 5:13, which meant the Ambien she had taken while watching Letterman had helped her to only five hours' sleep.

Her husband, Clive, turned over and asked: "Are you all right, Em?"

"Just a bad dream, honey. Go to sleep."

Four nights in a row now the owl had awakened her with dreams of dead bodies and children gasping for breath.

Discipline, she said to herself. *Mental discipline is imperative.*

But her brain associated discipline with responsibility, and hers was enormous. As the head of NCTS, it was her job to protect every citizen of the United States from attack.

Within seconds, sundry problems rushed to the surface: Kourani, al-Qaeda activities in Anbar Province west of Baghdad, a spike in cell phone traffic from Anbar to North Waziristan—a known al-Qaeda stronghold in the eastern tribal region of Pakistan.

What does it all mean? Has al-Qaeda actually gotten their hands on a chemical device or dirty bomb?

She'd underlined reports, queried the experts, attended meetings at all the intelligence agencies and the NSC, but she still had no idea of the answer. *What have we missed? WHAT?*

"Hoo! Hoo!" the owl called again.

It seemed unfair, cruel—the years of study and service in the U.S. Army; the long weeks and months away from her family; the sacrifice; the hard work all for naught. She faced a crucible. *History will judge me by my performance now.*

"Hoo."

Her mind flashed to an image of bodies exploding in the street, then traveled back to a paper she'd written as a West Point cadet— "The Political Fallout of the Bubonic Plague." It haunted her now, the story of how the Black Death had spread through Europe and Asia in the fourteenth century, resulting in 75 million deaths. Muslims and Jews had been blamed and persecuted.

She remembered the words of one eyewitness: "Father abandoned child, wife husband, one brother another; for this illness seemed to strike through the breath and sight. And so they died. And none could be found to bury the dead for money or friendship. And so many died that all believed it was the end of the world."

What else can I do? What?

Five nights of interrupted sleep had pushed her to her limits. With guilt closing in, she imagined escaping to Maui with her husband. Piña coladas, orange blossoms, the warm sun drawing stress-induced poisons out of her skin.

Please, stop!

Pulling on a robe, General Jasper slid open the patio door and stepped into the raw night air. "Hoo," the owl called mockingly.

She saw it gazing back at her from a maple branch fifteen feet overhead.

"Hoo."

"Go away!"

"Hoo!"

The bird seemed to be trying to speak to her. "What do you want?"

The regal gray owl cocked its head lower.

"Tell me!" she shouted.

The owl didn't move. "Hoo! Hoo!"

MATT SAT UP in the Tashkent hospital bed, thinking: *Oleg Urakov is the key. He worked for Soviet Biopreparat. Traveled to Uzbekistan on July eighth with one of Kourani's agents, Kasemloo. On the fourteenth, the three of them went to Rebirth Island. They didn't go for a picnic. Kasemloo died. Urakov's dying. I gotta get off my ass.*

He reached for his briefcase. *Only one problem. How do I get to Moscow without a visa?* Now that General Jasper had ordered him back to headquarters, a visa through official channels was out of the question. And he had to be in New York City in two days.

The contents of the briefcase didn't provide much promise—a passport made out to John Paul Morgan, a GSM international cell phone, his coded address book.

A nurse in a grayish blue uniform entered to remove the breakfast tray.

"Internet?" Matt asked.

"Wat?" she grunted back.

He mimed typing on a computer. "E-mail. Computer."

She held up two fingers and pointed downstairs.

"Thank you," he said in Russian.

On the second floor behind the nurses' station, he found the Dell, typed in www.google.com and entered "Russian brides and tours." More than a dozen sites popped up offering mail-order brides and tours for Western bachelors. Surfing through several, he settled on one called Russian Brides Café and composed an e-mail saying he was a successful U.S. businessman currently traveling in Central Asia and interested in being included in the next bachelors' expedition to Moscow. He explained that he was willing to join a tour immediately if his visa could be expedited.

When he logged into his e-mail an hour later, Matt found a response with a telephone number to call. The price: $3,500, excluding airfare.

It took fifty dollars to get one of the nurses to connect him to the number in Moscow. A Russian woman with a slight British accent identified herself as Luda Kolchaveska.

"Mr. Morgan, we would be delighted to host you," she gushed over the phone in English. "But we usually don't have individuals joining the tour at midpoint. Our current group of guests just spent four days in St. Petersburg and is scheduled to arrive here tomorrow."

"I would like to join them in Moscow," Matt insisted.

Ms. Kolchaveska was a good businesswoman. "We have assembled a group of remarkable young women," she said. "Are you anxious to find a bride?"

"You bet."

"Tell me a little about yourself."

"I'm a successful businessman in my early forties. My wife passed away last year. She wasn't able to have children."

"I think you'll be very pleased with our girls. Very beautiful and intelligent. Clean, healthy. No hang-ups."

"Sounds like heaven."

"This will please you, Mr. Morgan?"

"I'm in a hurry."

"We will have to charge an extra five hundred euros to facilitate an emergency visa. And we will have to bill you for the whole price of the tour."

Matt didn't hesitate. "That won't be a problem."

"Good. Where are you now?"

"Tashkent."

"That's easy. Go to the Aeroflot desk at the airport approximately four hours before your flight. Call me from there and I will arrange for the visa. At that time you will tell me when you will arrive in Moscow so I can have an expediter assist you in clearing immigration and delivering you to your hotel."

"Thank you," Matt said. "I'm going to call a taxi now."

Instead, he reached Phil at the embassy and told him he needed a car and driver to take him to the airport.

"You sure you're well enough to travel all the way to DC?" Rachel's deputy asked.

"I'll rest on the plane."

Phil hesitated. "Maybe it's best to have Major Dubois, the military doctor who's taking care of Rachel, have a look at you first."

"No need, Phil. I'm raring to go."

"Okay, Rambo. The car will be there shortly. I guess Oleg Urakov will have to wait."

"Any news on that front?"

"We're still trying to confirm that he checked into the Buteyko Clinic in Moscow," Phil answered.

"Give my best to Rachel next time you see her. Tell her I'll stay in touch."

Three and a half hours later, Matt stood at the Aeroflot counter at Tashkent International Airport listening to a ticket agent tell him that his visa had been approved and would be issued on his arrival in Moscow. In the reflection in the mirror behind the clerk, he saw Phil's blond head pop over the top of a black sedan.

He's onto me, he thought, and considered ducking around a corner.

Phil thrust his knees out as he crossed straight to Matt. "What are you doing at the Aeroflot counter?"

Matt lied: "I booked a flight through Moscow."

Phil leaned into his ear. "We have to talk."

Now what?

A Russian version of "Billy Jean" blared over the coffee kiosk stereo. Phil undid the clasp on a manila envelop and said: "This just came in from Burris in Kabul. He got it from a friend of yours. An Afghan."

"Tariq?"

Matt studied the computer printout of a young boy on a bike. "Is this all?"

Phil fished deeper. "There's a name. Javed Mohammed; eighteen years old; lives in France. Your friend said, and I quote: 'The boy is the grandson of Mullah Kourani. If you locate the boy, he may be willing to exchange information for help getting into the U.S.' "

Matt's eyes buzzed. "No address?"

"No address."

"France is a big country." He tugged Phil's elbow. "I need to use your phone."

"The Inmarsat's in the trunk."

Matt consulted the coded entries in his book and dialed a number. On the other side of the continent, in a garret across from the Odéon Theatre on the Left Bank of Paris, a tall, dapper Argentine answered the phone. "BCA. Bon jour."

"Is this my friend Guillermo Moncada?"

The Argentine shifted to heavily accented English. "Matt, is that you? Did you call to wish me a happy birthday?"

"Is it your birthday, ché?"

"Tomorrow."

"Then happy birthday tomorrow, Guillermo, and a big abrazo."

"Thanks."

"Now I need to ask you a favor."

"We can balance the ledger. Go ahead."

Eight years ago Matt had rescued Guillermo from a Serbian arms dealer who wanted him dead.

"I'm looking for a kid named Javed Mohammed. I believe his last name is Kourani. Eighteen; lives in France with his mother; his grandfather was a Shia mullah."

Guillermo was a useful guy. He'd escaped from Argentina in the '70s during the Dirty War and used his skills as a political operative to create alliances and make deals. You wanted a woman who had slept with Fidel Castro, he could find her. You needed a Chinese minisub, he could get that for you, too.

"How soon do you need him?"

"Today, if possible."

"You're kidding, of course."

"Absolutely not."

"You caught me at a busy time, hermano. How can I reach you?"

"I'm on my way to Moscow, but I'll check my e-mail: bachman-turner@yahoo.com."

THE EIGHT-PERSON FBI surveillance team had been following Kourani around Vienna for days, from one tourist destination to another.

At 4 AM on the sixteenth, a female agent sipped espresso in the lobby and reread the *International Herald Tribune* while two male agents sat out front in a car listening to Joss Stone on BBC radio.

None of them saw Moshen Kourani descend the service elevator and enter the laundry van that had pulled into the loading dock. Nor did they see the van let him off at the Schwedenpatz underground station, where he took the green line to Kettenbrückengasse and entered a twelve-story apartment building.

It wasn't until five hours later that the FBI surveillance team spotted an Iranian with a familiar close-cropped salt-and-pepper beard emerge from the elevator and climb the mirrored stairs to the restaurant. "Scimitar is right on time," the female agent whispered into her headset. "He's heading for the buffet."

Scimitar was the FBI code name for Moshen Kourani.

"He looks like he might have put on a couple of pounds," the female agent noted.

"The veal schnitzel and strudel," came a response from the FBI agents in the sedan outside.

CHAPTER FIFTEEN

September 16

D awn was spreading its warm glow over the horizon as the Gulfstream 5 began its descent. Alan Beckman stopped transferring papers from foldout desk to briefcase and focused on the smooth line of the Saudi coast below.

The crew chief stuck his head out the cabin door and tucked long gray hair under his Mets cap. "Fifteen minutes," the chief said.

"Roger that."

Alan's recent trip to DC had underlined the difference between people who saw realities firsthand and focused on real goals, and those who had the luxury of distance. The latter had a tendency to shift their attention to internal political contingencies.

We suffer from a weird form of narcissism. If DC spends all its time studying itself in the mirror, how can we expect to engage other cultures successfully?

The jet jolted right. He would save the answer for later.

This was Alan's second trip back to the Persian Gulf since he'd served in Saudi Arabia at the start of his career. He'd returned ten years ago as chief of intelligence for the National Security Council, one of a series of glorified staff jobs he'd filled in DC.

As a staffer, Beckman had prepared numerous reports and briefing papers on Qatar, but this would be his first time on the ground.

He knew that since Emir Hamid bin Khalifa al-Thani had seized power from his father in '95, the country had made significant strides toward modernization, enfranchising women, drafting a new constitution, and launching the controversial Al Jazeera Arab-language television news channel.

This little piece of desert, home to less than a million people (only 200,000 of whom were citizens), possessed huge oil and natural gas reserves. It was also home to the U.S. Doha International Air Base (also known as Camp Snoopy), which served in 2003 as a staging area for the invasion of Iraq.

This will be the test of Kourani's intel, Alan said to himself. *We'll either bust the cell or someone will have tipped them off.*

NCTS had passed on everything it knew about the threat to the Qataris without revealing the source, since no one knew to what extent the Iranian Qods Force, or even MOIS, had penetrated the Qatari government. The last thing they needed was Kourani's name getting back to the Iranians.

The Qataris had taken the threat to heart. Back in March 2005 the Doha Players Theatre had been blasted by an al-Qaeda car bomb, killing one and badly injuring a dozen. And given the nature of the impending operation—a truck bomb to breach the hard line of CENTCOM's forward headquarters, followed by two VBEIDs (vehicular-borne improvised explosive devices)—it had been imperative to bring the Qataris into play.

"The attack will be launched from within the city of Doha," Alan read from the latest threat assessment report as his ears started to ache.

No kidding.

Looking through the sheen of modern spires and elaborate construction sites, Alan's thoughts turned to his son, Nathan, a second lieutenant with U.S. Army Intelligence in Iraq. He remembered a freckle-faced boy playing catch endlessly in the backyard, his eyes eager and open, and wished Nathan had gone to law school as originally planned.

We're in this fight together, he thought as the plane touched down, linking Nathan, himself, the Qataris, the United States, and those throughout the Middle East who valued personal freedom.

"Supposed to hit a hundred and ten today," the crew chief growled. "Hotter than a red-assed bee."

Alan grabbed his suitcase and leather briefcase and greeted the young, tall Qatari official waiting by the black Mercedes.

"Salaam aleikum," the young man said in Arabic.

"Wa-aleikum es-salaam."

In the welcome cool of the leather backseat, the young Qatari identified himself as the nephew of the foreign minister. "We'll use the intel you provided to raid several sites this evening," he announced in crisp Oxford English.

"I assume you've identified the principal leader."

"We have, sir," the Qatari answered. "He's been under physical and electronic surveillance. This has enabled us to confirm that the cell is prepared to attack tomorrow morning. We'll neutralize them tonight."

"Well done." Alan noticed that they had arrived at the Four Seasons Hotel. "Please inform His Excellency the foreign minister that I've participated in numerous raids on al-Qaeda sites and can provide specific expertise in explosive ordinance disposal. I'm ready to accompany your team tonight." Beneath the veneer of a Beltway bureaucrat, Alan was a highly trained EOD specialist and occasional lecturer at the Joint Improvised Explosives Device Defeat Organization (JIEDDO) and National War College.

The LED read 8:25 AM as Beckman entered the subtly toned hotel room with the forty-two-inch plasma TV. He showered, napped, ordered a light breakfast, and descended to the lobby at 11:55. As he stood measuring the cut of his new tan linen suit in the reflective glass, the black Mercedes pulled up again.

Alan sat beside the young Qatari, admiring the country's attempt to embrace modernity and wondering how much of the luxury he saw around him trickled down. *Another problem begging to be addressed,* he thought shifting his weight. *But not today.*

They passed through beautifully manicured avenues onto Qatari military headquarters. The tall man beside him said: "Given the seriousness of the threat, a special military team will be deployed, not the police. Our team has trained alongside your JSOC [Joint Special Operations Command] and the British SAS [Special Air Service]."

They entered a one-story sand-colored building, where Alan was introduced to a fit, genial man with a bristling black mustache— Brigadier General Abdullah Hamid bin Jasim al Thani. He mentioned he'd been educated at Britain's Sandhurst military academy and with a soft chuckle offered tea.

An orderly in a brilliant white uniform served Darjeeling, then lowered the lights. General Al-Thani spoke over the PowerPoint presentation projected onto a giant screen.

"A little more than a year ago, two Saudi Arabian businessmen established the JAFA Trading Company here in Doha for the purpose of planning and coordinating the operation, described in a telephone intercept as 'the Snoopy transaction.' One of the two men, Kahlid al Haznamwi, has a brother in custody in Saudi Arabia on terrorism charges. Saudi authorities believe that both men have previously been active in Al Anbar Province in Iraq."

The general sipped his tea. "We've ascertained that six months ago JAFA purchased a ten-ton diesel truck, now parked in a compound on the northern outskirts of the city along with several small trucks and SUVs. Suspicious. Six weeks ago, they received a shipment of so-called industrial equipment that I regret to say wasn't searched prior to delivery."

The general continued, laying out plans for the raid. Eight sites had been targeted, including the compound, residences of both Saudi principals, and rooming houses being used by five other men associated with JAFA.

"Mr. Beckman," the general said, "I'll ask you to accompany me to the primary site, since we believe this is the most likely location of the explosive material."

"I hope I'm allowed to spend some time with the entry team leader."

"Rest assured that will be arranged."

• • •

MATT LEFT TASHKENT knowing he was putting his NCTS career in jeopardy. But that didn't stop him from napping through most of the five-hour flight.

I'm onto something big, I can sense it, he thought, stepping into the Moscow terminal. *I can't let anyone stop me.* It was what his mother called his "bullheadedness" that allowed him to push all the doubting voices aside. His father's voice told him that the farther he stepped out on a limb, the more he invited disaster.

You'll see, old man.

With a do-or-die swagger, Matt was starting to enter Customs when a tall brunette in her early thirties blocked his path. With her long light brown hair and thick mascara she didn't look like a member of NCTS Security, but he couldn't be sure.

In slightly accented English she said: "Mr. Morgan, I'm Anya from Brides Café. Luda Kolchaveska sent me to welcome you."

"It's a pleasure."

"Now if you will give me your passport, I will make the necessary arrangements and meet you where you recover your baggage."

Twenty minutes later, suitcase in hand, Matt was the only passenger still waiting to enter Immigration. *Where did Anya go?* A uniformed Russian official approached, asking for his passport. Starting to feel exposed, Matt was trying to figure out what to say when Anya returned, applying pink lipstick. "Sorry for the delay," she said, smoothing her long hair. "Always complications."

With her heels counting time on the tile floor, they glided effortlessly through the bureaucratic labyrinth even though Matt's visa had been issued last-minute and his passport was festooned with entrance and exit stamps from Afghanistan, Uzbekistan, Romania, Sri Lanka, and Iraq. He figured the Russian secret police (the FSB) had copied it and would track him to his hotel.

"Your efficiency is a positive example of the entrepreneurial spirit of modern Russia," Matt said complimenting her and testing her at the same time.

She raised an eyebrow at him cynically. "If you say so." Then: "We try to make things enjoyable for our customers." Outside she handed him over to a kid with a shaved head and a ring in his nose. "Gennady will take you to your hotel."

A dense fog hung over the capital; traffic hummed. The Sheraton Palace Hotel on Tverskaya Street was a corner kick from Red Square. A thin man at the desk took Matt's passport and copied it. *Some things never change*, Matt thought, feeling out of place among businessmen with manicured nails and gray designer suits.

His dyed black hair had started to show its sandy roots. His blue blazer and khaki pants looked rumpled.

Greeting him in the pale yellow room was a fruit basket and a note: "Welcome to Moscow, Mr. Morgan. This afternoon at 2 PM, please come down to the lobby and you will be accompanied to our first event. There you will meet a number of your countrymen and a large number of eligible young and very lovely Russian women. We hope your future soon changes in ways beyond your most romantic dreams. Sincerely, Luda Kolchaveska."

So do I.

Normally Matt would have found humor in the fact that he was traveling as a bachelor in search of a Russian wife. But the desperation that crept from his stomach up to his throat made that impossible. The time away from his family hadn't helped; nor did the possible hundreds of thousands of U.S. casualties, nor the flashing red lights associated with the name Kourani. And for the last two weeks he'd been constantly under assault.

Mentally and physically exhausted, his right temple throbbing, Matt swallowed three Advils. He wanted to look up some things on the Internet, but suspected the hotel connections were monitored by the FSB. Instead, he stood under the warm shower, called the front desk to request a wake-up call in three hours, then lay down in bed.

In the still, silver light of the room, he took stock. No, he wasn't the brightest, best-educated officer. Yes, he had a tendency to become overly excited and aggressive. No, he wasn't the smoothest talker or the most politically astute. What distinguished him were his instincts, honed through years of running sources and operations. Somehow, mysteriously, beyond reason and words, he'd developed the ability to sense things and grope the rough outline of future events.

And his instincts now screamed: *Kourani can't be trusted!*

AT 0600 HOURS the armored Lincoln turned right on Persimmon Tree Road and parked in front of General Jasper's Tudor-style residence. She downed the last of the hazelnut coffee and stepped outside. A bare-chested African American bodyguard with a receiver in his ear covered her walk to the car. Bending to fit her six-foot frame through the door, General Jasper noticed that Shelly's hair seemed blacker and spikier than the day before.

"Morning, General."

"I'm sick of all this ambiguity. Let's establish some clarity."

"I agree, General."

"The more clearly we anticipate the threat, the better we can prepare."

"Alan Beckman is on the ground in Qatar," Shelly said, handing her boss the red folder she clutched in her lap.

"What's he told us so far?"

"The broad picture remains the same. Hopefully he'll be able to provide more details after the raid."

The limo turned west on the beltway with a large black Suburban with extra security directly behind.

"In the category of interesting but hardly to the point, we got a note from the CIA chief in Uzbekistan crediting Freed for his courage."

General Jasper asked: "Anything further from the military team that rescued them?"

"In terms of?"

"Identities of the men who attacked Freed and his companion."

"Nothing has been reported."

"Are the Kazakhs upset?"

"The bodies haven't been identified as Kazakhs, General."

"I believe we violated their airspace."

Shelly cleared her throat. "Correct. No protest has been filed. Doubtful either government will publicize the event."

General Jasper tried running her hand through the tight curls on her head. "Do me a favor. Make sure we keep Freed away from anything sensitive."

Shelly didn't know what she meant. "Excuse me, General?"

"See if you can arrange for a desk job counting staplers. The man seems to attract trouble wherever he goes."

"Yes."

"Where's Trouble now?"

"En route to DC."

"Have someone meet him at Dulles and bring him directly to me. Shackle him, if need be."

"Yes."

Grunting slightly, the general donned her reading glasses and reviewed the morning digest in her lap. Attacks in Iraq, combat operations in Helmand Province of Afghanistan, a new offensive by the FARC (Revolutionary Armed Forces of Colombia) in Colombia, and renewed counterinsurgency efforts by the Moroccans against Salafists operating outside of Casablanca. Without thinking, she dipped her left hand into her blazer pocket and popped the first antacid of the day.

"We've got two days till Kourani arrives," she reminded Shelly.

"CIA is checking his ETA."

General Jasper gazed out the window at the fall colors flying past. Labor Day through Thanksgiving was her favorite time of year. Her two children, Sarah and Carson, had been born in September. Now both were away—her daughter in medical school at Johns Hopkins, her son (the older of the two) raising a family in Seattle, where he did research in nanotechnology. In another two weeks she and Clive were scheduled to celebrate her birthday at their favorite Shenandoah inn.

Now she wondered how much the world would change by then. She thought about her grandchildren, Ned (three years) and Sally (three months), and asked herself why they had to reside in midsized U.S. cities. Shutting her eyes, she uttered a passage from Proverbs:

For the turning away of the simple will slay them,
And the complacency of fools will destroy them;
But whoever listens to me will dwell safely,
And will be secure, without fear of evil.

●   ●   ●

"ELIZABETH, WHERE DO you keep the towels?" Liz's mother called from the upstairs bathroom.

"In the cabinet next to the sink," Liz answered, but didn't budge. She tried to focus on the game Candy Land spread on the dining room table and an argument between Maggie (eight) and Samantha (six) over whether Maggie had landed on the right space.

"She cheated, Mommy. She didn't count right. She should be on Mr. Nut."

"Liar! I rolled an eight. Can't you count?"

It worried Liz that she hadn't heard from Matt in over a week. And she'd learned from Celia that Alan had been back and forth to Washington. This morning he left for Qatar.

She knew from her CIA training that something significant was going down. She yearned to be part of it; to put to use the skills she knew she had.

Her nerves jumped when her mother screamed: "I can't find them. I'm getting a chill!"

Under normal circumstances Liz would have scolded her mother, but today she felt compelled to hold things together. Since her mother had arrived that morning, she'd turned the household upside down, initiating half a dozen projects and abandoning them, including the game of Candy Land and the half-assembled turkey sandwich on the kitchen counter.

Liz had hoped for calm and sanity but had gotten chaos instead.

"Elizabeth, can you hear me?"

"In the cabinet next to the sink."

Ever since Liz's father had died suddenly of a heart attack when Liz was fourteen, her mother seemed to have lost her way, becoming a blizzard of movement as though compensating for her lost husband. But none of it seemed directed in a positive direction or toward an achievable goal.

Liz considered that now, trying not to lose her temper, nodding at the drawing of a catlike creature that three-year-old Nadia had thrust under her chin.

"Liz, I'm dripping wet!" her mother screamed.

"It's beautiful, honey," Liz said to her youngest.

"It's an alien."

"Very nice."

"Miss Casineau told us: you get what you get and you don't get upset."

"Wise words."

"LIZ!!!!"

"Continue without me," she said to Maggie and Samantha, getting to her feet.

"We can't, Mommy. It's a problem!"

"Then wait."

Liz struggled to hold on to her emotions. The person she wanted was Matt. He was the yin to complement her yang. He was the movement; she was the emotional body that received his energy and brought creation. To her way of thinking, the two of them made a whole.

A HALF DOZEN of General Jasper's top aides stood as she entered the oak-paneled conference room.

"Good morning, General."

"We good to go?" Jasper asked, looking like she'd aged a decade in the past week.

The tall Asian American watch officer nodded to a technician, who dimmed the lights and illuminated five large monitors representing the CIA, FBI, DOD (Department of Defense), Justice Department, State Department, and NSC (National Security Council). Firing up simultaneously was a camera that would record the general and those immediately seated to her left and right.

Five minutes later, at 6:32 AM, the preppy, bespectacled face of NSC director Stan Lescher appeared center-screen. "I'm going to say this one more time," he began, with the head of Homeland Security by his side. "We want everything that comes in. Everything! I don't give a damn about protecting sources and methods. The president can't make a sound decision without the facts. If I find out that anyone has held anything back, heads will roll."

"Just what we need, more threats," Shelly whispered into Jasper's ear.

"Here at the White House we're following the al-Qaeda threat like hawks," the NSC director continued.

"So are we," General Jasper said under her breath, seated in a brown leather chair with a mug of java in her fist.

Lescher addressed his first round of questions to the FBI's chief of counterterrorism, a bony-faced man in a yellow shirt. "Where's Kourani?"

"The Marriott Hotel in Vienna. I have a twenty-person team on the ground. He and the other four members of the Iranian delegation are booked on a Lufthansa flight that arrives in JFK at 3:48 PM on the eighteenth."

"How are we prepared on the debarking end?"

"Everything's in place at Kennedy: surveillance teams, agents, bomb squads, SWAT teams, rapid deployment. All contingencies are covered."

"We can't let Kourani out of our sight even when he takes a crap," Lescher said bluntly.

"We won't."

The NSC director was all business. "Talk to me about defensive preparations on the ground."

"We have hazmat and quick-response teams in five deploy points—Washington, Detroit, Jacksonville, Seattle, and San Diego—on twenty-four-hour alert. Local medical, law enforcement, and SWAT are active in thirty-eight midsized cities."

Lescher shifted gears again. "Rebirth Island."

"The specimens arrived at Fort Dietrich three hours ago," responded a three-star general from Defense.

"How long before we get an answer on what killed those rats?"

"Could be days," answered the three-star from DOD.

"Have we ID'd the men killed at Rebirth, the ones who fired on our people?"

"Uzbek officials recovered the bodies."

"That's not what I asked!"

"One of them has been tentatively identified as Juma Khuseinov."

General Jasper bolted to attention. "That's the man Freed reported on. Kourani was looking for him when he arrived in Kabul, Afghanistan, in July."

"So far the Uzbeks haven't provided us with copies of any personal documentation," said the CIA director of operations.

"Lean on them," Stan Lescher said.

"They're telling us that there are no identifiable traces linking those men to known terrorist groups or security services or governments."

General Jasper said: "If it is Juma Khuseinov, the Uzbeks are wrong. We have him associated with al-Qaeda and a number of narco-trafficking groups out of Uzbekistan."

"If the dead man is in fact Khuseinov, what does that mean?" NSC director Lescher asked.

For the next fifteen minutes several possibilities were kicked around, but nobody could agree on the new fact's significance.

"We've also got a lead on a Russian bioweapons expert named Oleg Urakov, formerly of Biopreparat, who we believe was seen with Kourani," General Jasper said into the microphone clipped to her lapel.

"Recommendations on locating him?"

The CIA director of operations (DO) spoke first. "Time's tight, so I say we go directly to the Russians and tell them we want immediate access because of the significant threat to the U.S."

General Jasper cleared her throat and said: "I support CIA's approach. Also, under Nunn-Lugar we destroyed Soviet chemical and nuclear weapons and also resettled a number of Soviet scientists in the U.S. Several live in the area. I'm sending people out this morning to interview all of those from Biopreparat. I'm hoping we can find out what Urakov worked on, or at least narrow down his areas of expertise."

"Sounds like a long shot, but worth a try."

"Also, we just received a report stating that an Oleg Urakov recently left the Buteyko Clinic in Moscow."

"Who picked that up?"

"A phone intercept from NSA," General Jasper said.

"Do we know what's wrong with him?"

"Only that he was in the hospital."

"Where is he now?"

NSC director Lescher, who seemed to be reading something out of view of the camera, abruptly shifted subjects. "How are you going to cover Kourani's travel to the U.S.?"

"We'll have an FBI team on the plane," answered the FBI's chief of counterterrorism.

"Inform me immediately of any significant developments," Lescher said quickly.

Jasper reminded him: "Alan Beckman has landed in Doha and is coordinating a raid with Qatari officials."

"According to my schedule, that will happen at approximately 1 PM our time," Lescher said. "This meeting is over. We all have important work to do. We'll talk again at noon."

General Jasper was about to say something to Shelly, when the DO asked if he could have a word with her when the others went off-line.

She waited a minute for technicians to set up the two-way link. Then the DO, a big man with a pale freckled face, began. "I just got off the secure line with my chief in Tashkent. She says Freed's actions were exemplary."

"That's good to hear."

"But it seems that you've seen fit to deploy him into Moscow without clearing it with my agency."

General Jasper cocked her head toward Shelly. "I have no idea what you're talking about."

"Freed is in Moscow," the DO repeated flatly.

General Jasper mouthed the word: "Unbelievable!"

"What do you want me to tell the Russians with regard to Urakov? Should I tell them we want their help and at the same time have sent our own man?"

General Jasper sounded annoyed: "First, I was unaware that Freed deplaned. He was ordered to return directly. Second, this is less than a perfect situation and time is of the essence. So tell them nothing. If this causes a flap, I'll fly to Moscow and explain that it was the NCTS, not CIA, that failed to coordinate with them. Our liaison relationship is not as deep as yours. We have less in terms of equities. I'll take the hit."

The DO nodded. "That sounds reasonable under the circumstances."

"We'll be in touch," said General Jasper before hitting the "Mute" button beside her seat and growling to Shelly: "I didn't enjoy that."

"That son-of-a-bitch."

CHAPTER SIXTEEN

September 16

Matt rose twenty minutes before the wake-up call and turned on CNN International. A tightly composed and coifed Hala Gorani introduced a story about stepped-up security in Seattle, San Diego, Dallas, and other cities where armed National Guard troops were seen patrolling the streets. A spokesman from Homeland Security was asked to explain why the threat level had been raised to Red.

"From time to time, we learn about a threat from one of our overseas sources, assess that threat, and respond to the best of our abilities. We err on the side of being overly cautious sometimes. We always ask the American people to be vigilant and report any suspicious activity to local authorities."

Scary shit.

Matt showered, shaved, and descended to the lobby just before 2 PM. Gennady, the driver with the shaved head and the ring through his nose, tapped Matt on the shoulder as he studied a tourist map.

Matt kept it open on his lap as they zoomed up Tverskaya to the Beaux Arts Le Royal Meridian Hotel. Milling in the Pskov Conference Hall were fifteen portly, balding Americans, ranging from their late forties up to almost eighty. Luda Kolshaveska, smiling in a tight

green dress, introduced Matt to the rest of the group. One was a
deli owner named Sal Barrone from Bayonne, New Jersey; another,
a rancher from West Texas; a third, a marketing director from the
Upper Peninsula of Michigan. *Sure*, Matt thought, *some Russian
woman wants to go to a place that's colder than Moscow.*

"You'll be a hit with the ladies," Luda whispered, pressing her dé-
colletage against Matt's elbow and slapping a name tag onto his
lapel. "All your accommodations are to your liking, I trust."

"Lovely. Yes."

Smelling strongly of jasmine, she guided him through double
doors to a larger room filled with young Russian women. In the dim
cocktail party light, he estimated two hundred. Immediately thirty
or so aggressively engaged men in conversation. Quickly leaning
into Matt were four slim girls in their twenties, teasing him with
questions in heavily accented English.

"What part of United States you live?"

"Are you athlete, Mr. Morgan? You appear to have very
strong body."

"Is this your first trip to Moscow?"

"You like me to show you the city? Very beautiful at night."

Fifteen minutes later Matt excused himself. "I need a drink."

"What do you desire?" a tall brunette asked, tugging on his arm.
"I love oral sex."

Matt spied a bar in the corner and held up his hand. "I'll be right
back." Slowly, he worked his way through, stopping to exchange
pleasantries with a number of the women, all of whom were beautifully dressed, all of whom shared a desperation to leave Russia, which
they said was cold, economically depressed, and rife with crime.
Some had even come with their own interpreters. Others carried
photo albums and laminated diplomas.

A young woman with green eyes asked Matt if he'd ever been
married.

He lied. "No. Not yet."

"You seem to me like someone who's been married."

"I'd like to start a family, but haven't had time."

A quarter of the women hung back, somewhat embarrassed. They waited at numbered tables that clung to the walls and continued into the adjoining room.

Matt asked the bartender the purpose of the tables.

"Speed dating," the Russian replied.

After twenty minutes of mixing, Luda announced via microphone that the more formal phase of the event would begin. The young women, who had been issued numbers, took turns at the tables. The older Americans hopped from one to another, spending a maximum of five minutes at each.

Matt plied each candidate with similar questions: "What do you do for a living? Do you have family in the military? What have you studied?"

The other men skipped the less attractive women. But Matt wasn't interested in looks. He searched for other qualities: affability, English language skill, and someone he thought he could convince to help him.

After an hour of speed dating, he sat at table forty-nine, before a woman with dark shoulder-length hair cut in bangs. She introduced herself as Zyoda, born in Moscow, raised in the Soviet Far East. She explained in a straightforward way that her father was a Soviet colonel who'd died recently. She was a twenty-eight-year-old nurse, divorced, with a five-year-old daughter.

Perfect, Matt thought. "Would you like to join me for dinner?" he asked.

Zyoda revealed a set of crooked white teeth and a neat little mole near the corner of her mouth. "When would be convenient?"

"Tonight."

She creased the space between her cornflower blue eyes. "I'm so sorry, but tonight is difficult. Perhaps we can do it tomorrow."

"Tonight is much better."

"There is a problem, Mr. Morgan. I have to pick up my daughter and make arrangements with a cousin to watch her."

"Why don't you bring her along?" Matt asked.

Zyoda seemed surprised. "Are you sure?"

"Yes." He leaned closer. "Let's leave now."

Her blue eyes brightened considerably. "Thank you very much."

AT 2000 HOURS Alan Beckman sat in the back of a black panel truck that slowly made its way down a dusty industrial street. Somewhere a radio broadcast a prayer in Arabic. Sitting across from him and on either side were ten Qatari men in black jumpsuits cradling M4s and wearing helmets and elbow and knee pads.

They stopped in front of a two-story concrete building, and their leader, a small man perched on the passenger seat, jumped out holding a Heckler & Koch G3 automatic rifle equipped with a laser light module.

The others quickly followed, ending with Alan carrying a small backpack and armed with his own 9mm Beretta. He crouched with the others along the wall.

From an SUV parked at the end of the road, Brigadier General Al-Thani gave the order via radio: "Hold teams two through seven," the general said, alert to the danger of multiple teams rushing in and getting caught in a crossfire.

The squad leader signaled to the first man in line, who leveled a large shotgun and destroyed the lock with a blast.

Ten miles away at the Qatari command center, the Qatari foreign minister and the defense minister watched with arms folded as events played out on a video monitor, captured by a camera mounted on the helmet of the third man in. They saw light green flashes and the shadowy figure of the team leader firing on two targets in the reception area. Other flashes flickered behind him like fireflies.

Alan crouched behind a pillar in the lobby as shots echoed from all sides. The two targets near reception were down. One had been caught reaching for his pistol. The second had a big red hole where his left eye had been.

Alan fished a plastic kit from his briefcase and, kneeling over the bodies, got to work. Using a white gauze pad, he wiped the hands and faces of the two dead Saudis. Then he sprayed the gauze with aerosol and held it to the light. *Negative*.

He used a second piece of gauze to wipe down the dead men again. This one he sprayed with a different can of aerosol. The gauze turned pink.

The Qatari team moved methodically, clearing one room after the other. Hurrying, Alan caught up with the team commander down a hall. "Brother. Brother," he shouted in Arabic, "we have to talk."

The return fire had petered out, so the commander ordered his men to halt.

"What?"

"The men who occupied this building were working with a nitrate-based explosive," Alan explained. "Either C-4, Semtex, or RDX."

The commander nodded even though he didn't know the difference.

"You've got to look out for booby traps. Let me help."

The commander nodded again. "Yes. Yes."

Out of Alan's backpack came two more aerosol cans marked "Silly Spray." He handed one to the commander, who looked amused. "Are you trying to make a joke?" he asked in Arabic.

Having led successful raids on al-Qaeda sites in Albania, Pakistan, and Sudan, Beckman knew what he was doing. He barked: "Follow me."

Alan moved forward carefully, spraying the can of light, stringy material fifteen feet in front of him. The Qataris followed behind, confused. Proceeding cautiously, spraying the whole time, Alan entered a large bay area. Outside, fifty feet past the entrance, rested a ten-ton truck and a covered pickup.

This time, instead of falling, the spray hung in the air eighteen inches from the ground.

Alan pointed: "Look!"

The commander's eyes widened on a trip wire his men would otherwise have missed.

Alan fired the spray left, then right, to see where the wire connected. In a dark crevice he found a 155mm shell waiting to explode.

The commander spoke through a helmet mike to other teams outside: "We've engaged four targets. All dead. We found evidence of explosives and one trip wire. I'm ordering my men to withdraw. A full EOD team needs to be deployed immediately."

The brigadier general answered from his command post down the street. "Come out so we can talk."

"It's going to be a very slow process," Alan said in Arabic when they reached General Al-Thani.

The general with the shiny black mustache shook everyone's hand. "The EOD team is on its way."

"Good."

"Raids are underway at the other sites."

Beckman said: "We're particularly interested in any men with knowledge of the impending attack on the U.S."

General Al-Thani narrowed his eyes. "I know."

The second time Alan entered the building, he saw blood smeared across the floor and thick swarms of flies. Alan doubted that the Qatari EOD team had much experience, but they seemed well trained, picking their way carefully room to room.

Their work revealed a second booby trap wired to the back entrance and five hundred pounds of Semtex in the smaller truck. In the back of the ten-ton sat a whopping two thousand pounds of Semtex wired to a detonator in the cab that would allow either driver or passenger to set it off by pulling a plunger.

The general was pleased once more when he saw Alan. "We have five suspects in custody. They're being questioned now."

"Let's go."

It was a hop and a skip to the airport, where the prisoners were being held. Turning sharply into the gate, the driver screeched on his brakes to avoid a camel.

They bounced between tarmacs and stopped in front of a low-slung building with several antennas on top. A half-dozen military vehicles were parked out front.

Entering the tiny reception room, they were confronted by an officer who came out shouting in Arabic: "We need a doctor!" A heavily armed guard led them into a windowless room that reeked of sweat. Strapped to metal chairs were two thin men stripped to the waist.

Both had badly swollen eyes and bruises.

"That one has been identified by the other as the explosives expert," a Qatari officer explained. "He'll get special attention."

"Tell them I'll send money to their families if they tell us about plans for any future attacks," Alan said.

The offer was posed separately in Arabic to each of the prisoners, but the answer was the same: "We want to kill Americans! Death to the United States!"

As Alan climbed into a truck for the drive to the embassy, the general said: "There are two members of the group and one vehicle unaccounted for."

Later that morning as he sat at a laptop sipping coffee and typing up his report, Alan heard the news: the missing vehicle, a Toyota truck, had driven into the lobby of the InterContinental Hotel in Doha, killing thirteen people, including a Sri Lankan Airlines flight crew that was checking out.

The euphoria he'd been feeding off of stopped.

SIX THOUSAND, NINE hundred miles away, the people at NCTS headquarters couldn't hear the screams for God's help, or see the ripped-open bodies, the guts spilled on the marble floor. They had larger concerns. Not thirteen or even a hundred dead, but tens of thousands.

The consensus of those gathered in General Jasper's office eating Chicago-style pizza and drinking sodas was that Moshen Kourani of the Qods Force had to be believed.

"Absolutely," Shelly said, clicking on CNN's *The Situation Room* and muting the sound. It was 1 AM the next day in Qatar. Wolf Blitzer reported on the bombing at the InterContinental Doha, but didn't mention the raids.

The good news was that Kourani's warning had helped prevent an al-Qaeda attack. The bad news: his increased credibility meant the follow-up threat to midsized U.S. cities was more acute.

That reality gripped General Jasper's stomach. She felt like she was about to be sick. "We've got to make every effort to accommodate Kourani. Everything. We can't afford any roadblocks."

People around the room nodded their agreement. Shelly said: "He lands in less than forty-eight hours."

Jasper groaned: "Where the fuck is Freed?"

ZYODA'S CHEST SWELLED with pride as she entered the elegant dining room with the handsome American by her side. Her good mood wasn't spoiled by the presence of her daughter, Irina, or by the thick men and heavily made-up middle-aged women who followed her with their eyes and whispered snidely.

She'd seen the same disapproving look on the face of the taxi driver who'd deposited them outside.

They were all wrong. She wasn't a prostitute. And she hadn't been paid by the American to have sex. So far, Matt hadn't even tried to touch her hand.

She wanted to say: "What's wrong with you people?" It seemed to her that cynicism had infected every human brain in Russia. People no long believed in friendship, love, good fortune. Everything, even love, had to involve an exchange of money.

Her languid blue eyes watched Matt unfold one of the embroidered cloth napkins and spread it on Irina's lap. *Such a gentleman*, she thought.

She listened with pleasure as five-year-old Irina explained the items on the menu to Matt in the English she'd learned at school. "They have rich meat stew à la Romanoff, breaded veal, beef Stroganoff."

Irina was a smart, poised girl, wise about people beyond her years. Her self-confidence and bright demeanor helped assuage Zyoda's guilt for working as a full-time nurse and getting pregnant by a businessman from Kiev who'd refused to marry her and offered little support. He was far from her mind now.

"This one is fried quail wrapped in bacon," the bright, young girl explained.

Matt asked her: "Who gave you that beautiful pink dress?"

"My mother made it."

"She's very talented," the American said, glancing up at Zyoda, who blushed.

The prices were shocking, but totally in keeping with the rich surroundings—gilded Empire-style chairs, crystal chandeliers, large vases filled with flowers, antique silver. There was even a pianist in the corner playing Rimsky-Korsakov.

"What would you like?" Matt asked gently.

For the first time since they'd picked her up at Zyoda's one-bedroom apartment, the girl with the gentle heart-shaped face looked sad. Matt looked on as the mother and daughter spoke back and forth in Russian.

"She says she's only interested in dessert," Zyoda said, shaking her head.

Matt smiled. "I'll let you try all of them, but you have to eat something first."

"Okay."

Zyoda was impressed by the ease with which Matt interacted with her daughter. Reaching across the table, she gripped his hand. "You haven't told us about yourself. Why did you choose to visit Moscow?"

"My father's a scientist," Matt explained. "He's traveled to Russia often and talks about it all the time—the people, the art, the culture. I've been thinking about visiting for a long time."

"Your father wants you to settle down?"

"He never stops talking about the warmth and beauty of Russian women."

"I hope we don't disappoint you."

"He also has a Russian friend, a fellow scientist, who's been ill. This man, Oleg Urakov, stopped answering his e-mail about a month ago. My father asked me to track him down."

"Maybe I can assist you," Zyoda offered.

"My father says he was a high official in the Soviet government. He might be suffering from advanced lung cancer."

"He's in Moscow?"

"I believe so."

She thought out loud: "Rare diseases and advanced forms of cancer. Most likely he's in Burdenko Military Hospital. We can start there."

After the food arrived—sole for Irina, quail for Zyoda, beef Stroganoff for Matt—they discussed music and movies.

"I'm a woman. I like love stories," Zyoda said. "Like *The Notebook, Ghost.*"

Matt hadn't seen either.

"They aren't very realistic, I know. But love stories often aren't realistic, if you know what I mean." She looked sad.

"The world is changing," Matt said. "Women have more opportunities. I believe that's good for everyone."

It was a little past nine o'clock when he paid the check in dollars. Zyoda asked if Matt would like to stop at her apartment for a cup of tea.

"I'd like that very much. But I have to stop to check my e-mail first."

"Money and business," she said brushing the dark bangs from her eyes.

"I don't understand."

"Men like to build things like businesses, and get things done."

He smiled warmly into her eyes. She waited for him to put his arm around her or take her hand. But he didn't. *He's too much of a gentleman,* she thought. *Not with Irina watching.*

ALL THROUGH DINNER, Matt's mind kept creeping back to Kourani. A part of his subconscious had reached the conclusion that the deputy director of Qods Force was behind a plan to kill thousands of Americans. *Why?*

The key, Matt thought, lay in Kourani's personal history. But too many pieces were missing.

Official NCTS and CIA channels had turned up nothing about the Iranian that shed light on a possible motive. *Kourani's nephew is our only chance.*

At the Internet café, Matt entered a booth and logged into his Yahoo account. There was no message from Guillermo. *Dammit! I told him I needed it right away.*

Circumstances didn't allow him to go to Paris himself. He needed someone he could depend on to talk to the boy within the next forty-eight hours. *Who? I could call Guillermo again, but knowing him the way I do, he'd still take his sweet time.*

Matt racked his brain trying to think of anyone he might know at the CIA station in Paris. He knew that if he called the station cold, they'd check with Washington, which would only cause more headaches and delays.

Then the idea popped in his head. *Liz!*

He quickly punched out an e-mail addressed to cheetah12@ europenet.com. "Dear Liz: I need your help. Please travel to Paris immediately. Attached is a photo of an Iranian student. I need you to track him down in the next 12 hours max. Guillermo knows what to do, but needs a kick in the ass. I'm on my own. This is extremely important. Hundreds of thousands of lives at stake. Love, M."

Checking to make sure he wasn't being watched, he slipped into a phone booth and called his home in Athens. When Liz answered, a familiar warmth spread through his chest.

"Mrs. Freed, this is Mr. Faison about the carpets you ordered."

Liz knew the code and played her part. "Which carpets are you talking about?"

"Specifically the one with the cheetah print."

"Oh, that."

"I suggest you pick it up immediately. It's very important."

"I will. Thank you."

"Have a good night."

Liz's heart pounded so hard she thought she would faint. Logging onto the Internet and entering a code, Liz's mind quickly shifted from mother, to wife, to field operative. "Javed Mohammed Kourani. Paris."

The girls were asleep. She found her mother in the study watching *Nip/Tuck* on DVD.

"I've decided to leave for DC as soon as possible. I need you to watch the girls."

"Why the sudden change of plans?"

"I'm meeting Matt. It will give us a chance to spend a few days together. We'll be back by Wednesday."

Her mother seemed confused. "That will be nice for you."

"I think so. The house is stocked. Call Celia if you need anything. The bus arrives 8:15 Monday morning to take Maggie and Samantha to school. Nadia has preschool on Tuesday. I'll arrange for a friend to pick her up."

"When are you leaving?"

"Early in the morning."

"So soon?"

Liz stopped. "Is that a problem?"

"No, darling. We'll be fine."

CHAPTER SEVENTEEN

September 16

M att tried to ignore the tension that swirled around the backseat of the taxi as it continued up large boulevards lit with huge modern lights, then turned into a warren of smaller darker streets. He couldn't tell if the erotic charge was the product of Zyoda's desperation to escape or the excitement her vulnerability created in him.

It came as a relief when they stopped in front of a drab concrete apartment building.

Zyoda said: "It's not big or beautiful," hiding her eyes.

Matt felt good from a security point of view. He'd watched carefully for surveillance and hadn't seen any cars following them. He also figured that it was safer for him not to return to the hotel.

Zyoda used three keys to open the locks on her front door. They entered a narrow L-shaped room with a sofa and two wooden chairs. A romanticized painting of kittens playing with a ball of yarn adorned one wall. On the other were a baby photo of Irina and a map of the Republic of Tuva. "This is the living room," she said.

The foot of the L opened to an alcove, which contained a small table. This served as the kitchen with a microwave, hot plate, and tiny sink.

"A new purchase," she announced, patting a miniature refrigerator.

The only bedroom featured a double bed, which mother and daughter shared.

"Please, be comfortable."

Matt sat on the red corduroy–covered sofa and figured that was where he'd sleep.

After tucking Irina into bed and praying with her, Zyoda returned with a tray of tea. She seemed softer and more delicate in the dark blue dress that stopped above her knees. For the first time Matt took in her figure—full breasts and strong legs—before looking up quickly at the kittens on the wall.

He sipped the tea, trying to forget what he'd just seen. "Tell me about the United States and where you live," Zyoda asked.

"I grew up in Virginia."

"Mount Vernon?" she asked excitedly, tucking her legs under her. "I read about George Washington in school."

"Quantico, the town I come from, is close. Something like thirty miles farther down the Potomac River."

"Miles?" She looked confused.

"About fifty kilometers."

"Of course." She grinned like a cat. "Did George Washington really cut down the cherry tree?"

"As far as I know, that story was invented by Mason L. Weems, an early Washington biographer."

Her grin widened; her eyes drank him in. "I think you're very educated."

"I love to read."

"Who are your favorite authors?"

"Shakespeare, Tolstoy, Graham Greene."

"What about Edgar Allan Poe, William Faulkner? Have you read *Intruder in the Dust*?"

"I don't think I know that one."

"A fabulous story about a white teenager who tries to save a black murderer who has been wrongly accused of killing a white man."

"I'll add it to my list."

"Did you know any black people when you grew up?"

"One of my best friends was Demarco Washington. We played ball together on the Warriors. He went on to become a star receiver at Penn State until he blew out his knee. Great guy."

"What's a receiver?" Zyoda asked.

Matt explained the basic rules of the game, then using a small pillow for a football, instructed her to go out for a pass. She caught it on her fingertips and asked: "Do I win?"

"No. You only score points if you get in the end zone."

"Where's the end zone?"

He told her that she had to get by the opposition, which would try to tackle her. She pressed the pillow against her bosom and tried to run past Matt to the other end of the room. She faked right; he countered and grabbed her around the hips.

Zyoda folded across his shoulder laughing hard, kicking her strong legs. The roundness of hips and behind under his hand warned him where this could lead. As he set her down on the sofa, she reached up and kissed him on the lips.

"I like you," she said panting.

"I like you, too."

He turned to disguise his embarrassment. "I need to use your bathroom."

When he returned, Zyoda stood on her tiptoes reaching for a blanket at the top of the closet. She caught him looking at her behind.

Matt said: "You have strong legs."

"Volleyball."

"You still play?"

Her eyes sparkled with excitement. "Of course."

Zyoda had opened the sofa bed while he was gone.

"You sleep here tonight," she offered. "In the morning, we can go to the hospital and find your father's friend."

He nodded, thinking he didn't want to lead her on, and said: "Or I can call a taxi."

"Maybe it's better if you stay here," Zyoda concluded.

She was right.

Zyoda went about her business barefoot, returning with a toothbrush and towel. She said: "I have a second cousin who is a singer at a club in Brighton Beach, New York. She sent me this tape." Then slipping it into a boom box, she left.

A plaintive voice filled the narrow room singing "When You Wish Upon a Star" in Russian. Matt flicked off the lights, stripped down to his underwear, and lay on the sofa bed. The girl segued into an up-tempo number, then a sad lament in Russian. Shadows played on the walls. He closed his eyes, thinking: *Tomorrow is important.*

"Goodnight, John," he heard her whisper. Half asleep, he felt her warm lips on his, then followed her with his eyes as she floated past in a green silk nightgown.

Sometime later, he opened his eyes as a door creaked open and closed. Until he recognized the kittens on the wall, he didn't know where he was. Bare feet padded toward him, then Zyoda's soft voice: "I couldn't sleep."

"Why?"

"I'm so excited about what happened today. Feel my heart."

She took his hand and pressed it against her silk-covered chest. He told himself to forget the soft outline of her breasts and concentrate on the thumping of her heart.

"You think I'll be okay?" she asked like a little girl.

Without thinking, he put his arm around her. Immediately he scolded himself: *Mistake.*

"I want you to like me," she whispered snuggling closer.

"You're an intelligent woman."

She looked up at him pleading. "Yes?"

"And attractive, too."

I don't want to lead her on, he thought, *but I need her unflinching support.* Then they kissed.

Through the thin walls he heard a couple fighting. A child screamed. Matt remembered an incident in Spain four years ago when a colleague had refused the advances of a female Basque journalist who was offering information about an ETA bombing. Eight people died. Their lives could have been saved.

"My daughter and I have to escape this," Zyoda whispered, grabbing his head and kissing him again. This time he let himself slip deeper into the thick swirl of feelings that threatened to pull him under.

"There's something I have to tell you."

She put her hand across her mouth and whispered: "Tomorrow."

"But—"

"Let's enjoy the moment while we have a chance."

I should have never put myself in this position, he said to himself, *but what choice did I have?*

Rising to her knees, she lifted the nightgown over her head.

Shit happens.

Her beauty hung in the moment like a precious balloon. It was the glow of her skin that dissolved the little resistance he had left.

When he reached out and touched her, the thin barrier between them popped. She shivered and yielded. The bold force within him did the rest. Heaving, moaning, sweating, diving into each other unfettered, they made love.

GENERAL JASPER GLANCED at her BlackBerry as she paced the gold carpet of the White House Roosevelt Room. She scrolled past messages from her husband, daughter, and various aides. Finding nothing new from Science & Technology, she checked the time: 10:52 PM.

A dramatic equestrian portrait of Teddy Roosevelt hung on one wall and a wise-looking FDR stared down at her from another. She'd heard that back in FDR's day the room had been decorated with stuffed fish and was known as "the morgue."

A harried aide rushed in and shouted: "You're here!"

"Yes, I am."

"They're all waiting," he said frantically, escorting her down a hallway into a warren of tight rooms where watch officers sat at computers monitoring incoming intel from Defense, CIA, State, NSA, et cetera.

"General, leave your BlackBerry," the aide said pointing to a lead-lined cabinet decked with various Bluetooth devices and cell phones. A tightly vibrating tension passed through the air into her skin.

Entering the small, dark Situation Room, she popped another antacid into her mouth and took her chair. The cool, cherry-paneled space was lined with plasma television monitors and packed with people—secretaries of Defense, State, Justice, the director of the CIA, their aides. NSC director Stan Lescher sat near the head of an oval table nervously sorting through papers.

They all stood as the president entered, looking like he hadn't slept for days. "Let's begin," he said, setting down a Diet Coke.

Lescher paraphrased a report NCTS had prepared about the successful operation in Doha, Qatar. Officials from the Department of Defense and CIA followed up with accounts of al-Qaeda operatives killed and others who were still being sought.

"Good work," the president said, then looking impatient, asked: "What's next?"

Lescher attempted to straighten his tie. "Next, Mr. President, is the question of how we handle Kourani and the Iranian delegation."

"What do you mean by 'handle'?"

"Mr. President, it goes like this. The five Iranians are carrying diplomatic passports and diplomatic visas issued by us. Do we ask the Austrians to treat them like diplomats and wave them through Security, or do we go through their belongings and carry-ons like everyone else?"

The president scowled deeper.

"If we do the latter," Lescher continued, "we risk tipping off the Iranians to the fact that we suspect something is up, which could put Kourani in danger. We also run the risk of alienating Kourani, who might be loath to supply further intelligence on a follow-up attack."

The president rubbed his chin. "You called an emergency meeting for this?"

As Lescher nodded, he shrank in his seat.

"Do we have any reason to distrust Kourani at this point?" the president asked in a booming voice.

All eyes turned to General Jasper, who faced the president and answered: "In my opinion, no, Mr. President. Kourani delivered vital intelligence on the Doha threat. He saved American lives."

"Then I think it behooves us to treat him like a friend. A fully accredited diplomat. Don't you?"

"Yes, Mr. President. I agree."

Lescher leaned forward eagerly. "What about your guy Freed, who was tracking Kourani's movements?"

The president's eyes widened considerably.

"Freed hasn't turned up any useful information," General Jasper answered bluntly. "He was tasked with retracing Kourani's movements prior to his contacting us at our embassy in Bucharest. He ascertained that Kourani and some of his associates had traveled to Uzbekistan, Kazakhstan, and a former Soviet biological testing site known as Rebirth Island."

"What was Kourani doing on Rebirth?" the president asked.

"One hypothesis we're working with is that he and his men were tracking al-Qaeda operatives who were interested in procuring biological weapons."

"I assume there are others."

"Yes, Mr. President. That will be one of the first things we ask him when we have him in our possession."

"What about the samples from Rebirth?" NSC director Lescher asked.

"Inconclusive so far. The animals collected most likely died from a toxin, possibly a poison, possibly a virus. Our scientists are working to isolate whatever it is."

"Why isn't this a priority?" the president growled.

"It has been, Mr. President, and remains one," General Jasper answered, trying to stay calm. "Our people are working round-the-clock. But it's delicate, difficult, and dangerous work."

The president shook his head and grumbled to himself. Lescher filled the tense moment with: "What's your best estimate on how much longer it will take?"

"One to four days."

The president pounded the table and left abruptly.

The twenty-odd cabinet officials and their aides spent the next hour discussing Doha, Kourani, security in various midsized cities around the country, and the preparations in New York.

Around midnight the president returned with another Diet Coke. Per Lescher's and General Jasper's recommendation, he decided that the secretary of State would ask Austrian officials to swab the Iranians' bags before they boarded the plane in Vienna. No request would be made to open their bags or inspect carry-on luggage. In all other respects, the Iranians would be treated like traveling diplomats.

Then the exhausted officials left, some to their homes and others, like General Jasper, to their headquarters, where they spent most of the night.

CHAPTER EIGHTEEN

September 17

Matt woke on the morning of the seventeenth to the smell of eggs cooking in butter. Irina stood over him in yellow pajamas clutching a teddy bear.

"Dobre yutrom," she said, her pigtails wagging. "Are you as hungry as Boris?"

"Who's Boris?" He sat up, remembering the softness of Zyoda's skin, which quickly filled him with shame.

"You're silly. Boris is the name of my bear."

Zyoda grinned from across the room as she stood over the hot plate in a tight pink T-shirt and jeans. "I read that Americans like big breakfasts. Is that correct?"

"Yes," he said stretching and realizing he wasn't wearing pants.

Little Irina plopped beside him and said: "Mommy likes you. You make her happy."

"I like her, too."

"Coffee or tea?"

"Coffee, please."

He pulled a sheet around him, recovered his pants from the floor, and retreated to the bathroom, where he showered and brushed his teeth.

"How long do you plan to stay in Moscow?" Zyoda asked when he returned to the table.

"A few days this time, but I'll return."

"When?"

"In a month. Maybe sooner."

"Today is Saturday."

His discomfort wanted to turn into panic. "September seventeenth."

"Visiting hours at the hospitals begin at nine o'clock."

He sat distracted by scenarios playing out in his head.

"You said your father's friend is an ex-Soviet official?"

"That's correct."

She nodded. "Burdenko Military Hospital is close by. We don't have far to go."

Yes, we do, he thought. *I have to talk to Urakov, communicate with Liz in Paris, send what I've learned back to headquarters, and get back to New York by tomorrow to meet Kourani.* It seemed impossible.

I have to, he said to himself. *There's no room for error. One step at a time.*

LIZ BOARDED THE jet, thinking of time. For some reason time and the loss of it haunted her all the way to Paris.

Paris. Paris. Paris. The city had been the site of pivotal events in her life: her honeymoon with Matt, the place she had lost her virginity to a skinny boy at nineteen, the city where she decided to join the CIA.

Facing the bathroom mirror, she studied herself. Twelve years had slipped past since she'd met Matt at the Farm. Twelve years ago, as a CIA officer in training, she'd imagined a different life—single, living in a city with an unpronounceable name, matching wits with interesting people.

Like a sudden gale, Matt's wild energy had pulled her in a different direction. As a result, she was a mother, a wife, a trusted adviser to a man who was in certain respects less sophisticated than she.

In some ways he remained an enigma. His primal force challenged, sometimes scared, and often excited her. She saw him driven by impulses he didn't understand—a servant to something beyond ideas and explanations.

As much as she loved her husband and her children, a part of her still yearned to be fulfilled. She saw it reflected back through the stark, wobbly fluorescent light. Even though her skin had lost some of its youthful glow, even if she was slightly heavier and the insipient lines made her look more serious, she still wanted to carve a little notch in human history.

Time nipped at Liz's heels even when she deboarded the plane. Shoulders back, chin up, pulling the efficient black suitcase behind her, telling herself to be open-minded and brave.

Stepping through the automatic doors, she heard someone call her name. "Elizabeth Freed. Liz!"

To her left she spotted the tall older man with the long patrician nose and sweep of gray brown hair, Guillermo Moncada. He smiled with a hint of a different kind of temptation. Flattering, yes. But one that she knew she would resist.

Minutes later, they sat in the back of his chauffeured Citroën stuck in traffic on the A1, blue flashing lights and sirens weaving around them, with none of the majesty of the city in sight.

"The good news is that I've located the boy," Guillermo said, pulling on a Gauloise and exhaling through a crack in the window. He had a seen-it-all, done-it-all attitude that made her feel like a little girl.

"That's very good news."

"The bad news is we can't go there now."

"Why?"

"Clichy-sous-Bois," he answered in a world-weary tone, pushing a copy of *Le Figaro* into her lap.

Liz hadn't used her French since college. But she remembered enough to translate the headline: "Youth Unrest Rips Eastern Suburbs."

"The *banlieues*," Guillermo groaned, flicking the cigarette into the smog-filled haze. "The same old story. Authorities are in place to maintain the status quo. In this case, that means high unemployment, racism, deteriorating services, a bad attitude by the police. A couple of boys are killed by accident, and the whole thing goes up. Puff!"

"Puff?"

"Riots, Liz. Burning cars, looting. Social unrest. A flame to the dry refuse of society, if you will."

"You sound like a radical."

"Only of the café," Guillermo said, touching her hand. His smile promised charm and good conversation. "I've reserved a room for you in a nice hotel. There are some good exhibits, especially one at the Pompidou Center. The weather is delightful this time of year. Relax for a couple of days until this thing cools down."

"I can't," Liz said.

Guillermo waved his hand gallantly. "Be reasonable. Don't be so American. Smell the flowers."

"Matt needs the information now."

"I love that man, but he's impossible. Men like him can change the world."

"I love him, too."

"We can't get in there, Liz. So forget it. Go shopping."

Typical Guillermo. Nothing was ever urgent. No wonder Matt had wanted her here.

Liz didn't want to disappoint her husband. Besides she'd been waiting twelve years for an opportunity like this. She said: "Matt's counting on us. He said it was important."

Guillermo glanced out the side window and lit another Gauloise, muttering: "L'obstacle nous fait grands."

"What's that mean?"

"Something from the French poet André Chénier."

"What?"

"Obstacles make us great."

"I agree."

THEY LEFT IRINA at a neighbor's apartment and climbed into a green cab. Zyoda gave the driver directions to the hospital, then turned to Matt and took his hand.

She wanted to tell him that the ancient Hindus believed life had four purposes: sensual pleasure (*kāma*), material success (*artha*), correct action (*dharma*), and salvation (*moksha*). It was her goal to achieve all four. But the big man with the dyed hair and bruise on his forehead looked troubled. She said: "Don't worry. We'll be there soon."

"I'm an American," Matt warned her. "I don't want to cause a scene."

"That won't be a problem. I'll handle everything. Relax and leave it to me."

She snuggled closer and wondered how she could ensnare him further. He seemed to be a good man and she didn't want to let him get away.

They exited in front of the dour mustard yellow building and stood in line. "What's your father's friend's name again?" Zyoda asked, fixing the collar of Matt's white polo shirt.

"Oleg Urakov," Matt answered, hoping she was right about the hospital.

When they reached the entrance, Zyoda worked her charm on one of the guards. Another with a badly scarred face and clipboard stared Matt up and down.

"He wants your passport," Zyoda said, opening a document that identified her as a citizen of the Russian Federation and gave her age, marital status, and place of residence.

Matt didn't want to leave a footprint but had no choice. As he watched the guard record Zyoda's name over his alias, he thought: *This will cause her trouble. I'll have to clear it up.*

He followed her strong legs into the large lobby, down a hallway to the wooden counter of an information kiosk. Politely, poised on tiptoes, she asked for help in locating Oleg, talking about him as though she'd known him her whole life.

A neatly dressed woman made a call, then thoughtfully replaced the receiver on the rotary phone. "Did you know that the patient you wish to see is in intensive care?" she inquired over her glasses.

Zyoda turned quickly back to Matt. "I was afraid of that."

"He's not allowed to see visitors."

"Would it be possible for me to talk to a doctor about his condition?"

"Are you a family member?" the woman asked pushing the frames to the bridge of her nose.

"I'm his niece," Zyoda answered.

"Immediate family only. I'm sorry."

Zyoda wouldn't give up. "My uncle lives by himself. No wife, no children, no brothers or sisters."

"Intensive care is on the fourth floor. Inquire there. Good luck."

In the elevator Matt asked Zyoda again what she did for a living. The day before at the reception she'd told him she was a nurse.

"I work in a clinic where we help rehabilitate people with injuries," Zyoda answered.

"A physical therapist?"

"Mostly for young people," she answered, her bottom lip glistening in the artificial light.

At the fourth floor, Matt pulled her into a stairway where he could talk with her privately. "My father told me he's afraid that Oleg has been injured in an industrial accident," he explained. "It's possible that Russian authorities are trying to conceal what happened."

She looked deep into Matt's brown eyes. "What are you trying to tell me?"

"I don't want to cause you problems. I think you should leave now."

She kissed him and took both his hands. "Maybe you're working for the police or your government," she said. "I don't care. I just want to know one thing."

"What?"

"Are you really a bachelor?"

"Yes, I am."

She kissed him again and led him by the hand out into the hallway, into the ICU, where she asked for a Dr. Turesheiva. She explained to the nurse in charge that she was a physical therapist and had been asked by Dr. Turesheiva to see one of his patients, Oleg Urakov.

"Dr. Turesheiva hasn't checked in yet," the very tall nurse replied. "But the patient is down the hall."

"With your permission, I'll go look in."

The tall nurse turned her attention to Matt dressed in the same slacks, polo shirt, and jacket he had worn the day before. "Who is this gentleman?" she asked in Russian.

Matt extended a hand. "I'm Dr. Jackson, visiting from Canada."

"I have to get Dr. Malekov's approval. Wait here."

Seconds after the nurse turned a corner, Matt nodded at Zyoda, who followed him past twenty or so rooms, all occupied by three or four patients. The door at the end had a yellow warning sign on it and a chart encased in a plastic envelope. Through the little square window they saw a man strapped on a bed inside a reverse pressure system with hoses in his mouth and up his nose and multiple IVs.

"What do you think?" Matt asked.

"He's almost dead," Zyoda whispered back. Opening the envelope, she removed the chart and read the names of medicines she'd never heard of before. "I think we should go before the nurse comes back."

Matt calmly removed the top page of the chart, folded it, and stuffed it in his pocket.

"The doctors will need that," Zyoda said looking frightened.

"I need it to save him and others," Matt explained.

Approaching the elevator, they were intercepted by the tall nurse. "Dr. Malekov wants to see you. He asked that you wait."

Zyoda turned to Matt, who pointed at his watch. "I'm sorry," he said. "We have an emergency."

"But Dr. Malekov is from the Ministry of Defense."

Quickly they entered the elevator and were out the front door. As they sped off in a taxi, Zyoda grabbed Matt's arm.

"Tell me. What are you doing? Please."

"I'll drop you off at your apartment; then I need to go to my hotel."

"Am I going to have trouble?" she asked, out of breath.

Matt tried to reassure her. "If anyone asks questions, tell them where we met. Tell them I'm staying at the Sheraton Palace Hotel."

"Will I see you?"

"Yes."

"You promise?"

"I promise." He meant it and would figure out later how to help. Now he unfolded Oleg's medical chart and handed it to Zyoda to read.

"What's wrong with him?" Matt asked in English.

"Kiss me first."

She grabbed his crotch and didn't want to let go. He pulled away and pointed at the chart. "Read," he said strongly. "We can do that later."

She took a deep breath. "The doctors aren't sure. They think he's suffering from a rare form of a disease. A strain they've never seen before."

"What's it called?"

"Tularemia."

Matt made her spell it out in English. She did the best she could.

"What are the symptoms?"

The determination in his voice excited and troubled her. Trembling, she returned to the chart and read: "Sudden fever, chills, incapacitating headache. The bacteria attack the lymph nodes, spleen, liver."

"What are they treating him with?"

"Massive doses of tetracycline."

"Is it working?"

Zyoda shook her head. "I'm frightened of what you're asking me."

"Is the tetracycline working, Zyoda?"

"A little bit. Not so good."

After they hugged hard and kissed, Matt got back in the taxi and instructed the driver to take him to the airport.

"Which one?" the driver asked in Russian.

"Domodedovo." He had to get to New York. Fast!

CHAPTER NINETEEN

September 17

Light rain began to fall as Liz and Guillermo wound their way north past Le Raincy on their way to Clichy-sous-Bois. This was a part of France most tourists never saw—one drab town after another with patches of green in between—a mind-numbing cavalcade of concrete apartment towers in different shapes and sizes, all in various states of decay. Gazing at walls covered with lurid graffiti, Liz couldn't help thinking of the people who lived inside.

She'd read that half the residents of the *banlieues* were under twenty-five. A third of eligible wage earners were unemployed.

These low-income developments were populated by immigrants and first- and second-generation Muslims from France's former colonies. They passed shops selling *shawarma* and kebabs, and a Beuger King Muslim.

In the polyglot of names and cultures Liz sensed the people's displacement. They'd traveled from as far away as Senegal, Algeria, Uganda, Lebanon. But what had they become? French? "How long will it take for these people to assimilate?" she asked Guillermo, who was smoking his fifth Gauloise.

He shook his mind free of the bossa nova rhythms oozing from the CD player. "Decades at least. Centuries?" He shrugged. "France isn't like the United States."

Definitions of race and class had seemed arbitrary to her at first. When seen in the context of world history, though, they'd started to make sense. She understood that what she was seeing was the result of thousands of years of wars, political struggles, religious movements, and changes brought by technology.

They passed a street littered with the burnt-out carcasses of cars; walls covered with slogans like *Libérez nos camarades!* and *Vérité et Justice.*

Guillermo leaned into the Chilean driver and said in Spanish: "Start looking for signs." They stopped to speak to a woman who held an umbrella over her gray burka and told them that Seine-Saint-Denis branched off two miles ahead.

Seconds after they turned, they were stopped at a police barricade. Scary-looking anticriminal police in black uniforms leaned inside the windows and asked their business. Behind them stood black police wagons (*panniers à salade*), water cannons, and CRS anti-riot troops from the Ministry of the Interior armed with helmets, shields, goggles, batons, submachine guns, and tear gas guns.

With the sour smell of burning rubber hanging in the air, Liz explained in rusty French that she was delivering emergency medicine to the nephew of a friend.

"You're not a journalist?" a gendarme asked aggressively.

"I'm an American. The boy's a friend of a friend."

"What's his name?" asked another cop poking his shaved head in the car.

"Javed Mohammed."

"What's his last name?"

"Kourani."

The cop looked for the name on a clipboard and shook his head. Liz showed them her U.S. passport and a vial of Zestril she kept in her purse to regulate her high blood pressure.

"You're from the U.S. Embassy?" the gendarme asked.

Liz lied: "Yes. The boy's health is important to us."

The gendarme poked his big chin at Guillermo. "Who's he?"

"My security officer."

"We have to check with the ministry."

"Of course."

Tense minutes passed during which Guillermo argued quietly that this was a terrible idea that would end in their arrest.

The gendarme returned with an older gendarme, who announced: "We've imposed a curfew in this area that starts at eight o'clock."

"I'll only be minutes," Liz pleaded.

"You go past here, we can't go with you."

"Let's try again tomorrow," Guillermo warned in English.

"You go at your own risk," the officer said, pointing to Guillermo. "If I were you, I'd send him."

"Thank you, officer, but I need to do this myself."

The policeman instructed Guillermo's driver to park behind their black van and wait while Liz walked the remaining two blocks to 93 Seine-Saint-Denis. A dozen teenage boys stood around the entrance listening to rap music and smoking cigarettes. Ten feet away, a boy with his back to them pissed onto an old mattress.

She asked a black kid in a hoodie if he knew Javed Mohammed. The boy shouted, "Javi! Javi!" and, holding his arms out like an airplane, executed a couple of loops. The others laughed.

"So you do know him?" Liz asked in French, trying not to show fear.

"We all know that fool," a tall kid with a ring in his nose shouted back. "Who's asking?"

"A friend of the family."

He bounced closer on his toes and sniffed inches from her face. "You smell sweet. American or English?"

Liz pointed at the building. "Where is he?"

"Up a tree!"

A boy with a broad brown face motioned for her to follow him through the dank lobby into the elevator. He kicked the top button with the heel of his boot and smiled with broken teeth. "The cops," he said in French. "They plan to kill all of us tonight."

At the top floor, Liz followed him to the right and over some parked tricycles, up a flight of stairs to a door. Liz stopped halfway. "Is this a joke?"

"No, it's the roof," the boy said, waving her forward. "Come!"

Up the last eight steps, through the battered metal door, she gulped the fresh air, not knowing what to expect. The boy bobbed his head to the music in his headphones and pointed to a small, improvised shacklike structure stuck in the corner. A smaller, thinner boy crouched beside it and reached inside.

"Javi?" she asked.

"The birdman of Seine-Saint-Denis."

He came out cradling a white bird, which he threw into the sky. Liz crossed the thirty feet, never taking her eyes off the boy, who looked up into the mist. He waved his arms like a conductor. Strange whistling sounds came from his mouth. *Maybe he really is crazy*, she said to herself, now ten feet away.

He ignored the crunch of her shoes, his face deep in concentration. Through the mist, she saw the wings of a dozen pigeons swoop overhead.

"Are they yours?" she asked in English.

"My children."

He had a sweet face with burning eyes, a smallish chin, and little mouth. When the birds returned, he told her each one's name, what he'd paid for it, its unique characteristics, and how long it had taken him to train it.

"You love them, don't you?" she asked.

"This keeps my mind in its right place."

"That's important at a time like this."

"The beauty of the birds, the sky, the way they fly. I'd rather not think about anything else."

Liz decided to take an honest approach. "I'm an American," she said. "I've come to ask you some questions about your uncle Moshen and your grandfather."

Javi looked far away. "I haven't seen my uncle Moshen for ages. He sends my mother money. My grandfather died before I was born."

"If you help me, I can help you."

Hands in his pockets, Javi started to shuffle away. "That's all I know."

"Maybe I can help you learn more about these birds."

He stopped and stared at her. "What do you know?"

"A young man like you should follow his passion."

"Maybe he should. Maybe he needs to step out of the confusion created by the so-called grownups and take charge of his own life."

"That's an excellent idea. I think I can help."

TULAREMIA. TULAREMIA. TULAREMIA. Matt kept repeating the name in his head as the British Airways jet ripped through the evening sky.

"Sit back. Relax. Our flying time to London is approximately four hours, five minutes." The captain spoke like John Gielgud reading *Hamlet.*

That meant a long layover in Heathrow before Flight 117 left for JFK. In the intervening time, Matt had much to do.

First, he tried to shake the guilt. It was bad enough that he'd slept with Zyoda. He'd explain that to Liz. Worse in his mind was the fact that he'd abandoned Zyoda and her daughter, leaving them to face Russian authorities alone.

His actions had violated one of his rules: never leave an asset or contact worse off for cooperating with you. *Once I get a chance, I have to set things right.*

Doubts pushed back: *What happens if I never get the chance? What happens if Liz doesn't understand? Maybe I've already screwed up my marriage.*

Matt pictured his father swirling a can of Schlitz and looking up at him, bitter resignation etched around his mouth. "You're an idiot. I knew it would happen."

A needy voice reminded him that his work for the clandestine service had never been fully acknowledged. *How many times have I been passed up for promotion because some higher-up took credit? Or someone in Washington pointed out that I violated some meaningless procedure?*

Matt felt for a minute that his father was right. The system was rigged against him. Life was cruel at its core.

I could lie to Liz. Leave Zyoda to work out things on her own.

The jet hit an air pocket, dropped two hundred feet, and bounced. The Asian woman next to him grabbed his arm.

NO! he admonished himself. *That's not who I am.*

The 747 was packed. He sat in back, sandwiched between the Asian woman now returning to *Midnight in the Garden of Good and Evil* in English and a pimply young man in his twenties watching *Saw II* on his laptop. Privacy was out of the question, but he couldn't wait.

Sliding his MasterCard through the slot in front of him, he dialed Guillermo Moncada's number on the AeroPhone. No answer. He picked at the meal, then dialed again. Nothing. He flipped through the twelve channels of music, then tried to follow some scenes from *Spider-Man 3*. When he dialed a third time, a secretary picked up and put him through to Guillermo's cell phone.

The Argentine's voice brought a sense of relief. "Matthew. My friend. I'm sitting in my car next to your charming wife. We're heading back to the city. Where are you now?"

"Somewhere over Germany on my way to London." Matt had to be careful. He didn't know who was sitting nearby.

"You should come to Paris. Meet us for dinner. I know a fabulous new French-Moroccan place just up boulevard Beaumarchais off Bastille."

"Not tonight. How's the boy?"

"The boy. Are you serious? You're not going to ask about your wife?"

Matt didn't have time to trade wisecracks with Guillermo. "What did he have to say?"

The Argentine got the message. "Here's Liz."

Husband and wife quickly dispensed with formalities, each holding back emotions, each sensing the burden of the other. They were trained professionals. They knew the drill.

"Javi. He calls himself Javi. He's a gentle soul," Liz said. "Confused, angry; feels he's been abandoned. Doesn't think the French are kind. Loves birds. Wants to go to Cornell to study ornithology. I told him we would try to help him."

"We will. Of course."

"Moshen Kourani is his uncle. His father, Hamid, was killed by the Taliban in Afghanistan. He's been living outside Paris with his mother since. Uncle Moshen sends them money. He's been trying to convince them to move back to Tehran."

This threw Matt. "I wonder why."

"He didn't say. The boy wants to study in the States."

"Okay."

"But his uncle hates the U.S."

"He said that?"

"Oh, yes."

"They speak often?"

"About once a month. His uncle called two days ago from Vienna."

"That fits."

"The boy's frustrated. He feels trapped."

"I got that."

"You sound upset."

Matt tried to fit the pieces together quickly. "Did he say why his uncle hates the United States?"

"He was very specific. Javi said his grandfather died when the USS *Vincennes* shot down Iran Air Flight 655 over the Persian Gulf."

Matt knew the incident well. Back in the summer of '88 the U.S. Navy guided missile cruiser *Vincennes* had mistakenly shot down an Iranian commercial airliner while battling several Iranian speed-boats in the Strait of Hormuz. All 290 people on board were killed.

"Shit."

"What's wrong, Matt?"

"This changes everything."

"Why?"

"I'll call you from New York."

ALAN BECKMAN'S BODY had been running on adrenaline for days. Now in the crowded 26 Federal Plaza conference room high over downtown New York City, it wanted to stop, eat, and rest.

FBI, Homeland Security, Defense Intelligence, CIA, and NYPD

officials had been discussing the arrival of Scimitar (Kourani) and the Iranian delegation for the past hour and a half. "Protective vigilance" was the phrase FBI special agent in charge (SAC) Rove Peterson kept repeating.

Standing ramrod straight at the front of the room, Rove Peterson outlined the route the Iranians would be taking to the Millennium UN Plaza Hotel, the number of plainclothes agents stationed inside the hotel and the security corridor around the UN building itself. "We won't let these guys out of our sight at any time. We're treating them like our children. We want 'em safe."

The lights dimmed, and a map of New York City was projected on a screen with two big red circles, one around JFK and the other around the UN. "All right. Let's go through the route step by step."

Beckman wanted to close his eyes. Instead, summoning his last gasp of will, he said, "I'm sorry, Rove. I think we're missing something."

A sour look came over Peterson's face. "What?"

"I'm concerned about the allocation of resources, particularly your counterterrorism people."

A dozen of the thirty-three people in the room groaned in frustration. Since Alan had arrived from Doha, he'd been second-guessing their plans without explaining why.

Once again, Alan talked about the fact that a majority of JTTF (FBI-NYPD Joint Terrorism Task Force) teams had been deployed to nearby midsized cities, including Hartford, New Haven, Newark, Trenton, Philadelphia, and Boston. The U.S. Marines CBIRF (Chemical Biological Incident Response Force) was on twenty-four-hour alert at Camp Lejeune, North Carolina.

SAC Rove Peterson cut him off. "It sounds like you want us to take an offensive posture against the Iranians. Are we defending them, Alan, or countering?"

"Maybe both."

Rove shook his head. "I don't get you, Alan. Your own people have concluded that the enemy in this instance is al-Qaeda."

"I'm not sure that's completely clear," Beckman said.

Rove Peterson picked up the two-hundred-page threat assessment report from NCTS and let it fall to the table with a bang. "For christsakes, Alan. Have you read your own report?"

"I have," Alan countered, emotion rising in his throat. "But there are too many unknowns. The situation could change."

"How?" the tall, female African American ASAC (FBI assistant special agent in charge) asked, trying to sound sympathetic.

"Our source may not be completely reliable," Alan answered. For reasons of security, officials in Washington had decided to withhold the identity of their source.

"What does that mean?"

All eyes turned to Alan, who bit his lip. He hated to be put in this position. If he revealed that a member of the Iranian delegation was their source, he could be dismissed. Even more serious charges could be brought against him if the source was ever compromised.

"You have something more to tell us about your source?" Peterson asked.

"I can't," Alan muttered under his breath.

"Then what the heck are you talking about, Alan? You want us to go out on a limb here and do what?"

The tension around the table grew. Alan felt it tighten around his chest. He struggled to breathe. "I . . . I . . . I don't know."

Rove's frustration poured out: "If you have something important to tell us, we want to know."

Alan couldn't breathe; his bottom lip started to tremble. "I . . . I . . . I don't know."

The ASAC saw that he was in trouble. She leaned forward concerned. "Alan. Are you okay?"

The room started spinning. He knew what was coming. He scolded himself for forgetting to eat and letting his blood sugar soar. At the same time he tried to will his lungs to work, his throat to open up. "I . . . I have type 2 diabetes. I need some . . . wa—" He blacked out.

•   •   •

Rain started to fall heavily as the Citroën Guillermo and Liz were riding in reached the A1. Guillermo asked the driver to take them directly to Le Bar à Huîtres, where he planned to order a large platter of Belon and Marenne oysters with mignonette sauce to go with a crisp Sancerre.

"Maybe we should start with some little *boudeuses de Bretagne*," he said. "They're small, you know, and named after a kind of stubbornly immature child that refuses to grow up."

Liz looked out at a passing motorcycle, thinking about Matt. Chocolate and oysters were two of her favorite things in the world. But neither of them interested her now.

"I hope you're hungry," Guillermo said. "The rain always stimulates my palate."

"I want you to take me to Charles de Gaulle."

"After we have dinner?"

"No, now."

"But—"

Something in the tone of her husband's voice had convinced her. She said: "I have to meet Matt in New York."

General Jasper was sitting at her desk poring over the interrogation reports from Qatar when Shelly burst in. "I asked for a few minutes of privacy."

Shelly sputtered around the wad of blueberry muffin in her mouth. "It's an emergency. Freed on line twelve."

"Son of a gun!" Jasper jabbed a finger in the direction of the phone by the sofa. "Listen on the other line."

As soon as Freed came over the line talking about vital information he had picked up in Moscow, General Jasper cut him off. "No more obfuscation, Freed. Where are you now?"

"I'm on my way back to New York."

"Where exactly?"

"I'm at the airport," Matt answered. "My plane leaves shortly. I don't have a lot of time."

"You're in big trouble, Freed. You disobeyed orders."

"I regret that, General, but it's of vital importance to the safety of our country that you hear what I have to say."

From her position near the sofa, Shelly ran a hand across her throat. Jasper lifted her chin and nodded. "We aren't on a secure line."

Matt quickly looked around the crowded terminal. The situation wasn't optimal. He stood at the last phone along the wall. He'd jammed wooden coffee stirrers into the two closest to him. He said: "I repeat, General. I don't have time."

"All right, quickly. What have you got?"

"Two things. First, genetically altered tularemia."

"What's that?"

"It's the biological agent that infected one of Mr. Kourani's associates, a former Soviet biotechnician who is dying in a hospital bed in Moscow. This man, named Oleg Urakov, accompanied Kourani to Rebirth Island in July. I suspect that it's the same biological agent that killed the sample we sent back."

"Tularemia?"

"In some genetically altered form."

General Jasper indicated to Shelly to write that down. Shelly, who was already making notations on a pad, nodded yes.

Matt continued: "I looked it up on the Internet. In 2002, former Soviet Biopreparat agents admitted in testimony to the United Nations Special Commission that one of the biological weapons they were developing was an especially virulent strain of tularemia that could be dispensed airborne or through the water. One of their scientists testified that a small amount could infect the entire population of the United States or Europe within a few days."

"Why are you telling me this, Freed?" Jasper asked.

"I believe it's the biological agent that Kourani is bringing with him to the U.S."

The general's heart stopped for a second. "What in the name of God are you talking about?"

"I believe Kourani is trying to bring tularemia into the U.S."

"That . . . that doesn't make sense."

"I'm almost positive that Kourani is double-crossing us, General."

"You're wrong, Freed. Have you heard the news from Qatar?"

Matt waited for the man with the briefcase to realize that the phone next to his was out of order. "Only what I read in the *Herald Tribune*."

"The information he supplied saved U.S. lives and property."

"I'm not surprised."

"You're not?"

"It's all part of his plan."

"What plan?"

"It gives him the credibility to set up something much more important."

General Jasper felt the blood pulsing in her temples. She took a deep breath. "Freed, I want you back here, immediately. When you're in my office, we'll talk."

The man with the briefcase wandered back and stood nearby reading a copy of *Sports Illustrated*. Matt said: "I'll call you back."

Five minutes later he called from a phone in the Admirals Club. This time the general heard glasses clinking in the background and wanted to know if Freed was in a bar.

"General, it's very important that you hear me out. There's no time!"

"I need to know your specific location."

"Listen to what I have to say first."

"Freed, have you been drinking?"

Matt spoke quickly. "The important thing here is Kourani."

But General Jasper kept interrupting. "That's why you need to be in New York—"

"He's been clever. Extremely clever."

"—now!"

"First, he gains our trust, which he's done by giving us Qatar. Then he tells us to prepare for an al-Qaeda attack on our soil."

"What are you trying to say?"

"What if the attack comes from Qods Force agents instead? What if they make it look like it's al-Qaeda?"

Shelly blurted out: "That's very twisted."

Matt pushed on: "He's set it up to look like the attack is coming from another source."

"All right," the general said, trying not to blow her stack. "Let's say for the sake of argument that Kourani is double-crossing us. Is he working with Qods Force or on his own?"

"Unclear."

"Then what are he and Qods Force trying to accomplish?"

"We know that there are constant struggles for power among Iranian religious and political elements. Some secular elements are trying to establish a political footing. An attack like the one I think Kourani is planning accomplishes three things. One, it shows fundamental Shiites around the world that we're vulnerable. Two, it directs potential U.S. rage at Sunni terrorist and political groups. Three, it solidifies Qods Force equities and those of their clerical supporters. Their interests, power, and importance advance as conflict heightens in the region. Honestly, we do not know enough about intra clerical political intrigue in Qom to determine exactly why a faction of mullahs may be pursuing such a path, but violence and terror is a tried and tested tool of Iranian Mullahs."

Shelly chimed in: "They'd be in an excellent position to exploit the chaos that ensues."

"Exactly."

"So you're saying we misread Kourani from the beginning," Jasper added.

"He misdirected us deliberately."

Shelly cut in. "Wouldn't the Iranians be taking an enormous risk?"

General Jasper asked: "What if he's caught?"

"Maybe Kourani is acting on his own, or maybe he's just pretending to. Either way, if he's caught, the Iranians can disavow any knowledge. They can say they knew that he was acting strangely and only later found out that he had approached us in Bucharest with a plan to defect."

"That's out there, Freed," General Jasper said. "What's his motive?"

"Revenge," Matt answered strongly.

"Revenge? For what?"

"Kourani hates us. I found out that his father, who was a mullah and a devotee of Ayatollah Beheshti, died when the USS *Vincennes* shot down Iran Air Flight 655 over the Persian Gulf in the summer of '88."

Shelly blurted out: "Oh, shit."

"That's significant," the general said, holding her forehead. "How did you find out?"

"From his nephew, who lives in Paris."

"This has huge implications. We're going to need proof."

Matt said: "Someone there must have a copy of the flight manifest. Look for his name."

"That won't be enough."

"There's no time, General. The plane must be stopped."

"What?"

"The plane carrying Kourani into the U.S. must be stopped."

"Do you know what you're saying?"

"Kourani, the whole delegation, has to be detained at JFK and placed in some kind of quarantine. Once he gets the tularemia into the country, we're screwed."

General Jasper shook her head. "We'll be taking an enormous diplomatic risk. Practically every world leader will be here as witnesses if we make a mistake."

"The risk is even bigger if that stuff is released. Look it up. Tularemia spreads like wildfire. Medical facilities will be overwhelmed. We could be looking at millions of casualties before it's contained."

CHAPTER TWENTY

September 18, Morning

There was a detectable buzz in the orange blossom–scented air of the lobby of the Vienna Marriott the early morning of the eighteenth. While the five-man Iranian delegation milled around the gift shop discussing the prospects of the Iranian national team in the upcoming Iran-Bahrain football match, a short aide from the embassy reviewed the bill.

"I hear Ali Karimi isn't playing," the silver-haired Iranian ambassador to the UN said, referring to the team's star forward, also known as "the Asian Maradona."

"But he has to. It's an important game."

"Strained ACL."

"That means disaster," the deputy minister of foreign affairs groused.

"I've heard this new kid from Persepolis is very skilled."

The Iranian aide at checkout calculated that the tab for room service could buy a small house in his hometown of Arak. He would keep this to himself as well as the four hundred dollars charged to the Iranian ambassador for Shalimar perfume.

As the tall, blond hotel clerk ran the Iranian Embassy AmEx card through the register, three black Mercedes appeared outside.

The five serious-looking men picked up their hand luggage and headed for the door, all wearing dark suits and shirts without ties. The Iranian ambassador to the UN and the deputy minister for foreign affairs got into the lead car. Kourani and the aide from the embassy loaded in the second. Two rougher-looking men, who were security officers, entered the third. One of them was stocky, with close-cropped white hair.

They had passed a pair of Western-looking women in patterned dresses at the hotel entrance, discussing the price of shoes. As the last limo door slammed shut, one of the women spoke into a cell phone: "Post One to Base. The clients are leaving in three limos. Scimitar is in car two."

A young man at the end of the block climbed on a motorcycle and picked up pursuit.

Fifteen miles south at the Vienna International Airport, five fit, clean-cut FBI agents (three men, two women) stood in front of the United Airlines counter. Agent in Charge Devere Johnson II checked the text message on his phone and announced: "Scimitar's on his way."

His deputy, Tina Chang, put away her iPod. "We're good."

"Our cover extends from this terminal to JFK. All clear?"

"Got it."

Back in downtown Vienna, the FBI agent dressed as a motorcycle messenger watched the black limos veer left onto the ramp to the A4 motorway. He continued straight ahead, and a silver Audi 2000 took his place. The FBI agent in the passenger seat of the Audi spoke into his cell phone: "Post Three to Base. En route to the airport. Proceeding as planned."

Approximately twenty minutes later, all three limos turned off at the Flughafen exit and slowed in front of the international terminal. Three members of the Iranian diplomatic staff greeted the special delegation with handshakes.

"Customs and Immigration have been handled," one of the staff members said before handing the men their boarding passes. The diplomats thanked them and proceeded alone to the First Class lounge.

As they passed the bar, a young male FBI agent watched the Iranians sit before a plasma TV, which rebroadcast a Davis Cup tennis match between Spain and France. "They're in the lounge," the agent said into the cell phone earpiece. "Boarding in thirty-six minutes. Counting down."

Later, he saw the five men being waved through Security. "There's Scimitar," Tina Chang whispered, as the man with the closely cropped salt-and-pepper beard passed. He was followed by the UN ambassador, the Iranian deputy foreign minister, and the two Iranian security officers.

"The last two look more like wrestlers. Especially the one with the white hair."

"Security," Tina said. "And they're probably armed."

ALAN BECKMAN AWOKE at 5 AM, yanked the IV from his arm, grabbed the vial of Metformin from the night table, and wearing the green hospital gown for a shirt (because he couldn't find his own), hailed a cab that whisked him down to Worth Street. Sometime during the long night, he'd had a brainstorm. Foreign operatives usually used the same alias multiple times.

Now, sitting at a spare computer in FBI headquarters at 26 Federal Plaza, he logged into the FBI database and punched in a code. Entering the name Fariel Golpaghani, he clicked Search. Two entries appeared on the screen. The first dated back to September 2000, when Fariel Golpaghani had spent five nights at the Hilton Hotel on Sixth Avenue. A cross-check of immigration records revealed that he'd been traveling as a member of the Iranian delegation to the opening of the UN General Assembly.

Alan zeroed in on the more recent stay. This took place in March 2002 and involved three nights at the Mayflower Hotel on Central Park West. The hotel had been completely rebuilt since, but FBI agent Holly O'Connor was able to retrieve the hotel's telephone records and outgoing calls from nearby pay phones.

Forty minutes' work turned up three calls made to a Muslim

name in the Bronx: Rafiq Haddad. INS records showed that Haddad was a naturalized citizen who had moved to the United States from Lebanon in 1989.

Around 10 AM, while Holly tracked down an address, Special Agent in Charge Rove Peterson passed by and stopped. "I didn't expect to see you, Alan."

"Today's the big day."

"How're you feeling?"

"A flare-up of my diabetes. I hadn't eaten for a day or so. I'm better."

"Look, I didn't mean to bust your chops, but—"

"Forget it. I think I might have something. I'll stop by your office."

First, he called headquarters and spoke to Shelly, who told him that Freed was on his way to New York.

"What flight's he on? When's he scheduled to land?"

Shelly wasn't able to provide either piece of information and didn't seem concerned.

Curious, Beckman thought, hurrying down the hall to Peterson's office. No one had told him about Freed's revelations to General Jasper the night before. The head of NCTS had decided to keep the circle small.

With O'Connor by his side, Alan Beckman retraced the discovery of Kourani's previous visits, step by step.

"So there seems to be a connection between Fariel Golpaghani, aka Kourani, and this guy named Rafiq Haddad," the special agent in charge said. "Now what?"

"We find Haddad."

Thirty minutes later, Beckman slammed a 9mm clip into the Glock provided by the FBI. Beside him NYPD detective Vinnie Danieli (now on assignment with the New York office of the FBI) complained about the Yankees as he gunned the Ford Taurus up FDR Drive to the Bruckner, to the Bronx River Parkway.

"It's the pitching I worry about," Danieli said, cruising past eighty. "You know what I'm saying?"

Alan nodded, taking him in. Danieli was a wily-looking character with warm eyes, wavy hair, and a long nose. "I mean, a hundred and sixty-two games a year, those arms get tired. Especially when you got some guys on the staff who should be knocking 'em back in Florida."

Beckman quickly scrolled through the messages on his cell phone. Nothing from Matt.

"All of 'em lie about their ages. A friend of mine told me that Clemens is like fifty-two."

As Alan's mind traveled back to Athens and his last face-to-face with Matt, Vinnie burned rubber past the carcass of a Ford Explorer that had been stripped of its seats and tires. "Cannibals," the NYPD detective muttered under his breath.

"What?"

"You gonna tell me what this is about?" Vinnie asked, offering Alan a stick of gum.

"We're looking for a guy named Rafiq Haddad."

"Haddad?"

"That's right."

"What are we gonna do with that bad boy when we find him?"

"I'm going to ask him a couple of questions."

"Sure you are," he said turning onto Allerton Avenue.

Alan popped a Metformin in his mouth and swallowed it with bottled water.

"Heartburn?" Vinnie asked.

"Diabetes."

"Take up racquetball," the detective said slapping his abs. "Keeps everything hard."

They passed a bodega with a couple of elderly Haitians out front and double-parked in front of 1225.

"I don't want the whole neighborhood to know we're coming," Alan said, getting out.

Vinnie smiled. "It's a pleasure working with you, Beckman."

"Let's go."

They entered a three-story 1920s structure with no elevator and scrambled up the worn marble stairs to the second floor. Number eleven sat at the end of the L-shaped hall to the right.

Alan knocked and leaned on the buzzer. No answer. He tried the doors on either side. Nothing.

"What do we do now?" Vinnie asked.

"I guess I try to pick it," Alan answered. "We're not trying to build a legal case."

Vinnie turned away and hurried down the stairs with "I'll get my friend."

Two minutes later he was back with a two-person metal ram he'd fetched from the trunk. "Meet Ethel. She's one tough bitch."

On the first try the door gave way with a loud crunch.

"Thanks, baby!" Vinnie said planting a kiss on the metal.

"Let's try to be discrete."

They scoured the little one-bedroom, finding books in Arabic and English—*The Kite Runner, The Bourne Identity*—CDs, family photos, an old *Playboy* featuring Pamela Anderson, and a framed photo of an imam.

Inside the hall closet, Vinnie Danieli found a packed suitcase. "Looks like your friend is planning to go on vacation," he said.

"He's not my friend."

"But he will be soon, won't he?" Vinnie asked with a wink.

In a pile of bills scattered haphazardly on a little desk, Alan found a delivery notice from DHL International. He pocketed it along with a photo of Rafiq posed on the deck of the *Intrepid*.

"Let's go."

"Don't forget to lock the door."

Downstairs in the laundry room Danieli found a middle-aged Jamaican woman who identified Rafiq Haddad from the photo. "He quiet man," she said. "Go about his bid-ness."

"Does he have friends? You know, amigos."

"He got a girl sometimes. Arab-lookin'. Pretty. That's all I know."

"You see him recently, like maybe washin' his shorts?"

"Maybe yesterday mornin'. Ya."

"You have any idea what Señor Rafiq does for a living?"

"I believe he work for one of those portable toilet company. I seen him sometimes with da truck."

Alan asked: "What kind of truck?"

"Big truck."

Vinnie raised an eyebrow. "Big truck full of shit?"

The Jamaican woman collapsed with laughter. Vinnie slung an arm around her. "Port-a-potty? Johnny-on-the-spot? Crap-in-a-trap?"

The Jamaican woman chuckled. "You bery funny."

"I bet you make a mean jerk chicken."

"I think it somethin' like Pot-in-da-sand."

"You're the best."

NOTHING IN GENERAL Jasper's long, and sometimes difficult, career had prepared her for this level of stress. Aching and bleary-eyed after one hour's sleep, she rose from the sofa in her office to take a call from the White House.

It took several seconds for her to recognize National Security director Stan Lescher's high-pitched voice. "The president and I keep going back and forth on this," Lescher said. "We just took a look at Freed's personnel file and frankly, General, he seems like a loose cannon."

"Wait . . . You got a copy of Freed's file?"

"I had someone in your shop send it over. But that's not the issue."

"It's not?" Under normal circumstances, she'd have been screaming at Lescher for requesting something from her agency without asking her first. But she found it hard to muster outrage this morning. Too many things were spinning out of control.

"The issue, General," Lescher started, his voice gaining an edge of indignation. "The issue you brought to the table last night with the information you got from Freed is: What to do about Kourani?"

It all came back like a nightmare, the long hours in the White House Situation Room facing the president, the vice president, Lescher, the heads of CIA, Defense, Homeland Security, State.

Frayed nerves, disbelief, questions about Freed's loyalty to his country, aspersions cast about the way she ran her shop.

General Jasper understood that people generally didn't respond well to pressure, but this was too much. Sandwiched between meetings, she'd received news that her top man in New York, Alan Beckman, had collapsed from a drop in blood sugar and was recuperating at St. Vincent's Hospital.

Somewhere around 5 AM, after NSC director Lescher had assaulted her competence, General Jasper had sat down to write her resignation. It provided the relief she needed to steal an hour's sleep.

Looking down at the resignation letter on her desk, she smiled. It seemed childish now. Ripping it in half, she tossed it in the trash, then saw the Post-it from Shelly: "The latest from Science & Tech. Read NOW!!!"

Attached was a report that concluded with "better than 70% certainty" that the samples recovered from the rodents on Rebirth Island matched the chemical profile of a genetically altered form of tularemia.

Lescher continued to talk. She cut him off to pass this on. All she heard back was hiss.

Not knowing if it originated from the telephone line or her head, she asked: "Stan, can you hear me? Are you still there?"

Another half a minute passed. She entertained the idea that she was in a dream.

Lescher's voice shattered that. "So . . . so the tularemia threat IS real?"

"Yes!"

He cut her off. "Why the hell didn't you tell us before?"

"Excuse me, Stan. I just found out."

Lescher launched into another assault. "The president and I still can't fathom how you could let a man like Freed disappear and then present his findings at the eleventh hour like he's some kind of Jedi warrior back from—"

She wasn't in the mood. "What's your point?"

"The president—"

The general interrupted again. "Stop your bellyaching, Stan!"

"How dare you—"

"Listen! The Iranians arrive at JFK in nine hours. You have to make a decision."

"I understand, yes. The consequences could be huge."

"What do you want to do?"

Stan backtracked. "I hate putting the president in this position."

Jasper knew that before assuming his current position at the White House, Lescher had been a professor of political science at Yale. Previously he'd served twelve years as a Foreign Service officer with State and, briefly, as a staffer at NSC. He owed his current position to his friendship with the president and the advisory role he'd played during the presidential campaign.

"Stan, the situation is what it is."

"Where's Freed?"

She felt as though she'd gained the upper hand. "On his way to JFK. But that hardly matters. We've got a decision to make. I suggest we make it now."

"I know that. I have to talk to the president."

Half an hour later, after she'd splashed water on her face, brushed her teeth, ordered coffee and a bottle of Maalox, and summoned the head of Science & Technology to her office, the phone rang again.

This time she met the president's deep, gruff voice. "General, I trust we're completely up-to-date."

"Mr. Lescher knows everything I know, Mr. President."

"Then we face one hell of a difficult decision."

"That's correct, sir."

She suspected Lescher was on another line listening in.

The president took a deep breath. "I want to hear your best advice."

"Given what we know now, I suggest we manufacture an excuse to isolate the plane when it arrives at Kennedy. That will give our people a chance to go through the plane and examine everything— luggage, personal effects, the passengers themselves."

"Including Kourani?"

"Including Kourani, very carefully and diplomatically, of course."

"The Iranians are a sensitive group. You know that, don't you?"

"I do, sir."

"They're likely to go ballistic."

"We can tell them that we did it for their own protection. A bomb threat was phoned in. We took steps to ensure the safety of their delegation."

The president said: "I think I agree. I'll call you."

Ten minutes later, Stan Lescher called back, raising questions about the risk they'd be taking with Kourani. "What if he refuses to talk to us further? Then where do we stand?"

"That's a chance we probably have to take."

"How well are we prepared on the ground?"

"We've been discussing that for days, Stan. You've been in all the meetings."

"Tell me again."

"The U.S. Marines CBIRF [Chemical Biological Incident Response Force] is on alert at Camp Lejeune, North Carolina. The FBI has hazmat and quick-response teams stationed at five deploy points—Washington, Detroit, Jacksonville, Seattle, and San Diego. They're on twenty-four-hour alert. Local medical, law enforcement, and SWAT are active in thirty-eight midsized cities ranked by category. Full evacuation plans are in place for the top fifteen."

"Where, for example, did you put Cincinnati?"

"Category A."

"San Diego?"

"A."

"Portland, Oregon?"

"B."

"You sure?"

Losing patience, General Jasper said: "You've got the documentation, Stan. We're running out of time."

"Don't you dare push the president," Lescher shot back. "We've got nine hours."

"Eight and a half. And we need time to execute a plan of action."

"How much time do you need?"

"Three to four hours at least."

"You'll get it."

"Good."

"I'll call back."

CHAPTER TWENTY-ONE

September 18, Afternoon

Alan Beckman called DHL International from the car. After being transferred five times and put on hold, he spoke to a supervisor who said that the tracking number on the delivery notice Alan found in Haddad's apartment corresponded to three large boxes that had been shipped from the Russian Republic to a Mail Boxes Etc. on Third Avenue and Eighty-ninth Street. The recipient: Rafi Fragrances, Inc.

Vinnie Danieli got them to Mail Boxes Etc. in a flash. The eyes of the young Indian-looking man behind the counter fluttered like butterfly wings when he saw Danieli's FBI badge.

"Have you seen this man in here recently?" Alan asked, showing the clerk the photo of Haddad.

"I don't think so."

"Look again. He came here about three weeks ago to pick up three boxes shipped DHL Worldwide Priority."

Danieli was already behind the counter, punching keys on the computer. The young clerk took over. "I can do that."

"Be my guest."

The clerk confirmed that Rafiq Haddad had signed for three boxes delivered to Rafi Fragrances from an address in Moscow on September 3.

"Can you tell me what was in them?" Alan asked.

The clerk shook his head.

"It could be important."

He was a chubby young man with gold-colored eyes. "I'm not allowed to release that information."

"Didn't the shipper have to file a customs declaration?" Alan asked.

The clerk ran a hand through his short curly hair and asked in a shaky voice: "You guys are FBI, right?"

"Yes, we are."

"Aren't you supposed to have a search warrant?"

Vinnie got in his face. "This is the wrong time to play games. Are you sure you want to mess with—"

"Hey!"

Alan asked Vinnie to watch the door. Then he pulled the young clerk aside. "What did you say your name was again?"

"Daya. It means 'mercy.' "

"Daya what?"

"Narayan."

"You related to R. K. Narayan, author of *The English Patient*?"

"He wrote *The English Teacher*. He's my father's second cousin."

Vinnie, meanwhile, hustled the remaining two customers out and locked the door.

"You see, Daya, we have a potentially dangerous situation here," Alan continued in a reassuring voice. "I work for the National Counterterrorism Service. You've heard of it?"

Daya nodded.

"I need your help looking up that customs declaration."

The clerk said: "Maybe it would be easier if you showed me a search warrant first."

"The thing is, Daya, we don't have time. And a lot of lives are at stake."

The clerk thought about it a minute. "This is like a national security matter?"

"It is."

"I lost a cousin in a train bombing in India."

"We don't want something like that to happen here. Do we?"

Daya went back to the computer and looked it up. According to the customs form filled out by the sender, the three boxes contained "fragrance aerosol."

"Were these boxes ever examined?" Vinnie wanted to know.

"Probably not. Our electronic pre-alert system allows things to be cleared as they're shipped."

"Nice system."

"I just work here."

"Thanks."

AT 12:32 PM, the White House made the decision to stop and search the Iranian UN delegation. General Jasper immediately passed the order on to the FBI, which relayed it to 26 Federal Plaza.

Special Agent in Charge Rove Peterson took the call. "We have a gigantic problem," the deputy director of the FBI told him. "Get everything you can to JFK immediately. Inform your people on board that plane that their target, the man we've been calling Scimitar, whose real name is Moshen Kourani, might be carrying a bioweapon. Communicate this to your people directly."

"Yes, sir."

"The target needs to be put under control once the plane is on the ground. Your people need to separate him from the passengers and crew. Don't let him gain access to his hand luggage. Don't leave him unattended for a second, not even to use the john."

"Check."

"Hold him alone in First Class."

"What do we do with the rest of the passengers?"

"They have to be escorted to a special quarantine area and searched. That includes the crew. No one—no passenger, pilot, or crew member—will be allowed to touch their hand luggage. No exceptions! They will remain in quarantine until every inch of the plane and all the luggage on board are searched."

"Understood."

"This is the most important call of your life."

"Yes, sir."

"I suggest you use your very best people."

"I'll supervise the operation myself."

"Get as many hazmat teams out to JFK as you can. Tell them they might have to handle a virulent form of tularemia. Instruct them to bring as much tetracycline as they can get their hands on. If there's exposure of any kind, they should administer massive doses of the drug immediately. Are you taking this all down?"

"Yes, sir."

"I'll be running everything from the crisis center here at FBI headquarters in Washington. I'll stay here, throughout."

"I'll keep you informed."

"Act fast. Decisively. I'll be in constant contact with the White House."

"Yes, sir."

"Hundreds of thousands of lives are at stake here, Peterson. Get this right."

GENERAL JASPER WAS so pumped up with adrenaline that she felt she could run all the way to New York. Instead, she had a helicopter ferry her to Andrews Air Force Base, where she boarded a military jet. As the plane sat on the runway waiting for a team of biohazard experts, she telephoned Alan Beckman, who was speeding down FDR Drive.

"Alan," she said, "wherever you are now, stop what you're doing and get to Kennedy Airport as soon as you can. This is an emergency. The president has made the decision to stop Kourani and search the plane. I want you there to work with the FBI."

"Wait a second." He put his hand over the receiver and told Vinnie to head to JFK. "Fast!"

"You got it!" Vinnie reached out the window, stuck a flashing blue light onto the roof, hung a yoo-ee at Twenty-third Street, then tore uptown toward the Triborough Bridge.

"What's the exact destination?" Alan asked Jasper.

"Opposite the UPS cargo terminal, outside hangar 12."

"Hangar 12!"

Vinnie floored it.

"Alan!" General Jasper shouted. "Alan?"

"What?"

"Get your body on that plane! I want you with Kourani."

"Yes, ma'am."

"I want you to handle him. We've got to be tough and delicate at the same time. I don't trust the FBI."

"But why are we stopping Kourani?"

"Freed reported that Kourani's been trying to get his hands on a biological agent known as tularemia."

Alan Beckman smiled proudly and looked at his watch, which read 1:16. "I'm on my way now."

Freed came through, he thought. *All right!*

He turned to Vinnie, who grinned out the side of his mouth and asked: "What's cookin'?"

"Just get us there in one piece."

"We should hang together more often. This rocks!"

UNITED AIRLINES FLIGHT 352 was scheduled to touch down at Kennedy at 3:48 PM. From the perspective of Devere Johnson II, the FBI team leader onboard, passage over the Atlantic had been smooth. The five members of the Iranian delegation seated in First Class had enjoyed a meal of roast quail with a Madeira wine sauce, dill potatoes, asparagus, and cappuccino sherbet served in a dark chocolate shell.

The silver-haired UN ambassador appeared to be deep into *Chaos and Violence,* by Professor Stanley Hoffman of Harvard. The deputy foreign minister sat typing on his laptop. Scimitar (code name for Kourani)—the quiet one with the salt-and-pepper beard—seemed to be asleep. The two security officers seated directly behind them watched the in-flight movie, *Ocean's Thirteen.*

Johnson thought: *Piece of cake.* In another hour and fifteen minutes they'd be touching down at Kennedy, where a local FBI team would pick up the Iranians.

Johnson, who secretly hated flying, thought ahead to his wife and sons in Ditmas Park, Brooklyn, as he opened the special NBA preview issue of *Sports Illustrated*.

His Knicks were picked to finish next to last in the East. *Damn!*

Big Patrick Ewing had been Johnson's hero as a kid growing up in Forest Hills, Queens. Part of that had to do with the fact that Ewing had emigrated from Kingston, Jamaica, at the age of thirteen, just like Johnson's dad. Devere and both of his brothers had joined the New York City Police Department after graduating from college. Devere was the only one recruited by the FBI.

Tomorrow, his oldest son, Devy, would be trying out for his middle school basketball team. At twelve years, two months, Devere Johnson III was already six foot one.

At 1:25 PM EST, the pilot of the Boeing 777 received an emergency call from flight control at Kennedy. Not knowing that there was a special FBI surveillance team onboard, he summoned the air marshal—a burly former defensive lineman for the University of Nebraska named Bud Pine—who was seated in the first row of Coach.

Pine spoke briefly to Rove Peterson of the FBI, who asked him to get the head of the onboard FBI surveillance team.

Pine found him with a copy of *Sports Illustrated* in seat 14C.

"I'm the air marshal. You're needed up front."

"Why?" Devere Johnson asked.

"Emergency call from a guy named Peterson from the FBI."

Johnson didn't like the idea of walking past the Iranians in the company of the marshal, but he had no choice.

Over the cockpit phone Johnson got his orders from Special Agent in Charge Peterson, who asked him to repeat them so he'd know they'd been clearly received. Johnson said: "I'd rather not do that, sir. Not in my current situation."

"Okay, then. I'll repeat them." He did.

Then the surveillance team leader turned to the pilot, a thin, nervous-looking guy with thick lips.

"The tower's gonna give you clearance to land at runway 13L."

"13L. Why?"

"We're involved in a special situation."

"What's that mean?"

"It's simple. When we land, you're gonna taxi northwest toward the UPS cargo terminal. You'll park in a designated place outside hangar 12. You know where that is?"

"I think so," he said, looking at his copilot, who shook his head. "I need to know. Is the aircraft in some kind of danger?"

"No," Johnson answered. "But there might be a problem with something one of the passengers is carrying. This aircraft isn't the target. I repeat: we're not the target. My team is going to carry out a search once we're on the ground."

The pilot swallowed hard. "Okay."

"No need for you to say anything now. Treat this as an ordinary flight. Once we land, I'll make a special announcement."

"Fine."

The cockpit had become crowded with Bud Pine, two pilots, the head of the flight crew, and one of her assistants. "I want everyone to stay calm," Johnson said in a deep voice. "We're gonna treat this like a normal flight until we reach the ground."

After waiting for Bud and the two flight attendants to leave one by one, Devere Johnson stopped to use the lavatory and casually returned to his seat.

His deputy, Tina Chang, seated to his left, leaned over and whispered: "What's up?"

With his blood pressure rising and tension pinching his neck, Johnson removed a legal pad from his briefcase and starting writing instructions. *Please, God, get us through this*, he said to himself. *You know best.*

He had critical decisions to make.

MATT FREED LISTENED as the pilot of British Airways Flight 117 spoke over the PA: "Please move your seats to their upright position and fasten your seat belts as we begin our descent into JFK." He'd spent the entire seven-hour, thirty-five-minute flight ruminating about his life, career, family.

We're scattered all over the world, he thought—*Liz in Paris; our children in Athens; one sister married to a Frenchman living outside of Knoxville; another working in Seattle; my mother in Hollywood, Florida; my father dead.*

Matt remembered talking to him a week after graduating at the bottom of his high school class, a month before doctors discovered that cancer was eating his lungs. Together they carried fly rods and tackle to the back of the truck. Matt stopped and told his father that he was thinking of joining the Marines.

The old man had spit into the long grass. "Why? So you can become cannon fodder for some old farts?"

"Dad—"

"You think those fuckers care about you or anybody else? The less you have to do with them, the better off you'll be."

"We'll see."

"Don't be a fool."

The words still stung. A part of him still loved his father in spite of everything. *I'll call my mom when I reach New York.*

The pain and sadness of his childhood pushed to the surface of his consciousness. But he willed them away and focused on problems at the NCTS instead.

Removing a small notebook from his pocket, Matt wrote: (1) Officers are rewarded for avoiding risks. (2) Headquarters needs to develop a better sense of the challenges faced in the field and how to support their needs. (3) We have to recruit and train more officers fluent in local cultures and languages, particularly Arabic and Farsi.

He realized that these were the exact same concerns he'd carried for the last eight years.

How long can we continue to dodge bullets? Will we ever learn?

He started to wonder if the Kourani case would enhance his position in the NCTS. If things went his way, he wanted to command the new NCTS platform that was going to be created in South Asia.

His mind whirring faster, Matt started to spin out a plan to present his case for reforming NCTS to the leaders of the Senate Select Committee on Intelligence and the president. As the jet banked over northern Long Island, he stopped.

There were practicalities to consider. *What will we do once we have Kourani? How will we handle the Iranian government?*

Matt stuffed an uneaten sandwich into the seat pocket in front of him and exited the plane with the rest of the passengers. Passing ads for movies and products that were unfamiliar, he remembered Liz in Paris.

I wonder how she's doing. I have to think clearly. Calm down.

He fired up his cell. *I'll tell Alan to get emergency visas for Zyoda and her daughter. We might have to intercede with Russian authorities on their behalf.*

Curiously, there were no recent messages from headquarters or Alan Beckman. Nor did he find anyone waiting when he exited Immigration.

That's strange.

He speed-dialed General Jasper's office and waited while an aide put him on hold.

"Matt Freed here. Just arrived in New York City. I'm awaiting orders."

"Who did you say you were again?" the male aide asked.

"Matt Freed of Odysseus base."

Matt's name didn't seem to register.

"Look. General Jasper asked me to contact her as soon as I landed. I need you to put me through."

"I'm sorry, Mr. Freed. That's not possible. I'll have to take a message."

"Is there someone else there I can talk to?"

"I'll need a specific name, sir."

Matt tried Alan Beckman's cell phone twice, then left a message. As he exited Terminal 4 pulling his bag, Alan called back. "Matt, where the hell are you?"

"Just landed at Kennedy. Where are you?"

Alan snapped: "Give me your exact location."

"Outside Terminal four. I'm waiting for a cab to take me to 26 Federal Plaza."

"Where? What door?"

"Door three. What's going on?"

"DON'T MOVE!"

He hung up, called Liz's cell phone, and left a message: "It's a little after two, I just arrived at Kennedy. I'll call you as soon as I can. I love you."

He was about to call his children in Athens when a dark sedan screeched to a stop in front of him and a dark-haired guy leaned across the front seat. "You Matt Freed?"

"Yes. Who are you?"

"Vinnie. Get in!"

Before he'd even shut the door, they tore off. Even though the circumstances were unusual, it felt good to be back in the States.

"What's the hurry?" Matt asked, leaning back and smelling the air.

"You'll find out soon. Alan says you're the man."

They drove against traffic, horn blaring, siren flashing, and cut down a "Restricted" road onto the tarmac.

"Who the hell are you, anyway?"

"Vinnie Danieli, NYPD, on loan to FBI."

"Nice to meet you, Vinnie. You gonna tell me where we're going?"

"I'm taking you to Disneyland. Hold on."

Matt saw a terrific jumble of emergency vehicles, police cruisers, and medical vans parked ahead. "What the hell's this?" he shouted over the blare of a passenger jet taxiing past.

"It's the reception committee for your Iranian friend."

"Kourani?"

"Yeah!"

"Where's Alan?" Matt shouted. "Alan Beckman. Is he here?"

"You bet."

They stopped outside a security perimeter maintained by Port Authority police in SWAT gear. Vinnie flashed his FBI badge to get them through. Running together past a line of buses, men and women in hazmat suits, medical teams operating out of the back of emergency vehicles, they arrived at an inner perimeter manned by FBI agents.

"No one else comes in," the female ASAC (FBI assistant special agent in charge) said.

"Bullshit!" Matt shouted, nostrils flaring, as he reached for his wallet.

"I said: No one."

An out-of-breath Vinnie slapped the shoulder of the big man beside him. "Matt Freed."

The ASAC recognized the name and nodded. "Nice to meet you, Freed. Over there." She gestured toward a large police van with "Command Post" stenciled on its side.

They don't need all this, Matt thought, searching for General Jasper's curly head inside the van. He found her in seconds, with Beckman buzzing by her side.

"Freed, you made it. Good!"

"What do you want me to do?" asked Matt, feeding off the excitement.

Alan said: "I was just telling the general that a past associate of Kourani recently had three large boxes shipped to him from Moscow."

"Have you located them?"

Someone shouted: "The plane just landed!"

General Jasper turned to Beckman and said: "We'll take this up later."

"General—"

"Wait for a signal from the FBI team on the plane," she explained. "Once Kourani has been secured, they'll let the other passengers out and Alan will go in."

Matt said: "I'll go in with him."

General Jasper shot back: "No, Freed! You wait here with me."

"But I know him."
"Listen, Freed—"
"General, please."
"You stay with me!"
"That's—" He wanted to shout "bullshit," but held back.

CHAPTER TWENTY-TWO

September 18, Afternoon

The five members of the Iranian delegation sat in their seats and prayed to Allah. Twelve rows behind them in Coach, Devere Johnson II watched through the porthole window as they descended over Jamaica Park, then South Ozone. He'd received his first bloody nose there in Drew Memorial Park from a skinny kid who'd punched him and tried to steal his bike.

As they hit the runway he checked his watch for the fifteenth time: 3:45 PM. United Flight 352 had landed three minutes ahead of schedule.

Organization. Discipline. One step at a time, he reminded himself, trying to ignore the high blood pressure that had started pulsing in his head. He unbuckled the seat belt and whispered to his deputy, Tina Chang, "Remember, you and the air marshal isolate Scimitar. I'll join you as soon as I help get the rest of the passengers out of First Class."

"The marshal's the big guy in row ten, right?"

"Name's Bud Pine."

"You want us to cuff Scimitar?"

"Order him to stand with his hands on his head. Don't let him touch anything. Don't let him move."

"What if the target's uncooperative?"

"Then cuff him. Use force if necessary. Under no circumstances should you allow him to reach for anything on his body or in his hand luggage. He might be carrying some sort of device."

"A device? What kind?"

"I don't know."

"Scimitar speaks English?"

Johnson nodded. "Affirmative. I've got to go."

He passed quickly through First Class into the cockpit.

"The t-t-tower said hangar twelve," the pilot stammered, looking as though his eyeballs were about to launch out of his head.

Johnson flashed him a thumbs-up. "Good job."

Reminding himself to project authority, Johnson grabbed the mike, took a deep breath, and spoke in a carefully controlled voice: "Ladies and gentlemen. Ground security has informed us that as an added precaution we'll be taking special steps to clear the aircraft. I ask you to listen carefully. Everyone remain in your seats. Security agents will soon identify themselves to you and help you disembark. We're going to ask everyone to leave all their personal belongings—hand luggage, purses, laptops, books, everything—behind and leave the aircraft in an orderly manner. Once security agents give the signal, we'll ask everyone in First Class to exit out the front doorway. Coach passengers will exit out of the rear doorway. Your hand luggage, purses, et cetera will be returned to you once you are outside the aircraft and all its contents have been thoroughly searched. Please remain in your seats and await instructions. I apologize for the inconvenience and thank you for your cooperation."

Johnson turned to the chief flight attendant, who said: "Very good."

A tense, unsettled feeling immediately gripped the plane. As the jet slowly passed several passenger terminals, anxiety grew.

Tina Chang found big Bud Pine and cut through the curtain into First Class. An elderly couple were already on their feet, complaining. Tina flashed her FBI badge and spoke firmly: "FBI. I'm going to ask all of you to take your seats until the plane has come to a complete halt and you're instructed to stand."

A man with a German accent protested in broken English. Tina put a hand on his shoulder and pressed him into his seat. "Remain in your seat!"

As soon as Tina reached row 4, the Iranian UN ambassador started to complain. "I want an explanation," he shouted.

"Please, remain in your seat."

"Do you know who I am?"

"Yes, I do, Mr. Ambassador."

Bud Pine shouted: "Sit down!"

Through the cockpit window, Johnson watched ground personnel direct the big jet into a large circle made of metal pylons. Surrounding it stood ambulances, emergency vehicles, and emergency personnel in hazmat suits.

The flight attendant's voice came across the PA system confident and smooth. "Ladies and gentlemen. I'm going to remind all of you again to remain in your seats. No exceptions. Security personnel will have you out of the aircraft in a matter of minutes."

As soon as the engines were cut off, Johnson made another announcement from near the forward cabin door.

"Ladies and gentlemen," he said. "I'm going to ask all of you seated in First Class, with the exception of the diplomatic delegation seated in rows three and four, to stand."

Forty-two people jumped to their feet and started pressing forward. "Wait!" Johnson said firmly. "All of you, stop! We're going to do this in order. Row by row. I'm going to remind you to leave all your personal belongings behind. That's everything: jackets, sweaters, purses, computers, handbags."

The Iranian UN ambassador stared hard at Tina Chang standing over him and shouted: "I demand to know what's going on!"

"We'll have you out of here in a minute, sir. Please calm down."

As the last of the First Class passengers filed past, the deputy foreign minister, seated in the middle, got to his feet. "Excuse me," he said in Farsi.

Bud Pine shouted, "Sit down!" When the foreign minister refused, Pine drew a Taser. The two Iranian security officials in the row behind jumped to their minister's defense. "Don't anybody move!"

Chang wanted to scold the marshal, but didn't have time. The UN ambassador with the full head of silver hair stuck a finger in Bud's face. "I'm a fully accredited diplomat with the Iranian government. You stupid man, you're provoking an incident."

Bud Pine didn't budge. "Shut your mouth."

The ambassador complied, muttering something in Farsi as Johnson pushed by on his way to Coach. "We'll have you out of here in a minute, gentlemen."

"Sir," Tina said.

"I'll be right back."

Her focus didn't leave the man by the window, Scimitar (Kourani), who clutched a black leather bag in his lap and looked scared. "Sir," Tina said slowly, "I'm going to ask you to put the bag on the floor and stand."

Kourani turned to the ambassador seated next to him and looked confused. "He doesn't understand you," the ambassador brayed.

"I'll repeat it again: Drop the bag on the floor and stand."

A nervous Kourani stood with the bag.

Tina drew her gun. "No! Stop! I know you speak English. Put it down!"

Behind her, other FBI agents had started ushering passengers out of Coach. The flight attendant's voice poured loudly over the PA system: "Please cooperate and excuse the inconvenience. We'll have you out of the plane soon."

This only added to the confusion. Sweat quickly beaded all over Tina's face. "You heard the lady," Bud Pine shouted. "Drop the bag!"

"Please, set it down!"

Kourani didn't seem to understand. Visibly shaking, he paused in a half-crouch. The Iranian security officer with the close-cropped white hair leaned over the seat to try to help him. "Sit the fuck down!" Bud shouted.

The second Iranian security officer spat at Bud, who fired the Taser. Two probes attached to his shirt and zapped him with 26 watts of electricity.

Kourani turned abruptly toward the window as though he was about to set the leather bag down. With his right hand, he reached for something under his jacket. Bud Pine saw it was a pistol and leaned forward to apply the Taser.

Before he could reach him, Kourani pulled the trigger, putting two rounds into Pine's head. A third round hit Tina in the shoulder.

A part of her told her not to draw her gun. Another part said that if the Iranian detonated an explosive device, he would destroy the entire plane. She tried aiming for his shoulder, but two of the three rounds went through his chest. Kourani fell against the seat in front of him as the cabin filled with screams.

Tina felt herself losing consciousness. Devere Johnson shouted: "Down! Everyone down!"

Guns were pointed at the other Iranians as fear coursed through the plane and out onto the tarmac.

ALAN BECKMAN WAS standing on the top step of the FBI command center in a hazmat suit waiting for a signal from the plane when he heard the shots.

"What the hell was that?" he asked, turning to Jasper and watching the blood drain from her face. Seconds later, he was up the aluminum steps and in the plane.

Matt Freed tried to follow him, but was stopped. "I've got to see Kourani," he said to General Jasper.

"Control yourself, Freed. That's an order!"

"But—"

"Come with me into the hangar!"

They sat in a corner with Shelly and the head of NCTS's Near Eastern Division and discussed how best to handle Kourani, unaware that he was barely clinging to life.

Matt said: "I suggest we find a way to isolate him."

"How?"

"Tell him there's a problem with his passport. Invent something."

A harried-looking Rove Peterson stopped to announce: "We got three people wounded: one FBI, one air marshal, one Iranian."

Shelly said: "That's bad."

General Jasper felt sick to her stomach and excused herself. "I'll be right back."

Finding it impossible to sit still, Matt crossed to the other side of the football field–sized hangar where shaken passengers sat in rows of folding chairs with their hands in their laps.

"As long as you cooperate, we'll get you out of here soon," he heard a young FBI agent tell a middle-aged woman with blond hair stuffed under a Longhorns hat. "Name?"

"Janice Burrows."

"Seat number?"

"Twenty-three C."

"You traveling alone?"

"I'm traveling with my best friend, Barbara."

The heavyset woman beside her leaned forward and said: "We heard shots. What happened?"

"We're going to ask you not to talk about that. Right now it's a national security matter. In a few hours, I'm sure you'll hear about it on the news. Even then, we're asking everyone not to talk to the press. It's a complicated situation. We'll be in touch in a day or two and explain."

It all seemed unreal to Matt. A day ago he'd been in a Moscow hospital with Zyoda, stealing Oleg Urakov's medical chart. Now, like the other FBI and NCTS officers in the hangar, he was trying to understand what had transpired on the plane and what it meant. *We overreacted,* he said to himself. *Too many people. Too many goddamn trucks. Gave the wrong message. I would have handled it discretely. I should have been here to prepare.*

He listened as the young FBI agent recorded the length and purpose of each passenger's visit, the name of the New York City hotel they'd be staying in, and the number of bags and carry-on items they'd left on the plane.

Fucking useless, Matt thought, beginning to pace. He hated being pushed to the sidelines. *I've got to get in there. We're just marking time.*

•   •   •

ALAN BECKMAN SMELLED cordite the second he entered the cabin. The narrow space had filled with chaos: Iranians yelling threats and epithets; Devere Johnson II with blood all over his hands and shirt, shouting: "Where's the medical team? I got two officers down!"

Alan asked the identity of the wounded Iranian.

"I believe it's Scimitar," Johnson answered.

"Scimitar? We better hope not."

"I've got two people bleeding to death."

Seconds later, when an FBI medical team pronounced the Iranian dead, Alan felt something inside him shut down.

He moved automatically, clearing First Class, helping Johnson and the others wrestle the remaining Iranians out of the aircraft. He watched numbly as Bud Pine and Tina Chang were carried to a waiting helicopter for a ride to Queens County Hospital.

Then he carefully searched Kourani's body. Passport and wallet in the pants pocket confirmed the Iranian's identity. It was the letter in the jacket that got Alan's attention. He clutched it in his gloved hand as the corpse was zipped into a bag and carried away.

Beckman radioed the biohazard specialists: "All clear to inspect the plane."

He watched with arms crossed as men and women covered in plastic opened hand luggage and dumped purses on the floor. The mess sent him reeling back to the nursery rhyme: "All the king's horses and all the king's men couldn't put Humpty together again."

Someone announced that Bud Pine had died on the way to the hospital. Devere Johnson punched the back of a chair. "GOD-DAMMIT TO HELL!!!! You didn't tell us he was armed!"

"Pine?"

Johnson got in Alan's face. "No, the Iranian. Why didn't you warn us?"

"We didn't know."

"Who made the idiotic decision to let them pass through Security unchecked?"

"Not me."

"WHY?"

"Why what?

"Why were they allowed to pass through Security?"

"They're diplomats. We extend that courtesy to all diplomats."

"It's your fucking fault!"

OUTSIDE, THE REMAINING Iranians were herded into a waiting SUV and whisked to a nearby diplomatic lounge. The UN undersecretary-general for political affairs, the U.S. ambassador to the UN, and the mayor of New York City had been summoned to try to defuse their anger.

General Jasper stood with Shelly, Rove Peterson, and others waiting for something to soften the blow. Thirty tense minutes later, word came back that the fuselage had been inspected and nothing had been found in the carry-on bags. Another forty-minute search revealed nothing in checked luggage.

This was the third consecutive piece of bad news General Jasper dutifully passed on to the White House. The edge in Stan Lescher's voice could cut through steel. "General, do you have anything positive to tell the president?"

"All I can say is I'm deeply sorry. I feel as though I've personally let him down."

"Hands down, this has been our worst day ever," Lescher growled.

"I'm acutely aware of that."

"The president's a strong man. He's on the phone with the Iranian president now."

"He can blame it on me if he wants," Jasper offered.

"If only that meant something."

Jasper fumbled for words of encouragement. "The FBI team leader's still on the plane. Once he's out, we'll get a clearer picture of what went down."

"I doubt that will help. We're dealing with a diplomatic catastrophe of enormous proportions."

"I feel about an inch tall," General Jasper said, downing another antacid with a bottle of Evian handed to her by Shelly.

"We can't lose sight of the security situation," NSC director Lescher groaned. "What happens now?"

General Jasper hadn't had time to consider the future. She told Lescher she'd huddle with her people and call him back. That's when Beckman returned from the plane looking like his dog had just been run over by a truck.

"We're screwed."

"It is what it is, Alan," General Jasper said, trying to rally her people. "We've got to keep our heads."

"It gets worse."

Unfolding a piece of stationery stained with blood, Alan Beckman read the letter he'd found in Kourani's pocket. "Dear Mr. President and officials of the U.S. government," it started. "As you are aware, I assisted your government in blocking a terrorist attack in Qatar. I have tried to obtain the information needed to assist you in stopping a planned al-Qaeda attack against some of your midsized cities. Even though I believe this attack is imminent, I have been unable to develop more information. Also, my family has been unable to exit Iran. Under these circumstances I am not able to separate myself from my government. Trust that I will do my best to return to the United States as soon as my family is safely out of Iran. Please respect my wishes. Respectfully, Moshen Kourani."

Shelly, Alan, Rove Peterson, and a half-dozen others stood in a circle looking stunned. General Jasper took the letter and read it again. "I don't understand."

"It means Kourani had nothing," Alan answered. "And wasn't ready to defect."

"But the attack is still impending?" Peterson asked. "Isn't that right?"

Alan reread the relevant sentence out loud: "Even though I believe this attack is imminent, I have been unable to develop more information."

"Then we've got to rely on our defenses," General Jasper said.

She suggested FBI special-agent-in-charge Rove Peterson return to headquarters and start coordinating with his teams in the field.

"I'm leaving now to apologize to the Iranians. From there I'll go straight to Federal Plaza."

"Let's hope to God we catch a break."

No one bothered to talk to Matt, who stood at the far end of the hangar listening to the First Class passengers talk about what they'd seen on the plane. All had been outside when the shooting broke out. People seated across the aisle from the Iranians described five men in dark suits, reading and napping.

"Nothing unusual" was the oft-repeated phrase.

Seeing the despair on Alan Beckman's face, Matt started to cross. He was within a hundred feet of where General Jasper stood with Alan and Shelly when his phone rang. It was Liz.

"Hi, honey, I'm here," she said sounding tired but relieved. "Are you okay?"

"This is a real bad time."

"Why? What happened?"

"I'll tell you later."

"Where are you, Matt? I want to see you."

"Wait for me at Terminal four. I'll be there as soon as I can."

"News people are swarming all over the terminal asking people what they've heard and seen—"

"I'll talk to you later. I love you."

He snapped his phone shut. Shelly stood in his path and said: "I suggest you go somewhere and hide."

"Why?"

Anger rose scarlet in General Jasper's face. "Stay the hell out of my sight!"

"General, give me a minute to explain."

Alan wedged his body between them. "Kourani's dead."

Matt stopped for a moment as though he'd lost his breath.

Jasper spoke over her shoulder. "Tell Freed, per my orders, he's been placed on administrative leave effective immediately. I'll do the paperwork and see him when I get back to Washington. In the meantime, advise him to look for another line of work."

Shelly nodded. "Good idea."

Matt reached out to stop her. Two aides quickly muscled him away. "General, don't push me out."

"The rest of us will probably be joining you soon."

"There's more to this. I know it. We need to go through it step by step."

"I'm sure you're right, Freed," Jasper said pushing back her curls. "I take full responsibility. The president is furious. If you'll excuse me, I've got to call him with more bad news."

CHAPTER TWENTY-THREE

September 18, Late Afternoon

"Something stinks," Matt said out loud, folding the blood-stained letter and handing it back to his boss. "This doesn't sound like the Kourani I met."

Alan Beckman groaned: "Whatever he was planning is over now." He felt numb.

"Not necessarily."

"You're right. We've got a possible terrorist attack coming, and we don't know where." Behind them, FBI agents escorted passengers outside to waiting buses. Biohazard teams stripped off their hazmat gear and started packing it into trunks.

"Our country depends on us, Alan. We can't get soft in the head."

Alan's phone beeped. His red-lined eyes squinted at the screen. "I've got to take this."

It was Shelly telling him to meet General Jasper outside the diplomatic lounge where the U.S. ambassador to the UN, Rove Peterson, and she were preparing a statement to the press.

"I've been summoned."

Matt stopped him. "Wait, boss. We've got to talk."

"The president wants the general to prepare a statement."

Matt matched Alan's gait. "Screw the statement. This is more important."

Alan was in a hurry. "I'll catch up with you later."

"You're not seeing the whole picture, Alan."

Beckman's frustration flared. "Get some rest!"

"Fuck that!"

Alan turned at the exit and put a sympathetic arm on his second-in-command's shoulder. "I can't help you now. You heard the general."

"Why did Kourani wait to tell us now?" he asked following Beckman out the large bay opening where the 777 was being hooked to a truck. "Why didn't he say something in Vienna? Why was he on Rebirth digging up those canisters of tularemia?"

"Let it go, Matt."

"I CAN'T!"

Alan was torn. As much as he felt sympathy for his subordinate, he also had a job to do. "Your problem, compadre, not mine."

"Tell me about those boxes shipped from Russia."

"We'll take it from here." Alan paused before slamming the passenger door of the SUV. "You did what you thought was right even if you did piss off a lot of people along the way. I share the blame. Once things cool off, I'll sit down with the general."

"Dammit, Alan. Like I give a shit about that."

Beckman said, "We'll talk in DC. I'll buy dinner," and slammed the door shut.

WHAT'S WRONG WITH people?

Matt walked back to the hangar, hand on chin, sorting through information gathered all the way back to the assassination of General Moshiri in Oman, through Bucharest, Afghanistan, Uzbekistan, Rebirth Island, and Moscow. In some configuration the pieces fit together into a story that made sense.

How? That's the question. What was Kourani really up to? And where's the weapon?

He goaded himself to solve the puzzle as around him vehicles started up, gears ground, and metal chairs clanged.

Qods Force officers are careful and ruthless. Why would a man like Kourani come to us with an offer of information, take our money, then change his mind?

It didn't make sense. *If Kourani had survived the plane trip, what would have prevented us from blackmailing him? He had to know the Iranian government would have taken a great interest in watching a top Qods Force officer compromise his government on surveillance tape.*

His attention was pulled by a man passing in a black "Medical Examiners" jacket. Instinctively, Matt shouted: "Hey!"

The stoop-shouldered man carrying the cardboard cup of coffee stopped. "Hay is for horses. What'd you want?"

"Matt Freed, National Counterterrorism Service. I've been waiting to see the body. What's your name?"

The older man pointed to the name sewn on the breast pocket. "Borkowski, Simon."

"Simon, I need to see the Iranian. Let's make this quick." As with most instincts, there was little logic involved. Still Matt's mind worked to find some justification. *Maybe the body or the expression on his face will tell me something.*

Borkowski looked Matt over, then led the way to the back of a large van. Plucking a cell phone from his belt, he said, "I'm sure you are who you say you are, but I gotta do this by the book."

Matt said: "Simon, I'm the guy who's been tracking this bastard halfway around the world."

"So?"

"So I've got to take a last look at him, face-to-face."

"We're taking him in to be examined."

Matt didn't blink. "Two minutes. I won't touch anything."

Borkowski looked around and nodded. "No pictures."

"Whatever you say."

In the still darkness of the back of the van, Borkowski slipped on plastic gloves, then ripped open the zipper and pulled the two halves of the body bag apart. Then he clicked on a penlight clipped to his keys. "They're always disappointing."

"Who?"

"Stiffs."

Matt's eyes carefully scanned the familiar contours of the forehead, cheekbones, and jaw. A hint of a resigned smile clung to the corners of the lips. Lifting the left hand gently, he started to turn it over.

Borkowski barked: "I said: Don't touch." And shone the light in Matt's face.

"Point it at his arm."

"Why?"

"Point it!"

Borkowski complied.

Matt inhaled quickly: "No burn scar."

"What're you talking about?"

"This isn't him."

MATT CALLED CONTINUOUSLY for the next ten minutes—Alan, Shelly, General Jasper, Rove Peterson, NCTS headquarters—but no one answered. He left urgent messages with all of them: "I checked the body. It's not Kourani. Matt Freed here. Call me back immediately on my cell."

What now? he thought, lurching left, then right. He couldn't decide if he should dash to the diplomatic lounge or make more calls. *I've got to get to FBI headquarters! There will be people there who will listen. I'll make sure of that.*

Outside he found NYPD detective Vinnie Danieli tossing a couple of breathing masks into the trunk of a sedan. "Show's over," Vinnie said.

"No, it isn't."

Vinnie's attention perked up. "What do you mean, it isn't?"

"You'll see."

"Alan told me you might need a lift into town."

Matt asked if the detective minded stopping at Terminal 4 to pick up his wife.

"No problem, Kemo Sabe. Hop in."

•   •   •

PANDEMONIUM REIGNED OUTSIDE the diplomatic lounge as a hungry mob of gawkers, cameramen, soundmen, and reporters all jostled for position near the door. General Jasper, Rove Peterson, Alan Beckman, Shelly, and the others had to push themselves through.

"General! General, what's going on?" one reporter shouted.

Another thrust a microphone into her face. "Can you describe the events on United three fifty-two?"

"How many people were shot?" asked a third.

"Is it true that an Iranian diplomat was killed?"

Once inside, special-agent-in-charge Peterson blew his stack. "I want those son-of-a-bitches out of here! NOW!!!! This is insane."

A tall Port Authority sergeant suggested a small pressroom downstairs.

"Pack 'em in there. I don't care. Lock the door and make 'em wait."

Then Peterson and General Jasper walked over to express their condolences to the Iranian ambassador, who was huddled in the corner with the U.S. ambassador to the UN. Nobody noticed that the white-haired Iranian security guard with the C-shaped scar on his neck had slipped away.

"This was an assault on my country," the UN ambassador to Iran shouted, waving his hands like a sword. "An attack on the dignity of every Iranian citizen! An insult to Islam!"

The intelligent-looking U.S. ambassador, Max Grossman, tried to calm him down. "A terrible, terrible incident. We're all in shock. But the last thing we want to do is make things worse."

"There will be terrible repercussions," the Iranian shot back. "The poor man was assassinated before my eyes. It's practically an act of war!"

Grossman took special care with words. The ones the Iranian ambassador tossed around the room like grenades alarmed him. "Please, sir. Please. I know you're angry. But let's be prudent about what we say."

"I have to talk to the press!"

Grossman invited the conciliatory tone of General Jasper, who stood over the Iranian looking like she was about to cry. "Mr. Ambassador, I feel awful. I'm sorry. I want to apologize personally."

"Who is this woman?" the Iranian asked.

"General Emily Jasper of the NCTS."

The Iranian swept her aside. "Get out of my way!"

Outside, the Iranian's angry voice echoed down the airport hallways. "I'm tired of apologies. The consequences must be faced!"

In the diplomatic lounge, General Jasper took an urgent call from NSC director Stan Lescher. "With all the world leaders assembled in New York, this couldn't have come at a worse time."

"Stan, as much as I regret what's happened. I think I need to redirect my focus on the threat."

"The president is practically apoplectic."

"I'll submit my resignation when I get back," Jasper said.

"Let's talk about next steps."

General Jasper took a deep breath. "We're all at the airport. We need to get back to 26 Federal Plaza to regroup."

"Without Kourani we have no source."

"Correct."

"Any chance one of the other Iranians has anything to share?"

"I don't think that's a realistic expectation. Not now."

"Which means we have nothing. Correct?"

"Except for the lead about the possible use of tularemia."

"In light of what's happened, is that even relevant?"

Shifting contingencies overwhelmed Jasper's brain. She needed time to regroup. "Truthfully, I don't know. But as soon as this call is over, I'm going to make sure portable biohazard alert detectors are programmed to pick up tularemia."

"But we don't know where the attack is coming."

"The important thing to remember is that we're prepared," General Jasper said grasping for straws.

"What's your read on timing?" Lescher asked.

"Technically Eid al-Fitr starts at sundown, which is a few hours away, if we measure it using local time. In the Middle East, it's begun already, because they're seven or eight hours ahead."

"God help us."

"We're going to need a little luck."

Stan Lescher groaned: "Just what the president wants to hear."

FROM THE BACKSEAT of the Suburban roaring toward the Midtown Tunnel, Alan Beckman played back the message from Freed. "That's weird."

"What?"

Knowing that Matt wasn't General Jasper's favorite officer at the moment, he hesitated before he spoke. "General, Freed viewed the body and says it's not Kourani."

Jasper, who was listening to Rove Peterson, cut him off mid-sentence. "What? Freed did what?"

"He saw the body."

"Whose body?"

"Kourani's."

"When?"

"Sometime after we left the hangar."

She grabbed her head. "Didn't I put him on administrative leave?"

"Yes, you did."

"I'm starting to think the man's insane," Jasper started, trying to reestablish control. "First he goes on a personal crusade to prove that Kourani's a liar. Then he contributes to the death of the most important source we've had in years. Now he tells us that the man who died is not Kourani. I can't imagine what he's going to come up with next."

"God knows, General," Shelly added.

"He strikes me as increasingly desperate. Even dangerous. Am I being unfair?"

Rove Peterson raised his voice over the din of the tunnel: "We had surveillance all over Kourani in Bucharest and Vienna. My FBI teams didn't take their eyes off him. Whether his real name was Kourani or Joe Blow, the man we first identified in Bucharest is the man who got on the plane."

"My feeling, and I think it's held by the overwhelming majority of us at this point, is that Freed is no longer reliable," Jasper concluded.

Rove Peterson and Shelly agreed. The general turned back to face Alan: "You want to defend him?"

Beckman thought hard before he spoke. "I know Freed's been under a lot of pressure. I'm sure the events of this afternoon hit him hard. I'm not a psychiatrist and I can't categorize his state of mind. But I think we should hear what he has to say."

MOSHEN KOURANI HAD arrived via a Lufthansa flight to Newark the night of the sixteenth.

He'd spent the afternoon and evening of the seventeenth strolling down the East Side of Manhattan, appalled by the gluttony and greed. He passed men and woman adorned in fine clothes and diamonds, and women who proudly displayed themselves like prostitutes. In the faces of all races he beheld the sin of arrogance. *These people fail to express any humility to God.*

Now their false temples must come down, he said to himself as he paused near Central Park and faced the spires downtown. *They are built on the laws of Satan.*

Moshen knelt, faced the Kaaba, and prayed out loud:

Oh Thou whose witness is far removed from the oppressors, by Thy Strength, restrain my oppressor and my enemy from overwhelming me. With Thy Power, turn aside his sharpness from me. Let him be engaged in what immediately surrounds him. Render him powerless against that to which he is hostile. Oh Lord, imprint in my heart the likeness of what Thou hast stored for me of Thy Reward and of what Thou hast stored for my enemy by way of retribution and torment. Let this be the cause of my contentment with what Thou hast decreed and of trust in what Thou hast chosen. Amen, Lord of the Worlds! Verily Thou art the possessor of great excellence. Thou hast Power over everything.

Then he slowly made his way down Fifth Avenue toward Rockefeller Center. His father, Mullah Sheikh Kourani, had taken him here as a boy and pointed out how this monument to greed and oppression dwarfed the cathedral of Christian worship across the street.

"These are not people who cling to the heart of Allah," his father had told him.

He'd seen this throughout his life, in the United States' meddling in his country, their support of the Shah, their attachment to the sheikhs in Saudi Arabia and criminal leaders of Israel. It seemed boldly clear in the soft breeze that caressed his face like the affirming breath of his Lord.

It moved him toward Rockefeller Center and the ice skating rink he'd gazed into as a boy. And there it was, represented in gilded gold—the statue of Prometheus, the god who had stolen fire from Zeus. Incredible!

How stupid and self-involved are these infidels? he asked himself. *Don't they know that Prometheus was punished? Don't they understand that they must suffer a similar fate?*

DRIVING INTO MANHATTAN late in the afternoon of the eighteenth, Kourani heard the news over 1010 WINS. Shots had been fired on the jet that carried the UN Iranian delegation to New York. According to preliminary reports, the sky marshal and an Iranian diplomat had been killed.

The lighter-skinned man at the wheel of the truck turned up the volume and asked: "What has happened?"

"It changes nothing," Moshen answered, wondering if his brother Abbas had joined their eldest brother Hamid in martyrdom.

Instead of sadness, he felt emboldened and clear. To his mind this was a call from Allah.

MATT FREED'S MIND worked feverishly in the backseat of the sedan as he held his wife's hand. He pictured the carefully composed Iranian with the burning eyes. *Where's Moshen now? Is he working with Qods Force or operating on his own?*

Liz had seen her husband lost in concentration before, but never to this extent. Even as she'd talked excitedly about their children and Maggie's operation, a major part of him remained someplace else. She watched him shift in his seat repeatedly, crack his neck, groan, and turn abruptly toward the window like he was wrestling with himself.

"Can I help?" she whispered.

Matt sighed, gritted his teeth, and concluded: "He's here. I know he is."

"Who?"

Matt didn't answer.

"Matt, are you okay?"

He barely managed a nod. Most of his attention strained to answer questions: *Who was the man I met in Bucharest? Was he working for the Iranians or someone else?*

Over and over, his brain reached as far as it could, then got lost in a haze of assumptions. He was barely aware of the conversation between NYPD detective Vinnie Danieli at the wheel and Liz, which went something like this:

Liz: "We met at the country's most expensive matchmaking service."

Danieli: "What's that?"

"The Farm, the CIA's training facility."

"You're pulling my leg."

"Absolutely true. Right, Matt?"

Outside the window, Matt watched the spires of Manhattan fade into the evening haze against a backdrop of orange red. They looked like giant chess pieces. Moshen Kourani was four or five moves ahead of him and he was trying to catch up. He imagined his father nodding knowingly from the sidelines.

"You in the service, too?" Vinnie asked.

"I'm a housewife now, a mother. But we do live overseas."

"Must be an interesting life."

"Oh yes."

They followed the exit from the Triborough Bridge onto FDR Drive. Matt felt as though they were swirling into a darker world, a place where he would finally be forced to confront the fears of inadequacy planted by his father.

In his best Brooklynese, Vinnie asked: "Where you lovebirds stayin'?"

Liz turned to Matt, whose eyes followed an electronic billboard for the History Channel, which advertised a special on 9/11. "Honey, did you hear the question?"

Matt squeezed her hand. It seemed strange that she was there. He imagined his father looking back at him, saying: "Didn't I warn you it would come to something like this?"

He thought about all his fellow Americans going about their lives—eating dinner, washing their cars, children swinging in the backyard, playing Little League—unaware of the looming threat.

Defeat is out of the question, Matt reminded himself. *What does it have to offer? Disgrace? Alcoholism? Death?*

"Never!" he grunted under his breath at his father.

"Never what?" Liz whispered back.

VINNIE'S CELL PHONE rang. It was the ASAC (FBI assistant special agent in charge) telling him to be on the lookout for NCTS officer Matt Freed. "If you see him," she said, "bring him directly to headquarters. Rove Peterson and General Jasper want him off the streets before he causes more trouble. He might be hard to control."

"You got it," he answered, looking at Matt in the rearview mirror.

Vinnie wasn't anybody's fool. He'd heard Alan describe Matt's bravery and dedication. From his perspective, the big man riding in his backseat, the one that the ASAC wanted back at headquarters, had "solid" written all over him.

He said: "Yo, big man. What's up?"

Matt grabbed the back of the front seat and pulled himself closer to Vinnie's ear: "Look, I might need your help."

"Yeah?" Vinnie grew up in Bensonhurst. Ever since his first James Bond movie (*From Russia with Love*) at age six, he'd dreamed of working for the clandestine service. "That was the ASAC ordering me to bring you directly to headquarters."

"Then let me off here."

"I can't."

"I'm looking for someone who could be dangerous."

"Who's that?" Vinnie replied, knowing he was asking for trouble.

"We've been double-crossed," Matt said with intense conviction. "The Iranian who was shot on the plane wasn't the man we thought he was. I've got to find that man before he attacks us."

"Does headquarters know this?"

"I told them, but they can't accept it. They're still in shock."

Vinnie knew the difference between a bullshitter and the real deal. He'd grown up on the streets. "You got any idea where this guy is?"

Matt shook his head.

Liz leaned closer to her husband, who felt like he was on fire. "Is that the man whose father was killed over the Strait of Hormuz?"

"Yes."

"What's his name?" Vinnie asked.

"Kourani."

When Matt's cell phone rang he snapped: "Alan, I got the coroner to show me the—"

Alan Beckman cut him off. "The general wants you at 26 Federal Plaza. We're on our way there now."

"Alan! Listen."

"That's an order!" Alan hung up.

Matt slammed his forearm into the side of the back door, then dialed again. "Alan, this is important! Alan!" He didn't answer. "SHIT!"

They were flying through the East Side underpass approaching the exit for East Ninety-sixth Street. Liz squeezed her husband's arm. "Tell me, honey. What's going on?"

"I don't have time to explain." Matt spotted traffic snarling FDR Drive ahead of them. He shouted: "Turn off here!"

Rubber squealed against asphalt. Vinnie jerked the wheel to avoid a pothole the size of a baby carriage.

"Where we headed?" Liz asked.

"Twenty-six Federal Plaza."

Vinnie didn't like Second Avenue, so he zoomed farther west to Lexington. At the corner of Lex and Ninety-sixth, he stuck the blue light on the roof and pressed down harder on the gas. "This got anything to do with that Lebanese guy named Rafiq?" he asked.

"Who?"

The traffic thickened as they got into the eighties. Groups of people carrying picnic baskets and blankets seemed to be heading toward the park. "Dammit," Vinnie said. "I forgot."

"What?"

"Tonight's the free concert in Central Park."

Matt leaned forward. "What free concert?"

"Andrea Bocelli and Il Divo."

For some reason that seemed important. "Andrea Bocelli? You sure?" Matt asked.

"Yeah, the blind Italian singer," Vinnie answered before humming a few bars of "Con te partirò." "My wife loves him."

Matt's mind looped back to Tashkent and the two Andrea Bocelli CDs seen in Kourani's hotel room. It had always seemed odd to him. Now this: a free concert halfway around the world. It felt like a big leap, but a part of him begged him to jump. "Stop!"

"What the—?"

Matt leaned over and pointed at the curb. "Let me out!"

"What's a matter?"

"I need to get to Central Park."

"What for?" Vinnie asked.

"I'll jump."

As he swung the door open, Liz screamed: "Matt!"

"Wait a goddamn minute." Vinnie hung a right at Seventy-seventh and stopped.

But Matt was already out and pulling Liz. "Let's go!"

CHAPTER TWENTY-FOUR

September 18, Evening

Into the brisk evening air they ran, breathing hard, over Seventy-seventh then across Fifth Avenue and left, over the uneven stone walk under American elm trees, which formed a canopy against the biting sounds of the city. They joined the excitement of children and adults drawn to romantic music under the stars.

There was nothing idyllic about the cold sweat and desperation that crawled down Matt's back as he pushed through the crowd with Liz by his side. He didn't doubt that Vinnie was somewhere behind him notifying headquarters, giving chase, or both.

"Tickets?" barked a woman at the front—plump, middle-aged, with rosy cheeks and a fizz of red hair.

Matt reached for his wallet. "I'm with the NCTS."

"The . . . what?" she screeched looking askance at his rumpled pants and blazer.

"The National Counterterrorism Service," he said softly, hoping to avoid the ears of concertgoers pressing on all sides. "Can I talk to someone from security?"

"Security!" she screamed. Almost immediately two burly tattooed guys in black T-shirts squeezed Matt from the left and right.

"Why don't you come with us, sir?" a guard with garlic breath snarled.

One glance and Matt knew they'd never understand (1) his need to search the park and (2) his desire not to create panic. He was considering trying another entrance when an arm reached in front of him, brandishing a badge. "FBI. They're with me."

The security men stepped aside and let Matt, Liz, and Vinnie through.

"Thanks," Matt said, turning to confront the NYPD detective. "But don't try to stop me."

"Wait," Vinnie shouted grabbing at his sleeve. "There's something I need to tell you."

Before Vinnie got a chance to mention Rafiq Haddad or what he and Alan had learned, Matt bolted down the asphalt path, shouting: "Let's try the stage first."

A uniformed cop directed him to Eighty-first Street, center of the park. Hurrying, he jostled past concertgoers, who yelled back: "Hey! Look where you're going. Get a life!"

The stage glistened like a big white birthday cake, festooned with buckets of white roses. Matt overheard a stagehand say: "I hear he'll be dressed in black."

How nice, he thought, moving through the crowd, checking faces. Liz caught up with him, panting. Vinnie was right behind.

She said: "We can't help you if we don't know what he looks like."

"Ten minutes, then we're going to headquarters," Vinnie added, catching his breath. "Fair enough?"

"Fine," Matt answered. "He's Persian. Five foot ten. Mid-forties. Short salt-and-pepper hair. Neatly trimmed mustache and beard."

The three of them circled past the makeup trailers and wound their way through the first thirty rows of seated "special guests."

Near one of the video trucks, Matt sensed someone watching him. Turning quickly he saw a man with white hair duck behind a truck. *Could that be the man we saw getting out of the elevator in Dubai? What's he doing here?*

His instincts told him not to stop and think, but push forward. Vinnie kept up, talking in his ear. "What's your relationship to Alan Beckman?"

"He's my boss." Matt turned and circled back. The man with the white hair seemed to have vanished.

Vinnie said: "We went together to an address in the Bronx. He was looking for a Lebanese guy named Rafiq Haddad."

"What about him?"

"He's an associate of the other guy."

"Kourani?"

"Yeah."

"Did you find Rafiq Haddad?"

"We didn't get that far."

Liz caught up as Matt peered north and south, searching for a clue.

Vinnie said: "If there's a real threat, we should clear the park."

Matt frowned. "No one would believe us."

"I'd better call headquarters."

"I got a feeling he's here."

"Haddad?"

"Kourani. Let's go." He headed southwest, sniffing the air like a dog trying to pick up a scent.

Her high heels discarded, Liz followed in bare feet to West Drive, where Matt stopped and craned his head north. Vinnie's gaze drifted in the opposite direction toward a line of portable commodes lined up along the road farther south. "Hey."

Matt shouted: "This way."

"No, wait."

AROUND A BEND, past some trees, Vinnie spotted a white truck with a half-dozen Portosan units in back. Three men in gray overalls with protective masks over their faces were struggling to put one of the commodes into place.

When Vinnie got within fifty feet, a uniformed cop stopped him. "This area is closed," the cop said holding out his arm.

Vinnie flashed his badge. "FBI."

"You gotta use a toilet, try down near Sixty-fifth."

Something about the policeman's strange accent and the diffi-
culty with which the men were handling the commodes caused Vinnie to call out: "Rafiq!"

The man with the hand truck stopped, did a one-eighty, and hurried to the cab of the truck. Vinnie followed, with the policeman on
his heels.

"I told you this area is closed."

Vinnie ignored the cop and closed in on the man in the cab.

"Are you Rafiq?"

LIZ TURNED THE moment Vinnie reached the open door of the
truck. From two hundred feet, she watched in horror as the policeman drew something that looked like a knife and slashed it across
Vinnie's throat.

Her face turned white. "Matt!" she tried to scream, but nothing
came out. "Look!"

IN A SPLIT second, Matt took in the scene and started running,
hurling his body downhill while the three masked men dragged
Vinnie's body into the cab of the truck.

Liz yelled at his back: "Matt! He's not a real cop!"

Matt had already figured that out. *You son-of-a-bitch!*

"Hey, you! Stop!" the policeman shouted at Matt, drawing his gun.

Matt propelled himself forward, tackling the policeman at the
waist and slamming both of their bodies into the side of the truck.
The three masked men scurried inside and fired the engine as Matt
staggered to his feet.

Stars circling in his head, Matt saw the policeman on the ground,
mouth open, eyes closed. His pistol lay near the curb. Matt was
considering retrieving it when he heard gears grinding. The truck
lurched.

Not so fast! Grabbing on to the side of the truck, he used its momentum to swing his body to the driver's door. He met the closed
window and watched the man in the middle point.

Cocking his elbow back, Matt smashed the glass and, in one continuous motion, reached for the driver's throat.

"Matt!" Liz screamed. "Someone help!"

She saw him hanging on to the driver's throat and someone in the middle raise a gun. "Oh, my God! LET GO!!!!"

The momentum of the truck pushed it over the curb and into a tree. Then the gun went off. "MATT!!!!"

A cloud of blood burst from his right shoulder, but he held on.

Two dozen concertgoers bearing picnic baskets froze and watched in horror. Matt pushed his body halfway through the shattered driver's window. He squirmed farther in, throwing quick punches. Pushing past the driver's limp body, he grabbed the second's man wrist and twisted it savagely right until he heard the bones snap.

The man in the passenger seat reached over and sprayed something in his face. "Fuck!"

A thick, bitter smell filled his nose, and his eyes burned.

Matt reached blindly for the man in the passenger seat and grabbed his collar. Teeth sank into his arm. "Bastard!" Through watery eyes, he met Kourani's fierce glare.

"You're dead, Mr. Freed," Kourani shouted through the breathing mask.

"Not yet!"

Liz stood fifty feet away, watching the swarthy-skinned man jump from the cab, spray the canister in the direction of frightened onlookers, then toss it to the ground. Righting the straps of his backpack, he started in her direction.

All she could think of to do was to stand in his way and raise her arms. "Stop!"

Surprised for a second, Kourani lowered his shoulder and knocked her to the ground. From her back she saw him hop on the policeman's scooter and kick it started.

Matt stumbled up to her, wiping his eyes. "Liz!" he kneeled and lifted her shoulders. "Are you all right?"

Sitting on the pavement next to her husband, her lips trembling, she pointed in the direction of the man who got away. "Matt . . ."

Then she saw the blood dripping from her husband's shoulder. "You're hurt!"

His heart pounded relentlessly, bolstering his body with adrenaline, blotting out the pain. It was the heaviness creeping through his head and chest that worried him. He'd read somewhere on the Internet that certain virulent strains of tularemia could spread in minutes, especially if it entered through the mouth and eyes.

He said: "The stuff he sprayed is tularemia. Get tetracycline. A lot of it. For them!" He waved at the bystanders. "And you!"

"Yes. Yes."

"Then call in a biohazard team. Have them disarm whatever's in those toilets!"

"Matt . . ."

"I love you, Liz." He stood. "Make sure it happens."

She saw the unbending determination in his eyes. "I will. I love you, too!"

Standing over her, he glimpsed a white-haired man with a handkerchief over his mouth appear at the front of the crowd. He was of similar height and weight to the man in Dubai. *Is it him?* he wondered. But the face was hidden.

Matt ran north after Kourani, turning his head left to follow the white-haired man with his eyes. What he saw of the profile seemed to match. *Where does he fit in?* He watched the white-haired man enter a Lexus at Central Park West and head uptown. *Has he been tracking me all along?*

Facing north, Matt ran straight into three policemen closing in on scooters. They skidded to a stop. "What the hell happened?" one of them yelled. "Arms up!"

Matt grabbed one by the shoulders and pulled him off. "I'm with the government. NCTS!"

"Drop to the ground!!!"

Matt didn't have time to reach for his ID. He jumped on the scooter and took off.

The other two policemen drew their weapons. Liz shouted: "He's my husband! DON'T SHOOT!"

A dozen onlookers added a chorus: "He's a good guy! No! Don't!!!!"

That didn't stop a pair of plainclothes cops on foot from leveling their pistols and firing. Two bullets whizzed by Matt's right ear. Another ricocheted off the metal near his foot.

He turned sharply right and hopped the curb. Skidding down a grass slope, the scooter squirted from under him and smashed into a bench.

Disregarding the pain in his ankle, Matt righted the bike and took off. The shield over the front wheel dragged across the rim, sending up a stream of sparks.

He picked up speed along a walkway that cut through a row of trees draped with magnificent flame-orange leaves, then glimpsed a flash of Kourani's head before it disappeared down stone steps that led to the bridle path.

Hearing more shots, he ducked. Confused policemen near the reservoir crouched and fired.

"Out of my way!" he shouted to startled concertgoers ahead.

Experiencing chills and a powerful wave of nausea, he leaned to his right and retched. Which meant he didn't have time to slow for the steps ahead. The wheel hit the slab of concrete at the top step and the scooter went aloft.

Matt gripped the handlebars, rose off the seat, and braced himself. The scooter smacked the packed dirt with a clang. Somehow Matt managed to hold on.

His moment of exhilaration ended with the sight of Kourani jumping off his bike a hundred feet ahead and pointing a gun. He faced a choice: turn right into the woods, ditch the bike, or continue toward Kourani. He chose the latter, veering left, then right, dragging his feet to kick up dust, hugging his body as low to the scooter as possible.

Multiple rounds slammed into the metal; others flew past his head. Closing to fifteen feet, fourteen, thirteen, twelve, he let go and fell to the left. The scooter slid forward toward the Iranian, who threw himself into the brush along the embankment to avoid getting hit.

Matt's chest smacked the ground, knocking out his breath. For some reason his throat wouldn't open. *Is it the loss of blood or the spray?* His eyes and nostrils burned with dust.

With his last bit of strength, he pushed himself up and stumbled toward Kourani, who pulled something out of his backpack. It was a one-gallon can.

Tularemia, Matt thought, watching Kourani climb up the embankment to the reservoir, then climb across the six-foot-wide running path to the fence.

Seeing Matt staggering toward him, the Iranian grinned.

"The game is over," Kourani said pulling the mask aside.

Matt's eyes spun and caught glimpses of stars faint in the Prussian blue sky overhead. Holding on to a slender tree, he trembled as Kourani unscrewed the lid.

"Why?" Matt screamed, climbing toward him on his hands and knees.

"The point is to stop you," Kourani said calmly, setting the can aside and reaching for the pistol he'd stuck in his belt. "To fight the plague of Western civilization with a literal plague. Ironic," he sneered pointing the pistol down at Matt, whose arms and legs convulsed.

Matt tried to throw himself into Kourani's knees, but fell hopelessly short. Kourani snarled, "You're weak."

Looking up into the barrel of the gun, Matt imagined his father standing over him shaking his head. *I got this far, Dad. I'm not afraid.* Then, as in a dream, his father's head exploded in a mist of blood.

Matt blinked. When he opened his eyes again he saw Kourani fall against the fence and crumple. He blinked again.

Kourani hit the ground with a thud.

Then another man crossed his line of vision and pumped a second round into Kourani's head. Matt recognized the bristle of white hair and the C-shaped scar on his neck.

Mustering his fading strength, he asked: "Why?"

The Iranian answered. "Kourani was a zealot."

"Yes."

"We have to protect ourselves from these people."

The world grew muddled and dim.

"I was sent by my president. I represent the Iranian government. If you live, explain to your people what happened here."

"General Moshiri?"

"We are proud people, Mr. Freed. This is our business. We must take care of these things ourselves."

The words entered Matt's brain and unlocked a door to some kind of inner peace. He relaxed and let himself be taken.

THREE-QUARTERS OF A mile south, emergency medical services personnel and police tried to hustle Liz into a waiting ambulance, but she resisted. "Not yet!" she shouted. "Not until you check the toilets. Not until those people over there are helped."

She pointed to the several dozen people along the traverse who'd been sprayed by Kourani. "They need to be quarantined," she shouted. "They need to be treated immediately."

"We know."

"They were exposed to something called tularemia."

"What about you?"

"Me, too. They need to be given tetracycline immediately," she said holding on to the handle of the ambulance door.

"We'll handle everything, ma'am," the head of the EMS team said. "Let go!"

"Not until the biohazard team arrives to check the commodes."

A police lieutenant named Bastido barked: "Cooperate, lady. A team is coming."

In the background she heard the mayor over the PA system asking the crowd to be patient, telling them that there was a short delay due to "technical problems."

Two additional officers joined Lieutenant Phil Bastido, who changed his tone: "I'm asking you to please leave with me, ma'am. We'll get you to a hospital, have you checked. And if you don't mind, I'll ride with you and get a statement."

Liz pointed at the portable toilets. "What about them?"

"We put them out of service."

"Not good enough!"

When the biohazard team arrived five minutes later, they insisted that everyone leave the area. Liz stood with Lieutenant Bastido outside his police cruiser parked near the Museum of Natural History, where she swallowed two 500-milligram capsules of Achromycin (tetracycline) with a bottle of water.

Bastido told her that all the suspects had been apprehended and Matt was being treated at a nearby hospital. His condition: "critical." Liz was torn between her desire to be with her husband and the promise she'd made to see the job through.

A quarter of a mile away, four NYPD biohazard specialists clad in hazmat suits, hoods, and special breathing apparatus checked all twenty-four Portosans with portable McWhortle Bio-Hazard Alert Detectors.

"Negative for hazardous substances," came the report over Lieutenant Bastido's walkie-talkie.

"Ask them to check again," Liz said.

Bastido said: "We're moving the toilets to another location."

Liz was still protesting when two FBI officers arrived with questions: "What did you see exactly? What were you, your husband, and Detective Danieli doing in Central Park?"

She said she'd cooperate as long as she was allowed to talk to the head of the biohazard team first. Within seconds a Sergeant Woo was on the phone.

Liz asked him to describe in detail the procedure his team had followed.

"We checked the air, the deodorant liquid, the water, even the hand sanitizer. Negative for noxious or explosive substances. We've X-rayed the walls, seat, fragrance canisters, et cetera. No hidden explosives."

"What fragrance canisters?"

"The ones bolted to the ceilings."

"Sergeant, they could be loaded with a biological weapon. Please check them again."

A closer inspection of the canisters revealed tiny radio trans-mitters linked to a remote timer. NYPD bomb disposal specialists deactivated the devices four minutes before they were set to release into the air a very lethal genetically designed form of tularemia.

CHAPTER TWENTY-FIVE

September 21

Three days later, at five minutes to four in the afternoon, the presidential motorcade pulled in front of Mount Sinai Hospital on Fifth Avenue. Alighting from the row of black limousines were the president, NSC director Stan Lescher, General Emily Jasper, Alan Beckman, and numerous others.

The United States had barely escaped a major terrorist attack. Hundreds of thousands of people could have died or been infected. An inevitable U.S. counterattack could have provoked a Sunni-Shiite conflict that would have torn apart the Middle East and spread economic chaos.

Although the occasion was somber, the relief they all felt was huge.

Hospital and city officials escorted the president and his advisers up to a special eighth-floor quarantine area, where they met with Dr. J. P. Loventhal—director of the Division of Infectious Diseases. He explained that of the seventy-eight patients who'd been brought to the hospital, only one had died. Eight men and three women still suffered from "severe symptoms" but were out of danger. The remaining sixty-six were under observation and scheduled to be released by the end of the week.

"We were very, very lucky," he explained to the president. "Thanks to information supplied by Elizabeth Freed, tetracycline was administered immediately. She saved a lot of lives."

"We dodged a big bullet," the president said to General Jasper, taking her by the arm. "Thank you."

"The real kudos go to my team."

It had taken Rove Peterson, Alan Beckman, and their agents about nine and a half hours to uncover the mechanics of Kourani's operation. The Iranian government had cooperated, sharing information that showed Kourani represented a rogue element of the Qods Force bent on usurping power for a group of radical mullahs.

Despite the ugly incident on the United Airlines jet three days earlier, U.S.-Iranian relations were stabilized and returned to an uneasy standoff that had characterized the past thirty years.

"This is one occasion where I appreciate the irony," the president said with a sigh of relief.

"We need to do a better job of building relationships," General Jasper added, "especially with enemies and rivals. The more we know about them, the better we'll be able to advance our interests."

Tears appeared in the eyes of the country's top foreign policy makers as Liz Freed was brought out in a wheelchair. She sat up proudly as the president expressed the country's gratitude and handed her a Presidential Citizens Medal for "exemplary deeds or services for your country and fellow citizens."

"I'm not sure I deserve this," Liz said modestly.

"Let me know if you or your family needs anything," the president offered. "Are your children with you?"

"They're still with my mother in Athens. The girls fly here this weekend."

The president squeezed her hand. "The whole country thanks you and your family."

Thanks had previously been extended to Zyoda Reynek through the U.S. Embassy in Moscow. And emergency visas had been offered to her and her daughter Irina to come to the United States.

Next the president and his aides donned protective masks and gowns and were led into the quarantine section, where they exchanged best wishes with the sixty-six patients who were scheduled to be released at the end of the week.

Finally, Dr. Loventhal led them to a secure room at the end of the ward. There behind special glass and encased in a sealed plastic tent, Matthew Freed rested on a bed connected to tubes. The president's voice shook as he commended Matt for his "acts of uncommon valor under the most challenging and lethal circumstances."

"You put your own life, family, and career at risk to save hundreds of thousands of people from terrible suffering and death," the president said. "All of us stand before you today grateful for your strength and courage." He handed a box containing the Presidential Medal of Freedom to Liz.

They stood at the glass and watched in silence as Matthew Freed slowly pulled himself up. General Jasper's chin trembled as Matt raised his left hand and waved. They waved back and shouted words of encouragement.

The president asked Dr. Loventhal about Matt's prognosis.

"When he came in, I didn't think he had a chance. Severe loss of blood, high fever, bacteria attacking his lungs and liver, plus an assortment of recent wounds. But he's pretty much out of danger now."

"He won't go until he decides he's ready."

"Something like that," Loventhal said, looking over at Liz, her face pressed against the glass, silently mouthing words to her husband. "I'd say he has a lot to live for."